TO HOWARD PARKER —
A "DOER" AT SNAKE
MEADOW CLUB.

BEST WISHES,

Paul E. Chase

Meanderings of a Snake Meadow Editor

PAUL E. CHASE

authorHOUSE®

AuthorHouse™
1663 Liberty Drive
Bloomington, IN 47403
www.authorhouse.com
Phone: 1-800-839-8640

First published by AuthorHouse 1/12/2010

ISBN: 978-1-4490-2047-7 (e)
ISBN: 978-1-4490-2046-0 (sc)
ISBN: 978-1-4490-2045-3 (hc)

Printed in the United States of America
Bloomington, Indiana

This book is printed on acid-free paper.

Front Cover Image: From Marguerite Kirmse's Dogs in the Field, The Derrydale Press, Inc., 1935

Six of the chapters in this book first appeared as follows:

"No Finer Tribute" (in part) - April, May, June 1995 The Ruffed Grouse Society Magazine.
"Contentment" – The Double Gun Journal Index & Reader 1997-2005.
"Charlie & Dan" – by Jon Bradford Chase, The Double Gun Journal Index & Reader 1990-1996.
"Winter Woodcock" – Summer 2007, The Upland Almanac.
"For Woodcock and Other Things" – Volume 10 Issue 1 Spring 1999 The Double Gun Journal.
"North Country Musings" – Summer 2009, The Upland Almanac.

Steady Boy, Steady, **oil by**
Hy (Henry) Hintermeister, c. 1929
(study for calendar prepared for Kemper & Thomas)

This book is dedicated to my wife, Johann, whose
house-cleaning talents far surpass mine.

Table of Contents

Introduction

As the road passed my car window this morning, a maple tree showed it was changing its dress. This early sign has always shocked my wife, telling her another beloved summer was dying. I have learned not even to whisper of the observed changes and especially not to show my joy that another upland season is about to begin.

For many years each fall, the author and I headed north to meet birds coming toward us. These were all too brief trips stolen from obligations and duties. We earned livings, fed families, and eventually paid tuitions. Because time was always at a premium, we would meet mid-week on late afternoons and drive into the night toward our destination, western Maine.

As I read these essays, some touching on these hunts, I remember being on the ground together watching the dogs and anticipating the finds. In the beginning, we taught the guides that we would not leave wounded, hard-to-find birds that were down. We would put good dogs over the ground again and again in search. When dogs rebuffed commands to retrieve birds shot over ever-present water, one of us became the retriever. We would wade in, or in certain circumstances, would be lowered head first from the bank hopefully to fetch the bird. Even though we sought birds for the dogs and ourselves, we made it clear that being there in the field was the point.

The author helps us understand his hunting ethic by giving us insight into his heritage and who his heroes are. Through these descriptions, we see the basis for his standards. There was never a question as to why he believes in this sport and how it is to be played.

When he speaks of the land, he recalls an earlier ethic. This ethic, born on early New England hillsides, is still practiced by the author. He talks of the husbandry and devotion to his own land, and what it means for the birds. He decries the loss of open land and begrudgingly accepts the emasculation of it where birds are ever increasingly betrayed by development.

In describing his trips out of Connecticut, there seems to be a bittersweet acknowledgement that not long ago there was an abundance of birds in his lower lot and travel was not necessary. It's not that he doesn't love the uplands of Maine and Vermont but is perhaps saddened that his own house is no longer filled.

As in all great sports, the author recognizes the culture that surrounds them. He introduces us to writers and artists who have strived to portray the participation in the upland life. He wishes that we recognize and support these artists and writers that collectively enhance our own appreciation of what we can do. He also makes the point that we should care and contribute to the sport. Only if we care and conduct ourselves accordingly will there be upland sport for the future.

Once read, we see in these essays a degree of involvement that has happily dictated part of the author's life. As you turn these pages, you become privileged to be part of what someone loves.

It is mid-September and I have already seen that call to fall. My thoughts are always taken back to earlier days with the author when the maples stood in new dress, calling us north.

When you, too, are reminded that the season is abreast, take at least some of these stories with you. They will make getting there shorter, the dogs in front of you finer, and the covers fuller.

Ken Dugas, October 2008

Preface

This is a book of essays about upland hunting experiences, bird dogs, noteworthy authors who wrote books about upland hunting, celebrated entrepreneurs in the shotgun-producing industry, favorite upland painters whose subjects were dogs and men in the field, fine double shotguns, a few short stories and several miscellaneous subjects related to the upland shooting life. This book also offers historical, environmental, philosophical and aesthetical observations of a long-time rural landowner. A fellow bird hunter, Dick Curriden, of Greenville, Maine, also contributed sage words of a long-time sportsman, sometimes satirically, in the form of letters he sent to me over the years.

In 1998 I wrote a feature piece for *Double Gun Journal* that touched on many of the above topics. It was unusual subject matter for a publication that devotes a very large percentage of its material to high-end double barrel and single shot shotguns and rifles. My cousin Fred, who has a degree in writing from Wesleyan College, critiqued "Reflections on the New England Upland Sporting Life" and observed that the material was far too diverse and all-encompassing to be included in one article. The point that I wanted to make was that the actual hunting is only part of the equation of the upland shooting life, and that no serious practitioner of this traditional sport can ignore the fine art, books, history, and shotguns that are related to this pursuit. Put another way, there's a lot more than just "shoot 'em up." That's the "why" of this book.

As to all this other stuff being part of the equation of upland sport, some of my friends disagree. One, who has no financial inhibitions, travels to far places pursuing his hobby, in particular, his annual journey to Iceland for Atlantic salmon fishing. He "would rather do it than read about it" or collect images that display what others have experienced—the history. But given a choice, we would all rather "do it" if physically and financially able. Now that Harry is pretty much retired from the sporting life, I wonder if he feels the same way today. Like my friend, if you have no interest in the "peripherals" related to upland hunting, there's probably little reason to read this book.

So, it was with Cousin Fred's perception that I decided to write *Meanderings of a Snake Meadow Editor*. Actually, I have been gathering material for several years in the form of vignettes that appeared in *Snake Meadow Happenings*, a quarterly newsletter for the members of Snake Meadow Club, Inc., a highly respected and well-known hunting and fishing club located in northeastern Connecticut. As the long-time editor/writer of this publication, I felt compelled to put my "two cents" into every issue. Without exception, many of the essays appearing in *Meanderings* have been expanded, some significantly, from those lightly touched subjects included in the newsletters.

I never would have become interested in the upland sporting life were it not for my grandfather, Paul Glasbrenner. He told me of the days after 1899—the year he married and purchased my maternal great grandfather's family dairy farm—when he would set aside two weeks in the fall to hunt birds with his friends from Rhode Island. For a man who possessed a strong Puritan work ethic, two weeks was a long time to leave a working farm largely unattended—I surmise he had to rise about 4:00 a.m. just to perform the bare necessities. As I was very young, I've forgotten many of the stories he told me, but a few remain in my memory. Mostly, I remember that he made fun of their hunting experiences, such as the plethora of missed shots, misbehaved dogs, lost dogs, and the occasional empty game bag after a day-long hunt.

His friends were able to afford highly engraved American doubles, and my grandfather talked at great length about their fine shotguns. Somehow, the makers and details of their guns stuck with me, and in time and for a time I became a collector of medium to hi-grade American 20-bore doubles in fine condition, that is, until family responsibilities curtailed the lofty ambitions I once had. And when the occasional Prussian-made Charles Daly came my way, I was "forced" to rethink my focus, and most of the American-made 20 bores were sold or traded. The only one I really miss is a sweet 20-gauge Lefever Arms

Co. EE Grade with practically all the original finish, made about a century ago. How often do you see one of these gems in this condition? I cherish the several fine shotguns that remain in my collection.

Shortly after, I discovered sporting books and upland art that memorialized my grandfather's halcyon days and that reached into more modern times. I could afford to collect this stuff rather than going overboard with fine shotguns, I reasoned. I learned soon enough that the cream of collectible sporting books is very expensive; forget about original art—I'd be content to carefully select the few prints and etchings of favorite artists that have special meaning to me.

As to the books, I chose to concentrate on limited editions, signed first editions, and plain ol' firsts when limited editions weren't published. A first-class collection of sporting books needs a focal point, unless one has lots of room available. Even so, you can spend a lot of money and fill a lot of space with just upland books. I don't pretend to have the best, the most, or most valuable, such as the deluxe limited edition (seventy-five copies) of *Upland Game Bird Shooting in America,* published by the Derrydale Press in 1930. I settled for the regular limited edition (trade edition) of 850 copies in fine condition in the dust jacket. Still, I don't crave too many books that I don't already have. Being retired from gainful employment, some that I covet are beyond my financial reach—a select few possibly would command the price of a nice pre-owned automobile.

Like my Atlantic salmon fishing friend, I would much rather be in the field pursuing my sport, as opposed to being an arm-chair reader and casual viewer of sporting images. But I must admit that the other two endeavors are exciting. Far-away places are alluring, but I will settle for a day's drive into the coverts of northern New England and eastern Canada where grouse and woodcock fly and where high-headed, long-tailed setters flash through field and wood in their never ending quest to fulfill the dreams of their masters.

Formative Years

In the Beginning...

The kind captain made her little harbor his ship's resting place, and he and his men helped themselves to provisions that they desperately needed. Had she not complied, her life could have been threatened. He seemed civilized, but she had reason to be suspicious of his behavior. From the talk of the officers around the dinner table, it soon became evident that they were not law-abiding men; they were pirates!

On the other hand, in a strange sort of way, she welcomed the company.

Her husband Joshua spent much of his time on the mainland in New London, Connecticut, returning only every two or three weeks, and the care and responsibility of managing the farm fell on her shoulders. Their Block Island farm was a lonely vigil and not surprisingly, she longed for human interaction. Her servility and companionship were well rewarded, as the captain paid for what he took in gold. Not that she needed to be compensated; her husband was a successful merchant and a good provider.

This strange relationship lasted for several months until Joshua, upon returning home, questioned the depleted store of goods. She passed it off as a temporary loan to neighbors across the island.

And so, when the captain sailed into her harbor later on, she had to tell him that this convenience could not continue. Naturally, he was disappointed and upset, for he had come to rely on the security of her harbor and abode. The captain's displeasure soon subsided, and "he bade her hold out her apron," which he commenced to fill with "gold,

1

jewels, and other precious commodities," the bounty, no doubt, of his baneful plunders.

She—Mercy Sands Raymond—lived with her secret. Shortly after the death of Joshua in 1704, she, with her children removed their belongings from her lonely outpost and with a business partner and land speculator, Major John Merritt, purchased 1500 acres of land, hereinafter known as Raymond Hill, in the remote wilderness of Mohegan lands in the North Parish of New London, now Montville. She constructed thereon a dwelling house overlooking Long Island Sound, about eight miles distant.

The munificent provider of her good fortune, none other than the egregious Captain William Kidd, had met his fate at the gallows in London, England in 1701. The "Enrichment of the Apron" has been the source of pleasant conversation among family members over the years, the youngest of successive generations assuredly having been smitten by the romantic urge to explore the land for possible clues as to the whereabouts of untold riches. In truth, more than likely Kidd's nest egg provided the resources for her partnership and land purchases with Major Merritt, in itself unusual for a woman during those early times.

Henry Baker's *History of Montville* tells the reader that Mrs. Raymond died while visiting friends in Lyme, Connecticut—origin of the infamous tick-related disease—in 1741 and was buried there near the old stone church. I could never find her tombstone, but my son Jon, Montville's municipal historian, located the nondescript marker a few years ago at a burial ground never searched, in what is now East Lyme. I speculated as to why she was not interred in eponymous ground she gave for the Raymond Hill Cemetery that contained the North Parish's first church. Being several hours distant by horse and buggy and lacking body preservatives in those early times, it's possible that the reason for her distant burial requires no further explanation.

The early eighteenth century dwelling on Raymond Hill is my family homestead. The Raymonds continued to inhabit the property until about 1824 when the Bradford family, inhabitants of the town since 1717, purchased it. My grandfather married Julia Bradford—a direct lineal descendant of Governor William Bradford of Plymouth in the ninth generation—and farmed the land until about 1950. It was at this time that I formed a close relationship with my grandfather, spending uncountable weekends and vacations during grammar school, high school and beyond into college years at the "old homestead," as it came to be known. Soon after his death in 1960, my wife and I built a home on the farm property where we have remained to this day, keeping close watch on our ancestral dwelling.

Several of the essays that follow refer to this land—110 acres of woods, tillable fields, and regenerating pastures—that has been a joy and comfort all my life.

Excitement on the Farm

As I grow older, the poignant and formative days of youth stand clearly in my memory. My father was a successful financial man and he cared well for his family, but it was my grandfather who unknowingly pulled me from suburbia into the open arms of a beckoning land still disconnected from the jabs and forays of urbane influences.

He taught me real work, unlike the contrived physical regimen of city folk. He spoke to me in terms of actions rather than words and forced me to gather conclusions regarding life's purpose. His lifestyle was mostly devoid of the extreme ups and downs so characteristic of our generation, and his unspoken philosophy was to weigh heavily on the future path of my life's priorities.

I don't mean to infer that excitement never occurred.

He reveled in the telling of the time when, in the middle of the night, a disturbance in the henhouse prompted a look-see, the old double barrel shotgun in hand. Raucous and blood-curdling sounds emanated from inside the building. He unlatched the door, directed his lantern inside and peered into the gloom. A mass slaughter of half the population of Rhode Island Reds—he always kept about fifty—obviously had been consummated by the dark form crouched in the far corner of the dimly lighted building. Yup, shoot and ask questions later. The supposed "fox" turned out to be a prized animal from the mink farm—owned by the Graves family as I recall—down the hill, and worth $500 to its owner, a tidy sum back in the '40s when mink coats were much more popular than they are now. Gramp felt awful and offered to pay the owner for his "misdeed" but was refused.

3

I wondered, years later, if the retrieved shot-riddled hide was worth anything to Mr. Graves.

One early fall evening much later in time, we were all sitting out in the white Adirondack chairs in the stifling but somewhat dissipated heat of dusk watching the occasional auto drive by. This was a pastime that the older folks seemed to enjoy, excitement to them, I guess. Many of the travelers were known; their horns would honk in recognition, my grandfather and aunts would wave in return, and then speak the names of the occupant(s). One evening a deer could be seen emerging in the first orchard behind the tool shed. It crossed the road into the garden where it showed some interest in nibbling the few remaining vegetables before it jumped over the wall and disappeared below the henhouse. An exceptionally large doe, it was the first deer that any of us had seen in a long time. Back in the sixties deer were not very common in these parts and were hardly, if ever, encountered during the day. Today, deer are so prevalent that they are a menace on the roads and are so bold that they eat shrubbery in front of dwellings' portals.

A somewhat more egregious event was the basis for the mistaken odor of blood in my callow sixteen-year-old mind. I had spent an unusually hot June afternoon cutting sumac in the Stony Lot—what a waste; it just grows back. My maiden aunt, a long-time school principal, offered a ride in her brand new 1955 stick shift, V-8, 210 Chevrolet—she never got used to automatic except for her last Caprice—to Gardner Lake for a cooling swim. It was definitely a muscle car but only when I drove it alone! When we returned, all hell had broken loose. Ambulances, fire engines and swarms of humanity led us to believe that some terrible accident had befallen my eighty-five year-old mentor.

But then, there he was, shouting in stentorian voice, waving his cane, and directing traffic. Along with arthritis and other infirmities of advancing age, I never imagined Gramp could move so fast! We learned that a passenger car failed to negotiate the sharp turn in front of the farmhouse, rolled over several times, alternating between the top of the garden farm wall and the road. Its twisted and turbulent path resulted in the decapitation of the woman passenger. Brain matter and gore were scattered over the once-tranquil countryside, and the sweet fragrance of blood, as I thought it then to be, pervaded the air.

Needless to say, this horrible event formed a long-lasting impression, the sordid details of which I remember to this day.

The truth came the following June in tracing the source of the same odor wafting the breeze. The "blood" of my remembrance, conjuring the lurid event, is familiar to the late spring fisherman. Its summer fruit, on which grouse gorge, was gathered by women of yore and crushed into wine-colored jelly. I discovered it to be the innocuous pungency emanating from wild grapes.

"Bobwhite!"

It is emblematic for younger teens to hasten the coming of manhood by aspiring to accomplish some feat of renown, such as hitting the game-winning home run (with all the girls watching, of course), or perhaps less noteworthy or heroic, catching the first worm-enticed native trout out of Farmer Brown's "posted" brook.

As has been my wont to do, my youthful days stand in need of being transcribed into the annals of Time. In this case, the pursued was not always the four bases of baseball's diamond, but of bobwhites down back of the barn. I had just turned thirteen and had read all about the habits, so I thought, of the bird whose whistling, three-syllable supplication symbolized the coming of spring's transformation—and soon-to-be summer vacations!

Following Peewee League baseball/softball after school or Saturday mornings, often I would catch a ride to my grandfather's farm about seven miles distant from my suburban home. I helped with chores on the then mostly retired dairy farm, but there was spare time aplenty. One of my favorite pastimes was sneaking up on stonewall-perched bobwhite males to see how close I could approach—usually not less than twenty feet or so at best. While eating breakfast on Sunday mornings, I would listen to "Ah-bob-white" (my grandfather translated the familiar call to mean "some-more-wet") in the cool of early morning and rush outside to begin my skulk—that's if my maiden aunt didn't have plans to yank me off to the little church down the road. My, how nasally they sounded up close, much unlike the melodious call heard from afar. Contrary to the present scarcity, bobwhites were plentiful back in the 1950s.

Come October, I would be ready to take on the task. The 1889 Remington double had been carefully but apprehensively test fired under the watchful tutelage of its owner, my grandfather, who was 80-years-young at the time. The old Remington sported Damascus barrels, which I had read were not safe with smokeless ammunition. I wrapped a heavy coat around the breech the first time I fired it, thinking that my hands would be protected if it blew. Gramp scoffed at my concern for the safety of the old gun; he had hunted with it using light smokeless loads throughout the years with never a problem, and his father-in-law—my Great-Grandfather—shot it for a few years before it was passed down.

We started out, my exuberance crimped only by Gramp's arthritic legs. The retired and regenerating pastures had grown to an almost impassable mixture of Eastern red cedar, greenbrier (he called it bullbrier), and grape vines connected to and wrapped around every tree. The nascent bittersweet from the Orient that we all thought at the time was a most beautiful and natural growing vine, was not yet a problem in native landscapes. Fifty years later it had taken over the earth!

Even though we were on the beaten path, Gramp soon urged me to go on alone. "Go down to th' spring, Boy (he never called me by my given name), and go over to th' big white oak. There on the west bound'ry is where ya'll find some birds." I wondered how he knew that because he hadn't been down this way in a few years. With much effort, he managed to sit on the low-slung picnic rock to await the results of my foray.

I loaded the old Remington and started down the path in search of bobwhite, not knowing quite what to expect. The morning was quiet and peaceful, and it remained that way, that is until I reached the before-mentioned white oak. I had seen no birds flush, but there among the branches I saw movement, and then I spotted what appeared to be my quarry perched on a very dead lower branch about thirty yards distant. Before it could fly, I raised the old hammer gun, pulled back both hammers and let go the right barrel. The bird hit the ground with a "plop," and I ran to gather in the spoils. "Gramp, Gramp, I got it, I got it," I shouted as I rushed excitedly to my sitting mentor.

I thrust my bird into his outstretched reach. His gnarled hands parted the feathers as he studied my speckled-breasted bird with eyes starting to grow dim. By this time I suspected the truth and anxiously awaited his pronouncement. A cryptic smile crept over his swarthy face. "Boy, you jes' shot yerself a flika."

First Bird

In early November of 1954, when I was sixteen, I shot my first grouse. It was a late Saturday afternoon in Indian summer when I was off from school. After hurriedly wolfing down my mid-afternoon snack, I headed for the north acreage, past the first stonewall on the main path down the little hill toward the wooded swale where the running brook from adjacent land cuts through the middle. I was without a dog in those early days, and my grandfather no longer owned Red, the Irish setter.

Having read that Mr. Grouse can be a heavy feeder late in the day, my rambling took on the euphoric feeling of what was likely to happen. I made note of the gorgeous Indian summer day and reflected back in time…

It seems like yesterday when I was sitting in shirtsleeves in the doorway of the corn shed with my grandfather. My mentor said to me, as we looked over leafless, hazy valleys flowing into Long Island Sound, "This is Indian summer Boy, and it's the best time of year. Most people think it's any warm spell in October but that's wrong. To be Indian summer you gotta have haze in the distance after the first hard frost when the leaves are down, about the first two weeks in November. Cherish it, 'cuz you don't always get it."…

Suddenly the roar of wings that I had come to know interrupted the afternoon silence of my reverie. Brrpt, brrpt, brrpt. Supplications to the effect that this opportunity would not result in another inglorious miss, I swung the Model 870 pump but trailed the last of the three birds until a frantic swing-thru prompted me to pull the trigger. To my amazement, the bird tumbled to earth. It had finally happened! The bird landed just this side of the little stream and I rushed to gather up my prize.

It is difficult to sufficiently describe my emotion as I hurried up the barn lane into the cool calmness and ruddy glow of the dying day, suffused with wood smoke from the old homestead's kitchen stove. My grandfather would be proud because I had been trying to accomplish this feat for a long time. My thumping heartbeat betrayed the joy of shooting my first partridge on the wing, first ever for that matter.

As I passed the well curb, I could see my grandfather looking out the window leaning forward in his chair to better see me carrying my bird. I unlatched the door in the kitchen ell and he looked up from his rocking chair with a broad smile on his weathered face and quipped in his Yankee twang, "Gotcha a pa'tridge Boy?" As if he didn't know. There was an ever so slight roll and slur to the "t" in pa'tridge. To this day, I don't know who was happier, Gramp or I.

Several years later, I relived my jubilation and my grandfather's reserved celebration when reading Judge Nutting's rare 1889 tome, *The History of One Day Out of Seventeen Thousand,* in which the author relates the story of a young boy—the author—coming home from a day of hunting with his father in up-state New York. (Incidentally, this was the first book published in the U.S. devoted to just grouse hunting.) He was carrying his first partridge and viewed his mother in the distance watching them approach.

"Near the house, on the platform by the well, looking toward us stood my mother. Her right hand was shading her eyes and she appeared to be watching us anxiously. When I came near enough to see her plainly, she was smiling a happy welcome to father and me. Her dark hair was well brushed back from her face, which glowed with happiness. Her features were as calm, pure and sweet as given mortal to be. It seemed to me then, and it seems to me now, that she was the grandest, sweetest, and best woman in all the world."

My first grouse was a precious moment in my formative years, and Gramp was part of it. I felt that he was the most wonderful man alive when I handed him my bird. And of course, he wanted to know all the details; where on the property it fell to my gun, was it a clean wing shot, and how many other birds did I see.

I was proud, too, because as my mentor, he inspired me to love the land and to respect, appreciate, and protect its natural beauty. It's not something you sell like a commodity. As owner of the land, he made me understand that he was simply its steward for a brief period of time. The next generation would bear the same responsibility. The foregoing experience in my life was part of the beginning of that realization.

Raison d'être

> The World is too much with us; late and soon
> Getting and spending, we lay waste our powers
> Little we see in nature that is ours
> We have given our hearts away, a sordid boon.

William Wordsworth

The purpose for living is a complicated subject, and it is probably quite varied in every individual's case. I ponder the question often, just because maybe I'm not too sure what makes some people "tick." Woe to any man who cannot delight in life's blessings because of misplaced priorities in seeking life's fulfillment.

Loving or hating one's livelihood is important, considering that the vast majority of awake-hours are spent on the job. The Massachusetts upland painter, A. Lassell Ripley, perhaps paraphrasing the western sporting artist, Charles Russell, put it this way—"Any man that can make a living doing what he likes is lucky, and I am that. Anytime I cash in now, I win." Who can underestimate the love of spouse and family? A reason for living? Obviously.

Loyalty to one's religion and love of God are powerful ideals that sometimes transcend any formal list of forces that contribute to one's happiness. Too often, religious faith is something that is turned off when the spire pointing to Heaven is left behind on Sunday morning, not that church attendance, per se, makes a better person—far from it.

Many older folks live for their memories, especially if they are unable or unwilling to participate in a society turned sour from sweetness of unsullied times past.

The activities that we sportsmen pursue have a lot to do with life's fullness. I cannot imagine living my life without an English setter or two sharing practically every one of my days. They are a big part of my life. So strong are the bonds that I probably would hunt but little if it were not for dogs trained by my hand.

But it could be any diversion that gentles the soul and provides healing from man's selfishness and reality's rancor. To many, pride of family origin, public recognition, success in business, status, wealth and empowerment, are the guts that drive the will to live. To others, hate, greed, vindictiveness, excoriation and deceit provide the venue for life's "battle." One thing that I learned is that some do not change their malevolence. These are not kind people; their lives are a series of daily skirmishes that make up their war. They do not focus on the big picture. Recidivism abounds. Someone has vividly expressed—"The more people I get to know, the more I like my dog." So true!

The period of living is but a "flash in the pan" of Time, and so we all aspire to live a "full" life, whatever that means. Some are constantly on the go, spending money as if there were no tomorrow. Live for the moment. Nothing wrong with this I guess, but I relish life's subtle treasures, maybe for many reasons. Could it be that I'm too much of a cynic, with little conviction that mankind will alter his callous disrespect for the environment, or that social and vocational connections have caused a knee-jerk reaction that belittle human relations, compelling me to focus on the "un-monied" gifts of God's creation?

As I write these disconnected thoughts, my gaze is lifted up across the hills under June-blue skies, as yet unsaturated with summer's humidity, to glimpses of my life's treasures and keepsakes: the miracle of earthly rejuvenation through spring's spreading mantle that sentient human qualities allow us all to know if we are of such a mind; common bonds and lasting friendships; cool morning rambles into the contrasting luminous glow and shade of wooded bowers; whistling wings of longbills in cedar-laced, stone wall-edged pastures; a darting Killdeer plover's windswept jubilation in the clearing of a turbulent sky; saying kind words; praising good works; newly mown hay; a gurgling brook in a quiet setting; the marvel of a day; New England villages and their perfect blending of timeless colonial architecture with natural and unfettered surroundings devoid of development; fall's kaleidoscope (without the horde of leaf-peepers!); the stark beauty of winter's rural landscape; a granddaughter; family roots; the sprinkling of shadblow in April followed by apple blossoms' perfumed delight in May; apple cider and hazy Indian summers in November; Thanksgiving; giving thanks. There is much other enrichment in our enchanted world, all part of the big picture.

Yes, there are also material pleasures, but most fade into oblivion with the passage of Time. They become shackles to a world run amok with frenzied emulation.

No Finer Tribute

As I stood near the minister while he delivered the final words of committal—to which I listened but didn't hear— in the ancient burial ground, I couldn't help my blurred eyes being drawn beyond still-diaphanous sugar maples to the emerging panoply of spring on surrounding hills. The beautiful scene seemed, in a strange but meaningful way, to take the sting out of the loss of my mentor. He would have quietly reveled in this moment were he still mortal. Oh, what a legacy he left me.

How many times had life's ending played out in this early town cemetery over the last 300 years? Interred here were my ancestors resting in the rocky soil of the old churchyard. There was one difference now. My mentor was an interloper, a second-generation German who married my ninth-generation Mayflower/Bradford-descended grandmother, Julia Bradford, in 1899. Of his dissimilar ancestry I could not be more proud.

He was a simple and singular man, not one to join groups. To him, life was so precious that daily living was unblended rejoicing for his little corner of earth. His enjoyments were pure and uncomplicated and his thoughts without malice. No words of pretension, animosity, strident conjecture, or jealousy ever left his lips.

Physically strong as a bull but gentle and God-fearing, he took pleasure in watching a Hunter's Moon climb over valleys pierced with chimneys' smoky streams and glimmering windows of neighbors' farms.

He could lift a stout anvil by the horn with one hand. His hired farm worker, Prentice Williams, often goaded him into a little friendly competition with various feats of strength. At 5'11½" and weighing 220 pounds, my mentor had the reputation of being the strongest man in the county. His wrists were almost twice the size of the average man.

I often wondered, but never thought to ask, how far he had traveled from his life-long farm home. As a young single man working as foreman for James Manwaring, he once told of the time when he drove cattle as far west as the Connecticut River, maybe twenty miles distant—on foot. I suspect that was the extent of his life's wanderlust.

He often visited with Mr. Manwaring, for whom he held great respect—and for his maiden daughter, Ier, too. He sat with them on many occasions in their farmhouse, cracking walnuts on the arm of an eighteenth century ladder-back chair. His mischief was cause for a later inset repair three quarters of an inch square at arm's end. When he was in his seventies, he renewed his long-lost friendship with Dr. Ier and asked if he could purchase the old chair with so many memories. She agreed, and forty dollars sealed the deal. Even way back then it was worth considerably more, but both thought the price was fair.

He took care of his family the best way he could, working the land with a pair of draft horses and bare hands. But they never went without the necessities and the occasional material pleasure. He purchased a brand new car in 1938, his second auto. A Chevrolet sedan, he named it "Charlie" after one of his draft horses. I don't know about the horse, but Charlie II gave everyone a pretty rough ride, as my mentor never really mastered shifting gears.

A nearby brook yielded speckled trout in his younger days and from it he'd take a few in the course of a week during the spring—never more than he needed. They were always there—some of them a foot long—and thrived under his careful but unsophisticated husbandry.

And how he loved to chase "pa'tridge" with his Rhode Island friends, Whitman and Sweet. They came every year for two whole weeks. He put off his farm chores, just doing the bare necessities, and they hunted from dawn to dusk. Ah, the stories he told about their experiences.

His wife urged him to buy a little Parker back in the 1920s, but he couldn't justify spending the money. Why, his old pass-me-down Model 1889 Remington hammer double with the barrels sawed off to 28" suited him just fine.

As the Good Book closed and the small gathering slowly turned to leave the cemetery, I stopped and listened to the faint but unmistakable staccato and roll of a cock grouse drumming in the valley below. Nothing said by the good reverend could have been more fitting.

Amen.

Fact and Fiction

Contentment

A proud family has its legacy. Descended from the leader of the Plymouth Plantation Pilgrims, many became professional people of means and accomplishment – doctors, lawyers, bankers, legislators, and politicians. And there were farmers. In fact, many were connected with the "Great Farm" situated in the Mohegan Hills of New London County. A yearning of some to live simpler lives often overshadowed family pride in its progenitor and scions. This was wrought by the magic of the land and the beauty that it instilled in those who came under its spell…

This is a special day that the Lord has made, he thought, the day that he looked forward to all week. The chores were completed early, and the cloudless, azure November sky beckoned old Mr. Sun to rise up and spread warmth over the land where contented Jerseys grazed rock-strewn pastures. The sweet perfume of white oak burning in the kitchen stove seemed to take the chill from the cold, early morning air. An Indian summer day was just what he had ordered. Haze covered the distant hills overlooking Long Island Sound, and he estimated that the temperature might reach about 55° by early afternoon.

His friend arrived early with Molly, his young Gordon setter just turned three. She sat ramrod-straight in the buckboard, quivering with excitement sitting beside her master. Denison (S.D. for short) grabbed his Remington double from the corner in the horse barn and whistled for Sass (short for Sassafras), his aging white setter. (She always smelled of sassafras because she slept among the roots of the tree so-named between the barn and the woodshed.) Jotie, his young daughter, appeared at the ell door with his lunch, and he kissed her and bade her goodbye. George, awakened in his upper chamber by the barnyard din, pushed up the sash and waved to his father. "Don't worry about the milking tonight Pa, I'll do it. Good luck!" George never cared much for farming; he'd rather have a business in town someday. He liked to hunt on the old place though, in fact, he just ordered a new Parker direct from Meriden.

The two hunters ambled off down the lane, with both dogs stirred up like children on Christmas morn. The Gordon was really fired up. Sass, going on eleven, was a big setter, but was faster than most New England dogs. She really knew how to handle a pa'tridge. No doubt though, that today Molly was intimidating her. No problem. They'd both settle down some ere long.

S.D. glanced over at Buster, the barnyard bull tethered in the little three-corner lot between the lane and the barn, and a torturing sense of guilt passed through his whole body, just like when you seem to be living for the moment and then all of a sudden remember problems. He started thinking about his mounting debt and his ability to care for his growing family. Buster's snort brought his attention to another nagging problem. The one thing he had neglected to do in readying for this holiday was to trim old Buster's horns. His wife, Delia, had insisted and he had promised. No little wonder that S.D. always put it off—Buster was downright cantankerous! And he needed to be moved from his overgrazed turf. Maybe when he got home; tomorrow for sure...

The morning hunt took them east off the hill, around the big cedar swamp below Comstock Hill, and then west to the little brook just this side of the Maples' farm where they would break for lunch. Pa'tridge were plentiful this year, probably owing to the dry spring and the absence of one certain market hunter passing through. This local, Jake Vibber, accidentally shot a prize thoroughbred mare out on the Fitch place back in the fall of 1893. Claimed he'd never hunt again. The shooting was so good that by late forenoon they had moved about forty birds and taken a goodly share. The dogs, who always worked well as a brace, never performed better, even though young Molly bumped a few.

When they reached the brook near the swamp, S.D. removed a sack from his coat pocket and produced a tangle of fishing line and a few worms from its dirt-filled contents. He commenced to unravel the line and carefully floated the hooked worm into the little pool down beyond the stone bridge. Zap! A twelve-inch speckled beauty finally came to him after a frenzied contest that would have thrilled the most enthusiastic angler. He lined his pocket with a bed of sweet fern and carefully placed his prize atop the pa'tridges. He and Jotie loved trout. She'd cook it up and they'd share it for supper.

After lunch, the two friends headed up over the hill to neighboring north-slope pastures interspersed with little patches of brush and young pole timber. It was still wet from last night's cold rain, and if S.D. figured right, the northwesterly wind should have brought in a fall of woodcock. Well, I tell you, they were everywhere. They had never seen so many birds, and the dogs went crazy! Funny thing it was because the dogs never had a chance to set many of their birds. Once they'd wind a 'cock, another'd put up. Shooting was fast and furious, and clouds of spent power so filled the air, on account of the still day, that they had to stop so they could see the dogs and where they were at.

The next pasture up the hill was not as wet and a little more open. Soon Sass came to an abrupt halt a full thirty yards behind Moll, whose black and tan color was hard to see in the distant brushy undergrowth. Young Moll had set her bird and had jacked around to face the gunners. Sass instinctively pulled up, honoring her bracemate. "Now ain't that somethin'," S.D. mused. "Nuthin' wrong with this old dog's eyesight!" The pa'tridge they expected turned out to be a twenty-five-bird bevy of bobwhites, and they were only ten feet in front of Sass's nose! Yet it was Moll who first found the birds thirty yards away. Even though they were surprised by the flush of the big bevy, both hunters got a double on the rise, and for the rest of the afternoon they had the best singles shooting ever. They took nine birds but left plenty for seed.

He and his friend laughed and joked about some of their misses. Still, the day had been the best that S.D. had ever experienced in the field. Game was abundant and the dogs were just simply awesome. Lengthening shadows signaled the commencement of the long walk back over the farms of S.D.'s neighbors. He sure was grateful to the good Lord for allowing him to have the time away from work. Yessir, he was a lucky man and he felt at peace with the world.

17

Back home, just enough light remained to complete one of the unfinished chores. Although anxious to show Jotie his trout, he removed his game-laden coat, loosened the iron stake that tethered Buster, and led the snorting behemoth across the barnyard to his new piece of ground. The trimming would have to wait until tomorrow's daylight. He tentatively set the pin, probing for a rockless anchor. As he raised the sledge to drive it home, Buster's head swung around and caught him low on the right side. It only stung for a second, but then the enraged bull kept coming at him as he rolled on the ground trying to protect himself. The day faded and grew warmer, and his listless thoughts relapsed to the pleasant hours spent bird hunting with his friend....

Home Again

"The blue sky that now canopies the skyscraper where you hear the
phone bells and the typewriter keys that jangle your nerve-strings,
will furnish the blue skylight and a rainy day for you as you ride,
and studded with stars, will cover you when you and your
hobbyhorse need restful sleep at the journey's end."

From an essay entitled "Hobbies" included in *Snap Shots of Many Years,*
By Edward Russell Wilbur, 1929.

After S.D.'s untimely death as a result of being gored by the barnyard bull, the burden of running the "Great Farm"—as it was called in a local history book—was passed back to his father, Samuel, and S.D.'s son George. Sam was getting on in years, and George cared little for the demanding physical toil required of a New England farmer. Sam died a few years later and sister Jotie married Paul, who bought the farm, lock, stock and barrel. George was glad to be relieved of his family responsibilities, and he went off to make his lifework in business down in the valley. That was in 1899.

But George never lost his love for the ancient farmhouse, the surrounding land, and especially the bird hunting, which was as good as anywhere in the whole county. He cherished the carefree days he had spent afield with Paul and a fine chap, Horatio "Rashe" Bigelow, superintendent of the Norwich and Montville Street Railroad. Although Rashe later became well known and wrote about some interesting times hunting in eastern Connecticut in the towns of Groton, Voluntown and Bozrah, he never mentioned his Montville days in his books.

George had accomplished his goals. He owned an insurance agency and eventually becoming heavily and successfully involved in the business of politics. In fact, later he became High Sheriff of the county. However, as middle age languished he had become especially conscious of his reason for being. He had seen hate, greed, and deceit destroy lives. Mostly though, people were just too busy making money. For him, public recognition, success in business, status, wealth and empowerment had been important and, indeed, had been achieved over the years. One thing he learned is that some people do not change. Their lives are a series of daily quests of getting and spending, acquiring more worldly possessions that, he had thought, proved success. George knew there was more. He had tasted it in his early years on the farm.

And he missed keeping a bird dog or two. Paul had a setter, Mac, who George would take on rare occasions when time permitted. But life had become complicated and demanding, and Time was becoming a precious commodity. In addition, his dear wife of many years had grown ill with consumption and required ever-increasing care.

So it was with great anticipation when George was able to break away for an afternoon of bird hunting the coverts of his youth. In some years, pa'tridge were especially plentiful. Bobwhites and woodcock almost always provided a mixed bag. And how he loved Mac!

Along about this time, the state of Connecticut had begun to release pheasants. This really bothered him now, especially on Saturdays, when one had to contend with a steady swarm of hunters from the city who showed a blatant disregard for the land in general, especially stonewalls and bar ways. Why, just last month Paul told of a day when the bars in the Rogers pasture were left down by a hunter, and a cow and her calf got out. Both were killed instantly by a carload of pheasant hunters. Another time, he watched two hunters groundswatting ringnecks from the rumble seat of their machine. George thought these birds too beautiful to shoot. And now, it seemed, hunters would rush from cover to cover in their automobiles, pile out in great numbers, and unleash their repeaters on this new imported game bird from the Far East. "No hunting" postings became common. He believed it would take many years, if ever, for farmers to welcome this new breed of hunter back to their farms as in the old days.

On this fine but cold November day—it was the day before Thanksgiving—George started out in the late forenoon, whistled for Mac, and headed east. He swung around Comstock Hill and then came up over the top. The woodcock were gone now, but he moved a fair amount of pa'tridge. Mac bumped a few birds in between good, solid points, but George killed several in classic fashion within a short time as the day began to wane. He stopped to breathe heavily of the cold, pungent air and as he turned to look back at the distant purple hills to the east, he reflected on some of life's pleasures that were really important to him, simple things that had been gone from his life for too long—time to know the stark beauty of winter's landscape, white speckling of April's shadblow urging the sleepy land to wake up and give forth the green earth, the fresh smell of new-mown sweet hay in the swales, and hazy Indian summers when the leaves are down. He regretted his faithlessness of the long years.

His bag was full when it began snowing lightly. He detoured south to strike the road near the meetinghouse so that he could get back up to the farm before the weather worsened. Beckoning bells were tolling as he drew near the little country church, and he could see folks starting to arrive for the Thanksgiving eve service. He unloaded his Parker, buttoned up his jacket, and turned into the road. Suddenly his legs felt like jelly. The juggernaut of Time reversed, and he found himself being drawn back down a narrow path toward a big light, with a collage of his life's events waxing and waning in reverse. But why was Mac barking and licking his face? People came running and he knew the service was over...

Charlie & Dan

By Jon Bradford Chase

There are things that you can always count on back home, especially in November when "the frost is on the pumpkin and the corn is in the shock." When you walk across my barnyard just at dusk, when the crisp warmth of another Indian summer day ends and night envelopes the place in shadows 'neath of heel of Orion, there's always a woodcock or two that'll flitter through the twilight and into my old orchard if you'll just wait long enough. And if you've a mind to go out early, you can count on finding a pa'tridge in a certain place where an overgrown pasture slopes down to the bog at the edge of a grove of hickories (but I'll never tell anybody where that place it). And when the weather's just right, Charlie Parrish will take Old Dan for a hunt.

Charlie lives on that old place that's near the road to the old sawmill. It's a decrepit, falling-down place, the kind that city people are always trying to buy out from under you and make into a summer place. All in all, it was as fine a home a man could ask for, for him and his dog.

In his day, Old Dan (he was just Dan back then) had been the best bird dog in the whole county. He was all of a legend when he was really still but a pup. They used to say that he could find a bird a half-mile away and with the wind in the wrong direction. In those days, old Charlie was a good bit more able, too. They were one helluva a team.

When my father was living, he had plenty of stories about that dog and his master, and there's one I'll never forget. Charlie had Dan over on the Browning place (no, not where Doc Browning lives; this was his uncle's place, where Ike McAckern lives now). They were up on that hillside above the swamp. It's all woods now, but back then the old fields had been overgrown for about fifteen or twenty years and the brush and brambles held more woodcock that year than Carter had pills.

Well, they took a good bag that day, and Charlie was ready to head home when Dan went on point once more. Up flushed not one, but a pair of ruffed grouse. A chance to double, and at pa'tridge no less! Now of course that wasn't as rare in those days, but that was the first time it happened with Dan, that being his first autumn, in 1931. Charlie must have been a bit too excited when he fired his trusty old Lefever because the first bird dropped, but the second kept flying in that pathetic way they do, that jerking, crippled way when you've got lead in him but somehow not in the right place. You sometimes get a little sick inside, just for a second or two. But then you find it. And when you don't—well, that happens sometimes.

But Charlie! If there was one thing that could wrench his insides like nothing else, it was a hurt bird. Especially that day. He couldn't see where it dropped. They looked for it, him and Dan, until the man couldn't see anymore. And the thought of it gnawed at him, sickened him.

And the night got worse, for when he went out to milk his cows, the dog was gone. Dan would always follow Charlie around the barn and his master would play with him as he worked, sometimes even shooting a little of the good warm milk into the patient dog's waiting mouth. But he wasn't there tonight. Charlie stayed up late that night, and walked all around the pasture out back of the barn, blowing his whistle and calling Dan's name, but that dog was nowhere to be found. Now Charlie was concerned, but he was also getting pretty angry. Why, when he found that dog, he'd learn him not to run off!

When Charlie got up the next morning, he was so worked up his wife couldn't get him to eat any breakfast. Then he looked out the kitchen window and there was Dan, running 'round the yard in circles, chasing leaves in the wind. Charlie headed out to teach that damn dog a lesson he'd never forget. But as he went out the back door, something caught his eye and he looked down. Meanwhile the dog had bounded across the yard and jumped at his master in joy.

There on the back step was the lost pa'tridge.

Well, I tell you, that dog was known far and wide after that. More than a few men made Charlie offers that he would have been well to accept, with times getting bad and cash hard to come by. But there's no way that Charlie would ever have parted with Dan after that morning.

Dogs get old, and blind, and then their noses go. It's the hardest thing about having a dog. But men get old, too. And sometimes, a little strange. Oh, there are reasons. Charlie was never the same after the night that crazy fellow escaped from the state prison, bedded down in his barn for the night, and with a careless cigarette burned it to the ground. The following winter, Charlie's wife died. Charlie was never the same.

One day, in his fifteenth year, Old Dan died. By then he was blind, and could hardly even walk he had such bad arthritis, or whatever it is that dogs get. He just curled up, like he always did, at his master's feet and ceased to live.

Charlie, Old Charlie to us (or even Crazy Charlie), didn't take and bury him out back like he did all the other dogs he had had over the years. He had Old Dan stuffed, right on point with leg up and tail straight as an arrow, and kept him in the parlor next to the chair where his master would read at night. Of course, Charlie always used to read in the kitchen, feet on the stove, and his wife wouldn't allow him in the parlor at all, save for holidays. But then, she was dead now, too.

Old Dan stood in that corner, eternally on point, all year long. Except when Charlie took him hunting. Charlie's arthritis was bad and he'd just stand on the porch, having put the dog on the grass of few feet ahead of himself. And by and by twilight would come, and a woodcock or two would flitter through the dusk toward his orchard, which he could always count on happening if he waited long enough. And, of course, he waited, because the dog was on point and there just had to be a bird near.

If you'd happen by the place at twilight on an autumn evening, then, you'd see an old man shooting from his porch into the gathering darkness. You could count on it. There Charlie would be, standing in the moonlight 'neath the heel of Orion, both of them with their faithful dogs close by. And then Old Charlie would shuffle across the lawn and pick up the little brown bird that he'd hang up in the shed to season for a few days, and then maybe have on toast for breakfast. Then he'd put his gun away in its corner, and then he'd put old Dan away in his corner.

Sleigh Ride

> Announced by all the trumpets of the sky,
> Arrives the snow, and, driving o'er the fields,
> Seems nowhere to alight; the whited air
> Hides hills and woods, the river, and the heaven,
> And veils the farmhouse at the garden's end.
> The sled and traveler stopped, the courier's feet
> Delayed, all friends shut out, the housemates sit
> Around the radiant fireplace, enclosed
> In a tumultuous privacy of storm...

> From "Snowstorm"
> Ralph Waldo Emerson, 1803-1882

The life of this turn-of-the-twentieth-century farmer was not without anxiety, however far-removed from stresses of more modern times. But he had to support his young family, and winter's vagaries sometimes tested the mettle of this stalwart and enterprising young man. Although pretty much self-sufficient, he was overdue to fetch a few necessary items to sustain his family through the remaining winter months. A few hardware supplies and hinges to repair the barn door had waited far too long and were badly needed.

Several after-Christmas snows were fairly well packed and frozen to road surfaces that had been impassible till now. After finishing the early afternoon chores, he hitched up Beauty to the one-horse sleigh and prepared for the seven-mile journey to the city. It was raw and blowing when he left, and the smell of more snow filled the air. Not the best day to make the trip, he mused, but the old work horse trotted ever onward without hesitation over the familiar road down through the hollow. He just held the reins and thought about his little nagging problems that he never shared with anybody.

Surveying his land as he crossed the farm boundary, he surmised that life had been good to him. His three girls were enriching themselves with a good education and were starting to embrace promising careers that caused his wife Jotie and him to be proud. They loved the land too, but they were girls and would never carry on with farming. No matter, there would be grandchildren and hopefully a grandson to follow in his footsteps someday.

His reverie focused on the fall season just past. The two weeks spent with Rhode Island hunters Whitman and Sweet were memories he would never forget, especially the double on pa'tridge that Sweet managed with his 16-gauge CE grade LeFever. The dogs had settled down some from the previous fall, birds were plentiful, and Jotie prepared some delicious meals with the game the hunters brought back, especially woodcock, and that takes some doin'. The family was still eating the fruits of their labor—if you could call bird hunting work—in January. God, at times he felt so guilty partaking of all that pleasure—away from his chores.

When he turned left toward Norwich at the junction of Fitch Hill and the turnpike, the road was packed hard and icy from heavy use. Mostly sleighs ruled the route, but a few automobiles used the turnpike, the one visible today was stuck by the roadside. Beauty pulled his sleigh effortlessly, and they soon approached the city in record time.

Ere long, destination reached and provisions purchased, he headed back into what had now become an ominous, squalling mid-afternoon snowstorm. He felt better though, as scudding clouds finally whisked away to be replaced by luminous pink and orange glows on the western horizon. The sudden stillness of the clearing imparted a wholesome, fresh smell to the newly cleansed land. Rounding the big curve on Fitch Hill, he felt so good that he removed the jug of hard cider from its sack on the floor that Prentice Williams, his hired hand, had mistakenly left there. He drank heartily and heavily of the fiery potion, though he rarely imbibed.

It was not long before a booming tenor voice could be heard belting out "Rock of Ages" down through the "holler," as a neighbor, the local raconteur, gleefully recalled on one of his many story-telling occasions. He viewed his sprawling hilltop farm as he passed the old meetinghouse with 1722 over the front door. Life seemed good.

The alien resonance of trotting hooves on the frozen road scared up a pa'tridge in the little copse of cedars just beyond the two-room schoolhouse. He knew the brood. He and Whitman had taken a few birds from it back in early November.

The last half-mile went a little faster as Beauty stepped more sprightly in anticipation of home and the confines of her steamy stall. All was well, and the snowy landscape was enveloped by cheery bustle and glowing warmth of the old farmhouse kitchen.

Noteworthy Authors, Artists of the Uplands

Frank Forester's Nomenclature

I would venture a guess that not too many readers of contemporary sporting literature recognize the name Henry William Herbert. A British ex-patriot of Welsh royal blood, he was one of the most popular and prolific American sporting writers of the nineteenth century, having emigrated to the U.S. in 1831. He was much better known by his pseudonym, Frank Forester. A gentleman and a highly accomplished scholar who taught Greek in New York City, his early life was devoted to writing historical novels. He is known today, however, as the father of sporting literature.

In 1845, at age thirty-eight, his first sporting book appeared entitled *The Warwick Woodlands,* which was based on his gunning activities around Warwick, New York (a few miles northwest of New York City). Twelve more hunting and/or fishing titles appeared in rapid succession over the next several years; some were reprinted by the renowned Derrydale Press.

In the two-volume *Field Sports of the United States and British Provinces of North America,* first published in London in 1848, Forester deeply regrets summer woodcock shooting as being injurious to the native population, which, if shot out, would break the cycle of birds returning year after year to their birthing grounds. Obviously, he was right, but not until 1918 was summer woodcock shooting outlawed.

In thumbing through the Appendix of my first edition of *Field Sports,* Vol. II, I came across some interesting sporting nomenclature

that has been lost to callous misuse and/or the ever-evolving English language. Following is his partial list:
As to a single hatching of—

Turkeys	a *brood*	Grouse*	a *brood* (before they can fly)
Pheasants*	a *nide*	Grouse**	a *pack* (after)
Partridges*	a *covey*	Quail	a *bevy* (never a covey)
Woodcock	a *brood*	Ruffed Grouse	a covey
Snipe	a *brood*		

* Pheasants and Partridges were unknown in America
** Pinnated Grouse

As to large flocks of wildfowl—

Swans	a *whiteness*	Bitterns	a *sege*
Geese	a *gaggle*	Herons	a *sege*
Brant	a *gang*	Larks	an *exaltation*
Duck	a *team*		

(smaller number—a *plump*)

Widgeon	a *company* (or *trip*)
Teal	a *flock*
Snipe	a *whisp*
Plovers	a *flock* (also all shore birds)

As to several united hatchings of—

Grouse	a *pack*
Partridge	"
Quail	"

Further, two Grouse, Pheasants, Quail, are a *brace,* three are a *lease.* Two Woodcock, Snipe, Wildfowl, etc. are a *couple,* three are *a couple and a half.*

Two Pointers, Setters, Spaniels, Greyhounds, Terriers are a *brace;* three are a *lease.*

All other breeds are referred to in actual numbers.

To make Pointers or Setters stand ("whoa" today)	*toho!*
To make Pointers or Setters drop to shot	*charge!*
To make Pointers or Setters come behind	*heel!*
To make Pointers or Setters careful	*steady!*
To make Pointers or Setters rise from the charge	*hold up*
To make Pointers or Setters hunt for killed game	*seek dead!*
when found	*fetch!*

It is interesting to note that I use the anachronistic *charge* to make my setters lie down. I always presumed that the command meant for the dog to lie down while the fowling piece was being "charged." Evidently the command was also given after the flush for safety reasons. Hunters (some) and especially field trailers today would use "whoa" for steadiness after the flush and shot.

Forester's reference to larks being a game bird seems unusual. However, to this day they are considered to be tasty morsels in Italy and other countries.

Further, a male horse is never a stud, a reference he calls "vulgar squeamishness and "sheer nonsense." A *collection* of horses is a stud.

Forester's list goes on and on, and he states that to apply the wrong terms is a "bad sporting blunder."

He ends with an amusing clarification by calling the females "of a Dog, a *bitch*, not a *slut,* the use of the latter being far more objectionable…."

Men react differently to despondency over life's woes. As a result of his failed second marriage, he took his own life in 1858 at age fifty-one.

George Bird Evans, Sportsman, Gentleman

George Bird Evans was one of the all-time great upland writers. A prolific producer of prose, this famous sporting writer and gentleman wrote a small library of sporting books for the Amwell Press and his own, Old Hemlock Press. His life was a consummate love affair with upland sporting pursuits. In my humble opinion, no other upland writer achieved as much fame and respect during the last half of the 20ᵗʰ century, as did Evans. And no man on earth was more of a friend to ruffed grouse than George Bird Evans.

The Evanses forsook the vagaries of city living after George served as a Naval officer during World War II. George and his wife, Kay, lived a fairy tale life in the remote hills fifty miles north of the Canaan (pronounced Ka-nane') Valley of West Virginia, he as a writer/shooter, she as the faithful companion—she shared authorship with her husband on early mystery novels—who experienced and lived the sporting life. Kay shoots with a camera.

One mark of this great sporting writer and human being was his empathy for grouse and woodcock. A theme in some of his earlier books is that extended hunting seasons for grouse—for longer recreational enjoyment, as state officials would say—caused a dramatic reduction of grouse populations in West Virginia. He minced no words in his criticism of the West Virginia Dept. of Natural Resources.

Evans was equally known for his Old Hemlock line of English setters, known for their attractive conformation. The classic Old Hemlock strain is probably the most beautiful, along with the Ryman, among dual type English setters.

The sportsman can gain a broad education—I know I did—on earlier writers and shooters from the books that Evans' edited, namely *The Bird Dog Book, The Ruffed Grouse Book, The Woodcock Book, Men Who Shot,* and *George Bird Evans Introduces.* They are among some of my most treasured sporting books.

My wife and I enjoyed visiting Old Hemlock (also the name of their 18ᵗʰ century stone farmhouse) several years ago when we picked up an O.H. puppy, O.H. Best, sired by O.H. Quest. (Quest was Evans' personal gundog.) That little squiggling white belton puppy became part of our lives at that moment, and in time so did all the twenty some-odd sporting books that the Evanses produced over the years.

The Evanses had their own ideas with respect to naming puppies. They frowned on human names for their own setters, and when I proposed "Bess" for the name of my puppy, Kay immediately countered with "Best." And so Bess became Best, at least on her papers (but we always called her Bess).

Evans also distained the use of common nicknames for game birds, such as the commonly used "timberdoodle" for woodcock and "partridge" or "pat" for grouse. The former is demeaning and the latter two are misnomers. A grouse is a grouse, not a partridge (as in Hungarian partridge). Pay attention, New Englanders!

It was truly a portentous occasion, meeting the Evanses, O.H. Quest and Belton—about whom he so frequently wrote—and seeing and handling the famous Purdey. How he came to get it is the subject of his early book, *Recollections of a Shooting Guest*, an out-of-print collector's prize. It was only published in a limited edition and is probably the most valuable of all his books.

We talked about grouse populations and why famed biologist Gordon Gullion and others still hadn't discovered all the right reasons for cycles—biologists still haven't got a complete handle on it, the way I see it. Is covert fragmentation and maturing habitat the main cause for the long-term downward trend? How about protected predators such as hawks and owls, and ground critters such as skunks, and egg-sucking possums? Are they part of the equation?

Evans' prolific sentience of the undemanding earth reflected the solitude of his country, and I learned, back then, that there is indeed other turf to love other than my New England.

I enjoyed corresponding with the Evanses over the years. When I called on the phone, I always talked with Kay, not George. It appeared that she was very protective of George's time. She was always interested in my puppy's progress. As with many other fans, I'm sure, Kay and I became frequent correspondents. When George passed, I couldn't bring myself to intrude on Kay's privacy with verbal condolences until several weeks later with a long penned note.

Whenever I read the following poem by Don Titus, I am reminded of Evans and how a "thinking" bird might feel about falling to Evans' gun...

O, Hunter, when you come at last
And start me from some covert
place
And I am brought to ground
My body thrashing in the sorrow-

ing leaves,
Hold me in your hands
until I yield,
Praise me as a trophy fit
the hunt
And carry me home
in the great pocket of your coat.

Hilly

In early June of 1997 I learned of the death of Gene Hill, having received a copy of the lead story on the sports page of the *Bangor Daily News*—notice I said *lead story*, meaning it would have been improbable for this to appear in almost any local newspaper in such a prominent position—written by sportsman/artist/writer Tom Hennessey. One must realize that the *Bangor Daily News* is very well known for its coverage of hunting and fishing, primarily because publisher Rick Warren is/was a salmon camp owner in New Brunswick and a distinguished sportsman. Anyway, this lengthy commentary on Hill was a tribute to Hennessey's recently departed friend, one of the greats of sporting literature and probably the most loved writer of his generation. "Hilly," as he was known to his friends, was sixty-nine when he died, May 31. He had fought the valiant battle with cancer for several years.

Those who did not know him asked what Hill was really like in real life. A *poseur*? Never! Someone answered the question like this: "He was just like the little essays he wrote—unassuming and down-to-earth. My library is full of Hill's stuff, several books of which are illustrated by Hennessey. Hill's style has been described as self-deprecated, dry humor. He was the kind of writer who was everybody's favorite, never evoking controversy. Most sportsmen who have hunted of fished for more than a few years are familiar with Hill's well known columns "Mostly Tailfeathers" in *Sports Afield* and, more recently, "Hill Country" appearing in *Field & Stream*. Oddly, the terms "sporting" and "outdoor writer" were appellations he despised.

From rural New Jersey origins, his refined character and confidence synthesized well with his farm-boy shyness. Harvard educated, he found early in his professional career that the advertising field was not for him. It has been pronounced that Hill was one of the top essayists of his generation. His short story, "One," appearing in *Tears & Laughter,* is the best of its kind. Another favorite is "Pepper," also included in this title.

Hill generally shot 12 or 16 gauge shotguns, and most often used his Woodward or Beretta hi-grades. For smaller flying game, he often chose the 28, preferring the latter to the 20, which he described as "bitey." (I suspect he used this adjective to describe recoil of the heavier than 7/8-ounce loads for which the 20 is best suited.) He always claimed to be an average shot. The truth is that he was a formidable opponent on the trap and skeet fields.

He had a fetish for unusual hats as pictured in *Beyond Hill Country.* One, a monstrous affair with a broad brim, is reminiscent of Hoss Cartright's chapeau as seen in the television series, *Bonanza.*

First inspired by Ernie Schweibert's planned tribute—which he never delivered because his plane was late coming in from Europe—at Hill's commemorative wake, Amwell Press publisher Jim Rikhoff and Monica Sullivan (his right hand at Amwell), conceived a memorial to his friend, written by his friends, entitled *Beyond Hill Country... Gene Hill Remembered.* In addition to the fine writing of the many contributors—Schweibert, Rikhoff, Hennessey, Harry Tennison, Lamar Underwood, Jerry Warrington, David Petzal,, Jack Samson, Bob Brister and others—this book will become a collector's item in the limited edition. The subject matter, as you would suspect, is comprised of memories of Gene Hill fishing for trout and salmon and gunning for waterfowl, upland game and other humorous sketches of the man that everybody loved.

One essay that I cherish, "Voices from Woodcock Country," appeared in *The Whispering Wings of Autumn,* a joint effort with Steve Smith. It describes Hill's youthful fascination with old-time setters and the post-gunners of the Golden Age of shotgunning who owned them, the men who shot Bakers, LeFevers, Remingtons, Parkers, Smiths and Foxes. Someday he yearned to own a fine setter and one of the old American doubles like they shot. He revered the old timers' conversations around the pot-bellied stove of the local general store. Hill eventually acquired the dogs and the guns, but he could not prove to his mentors that he was like them now because they had long since passed on. He could only hope that the youth of today would look to him and be held in awe for those same possessions.

"That Hilly there, him and that Ben dog is about as good a pair
as you'll find anywhere when it comes to woodcock."

I believe he succeeded in passing on this legacy—and many more in the surfeit of fine literature he left to future generations of sportsmen.

Dave Petzal wrote an outstanding eulogy to Hill that first appeared in the December 1999 issue of Field & Stream. It also appeared as the last chapter in *Beyond Hill Country*. A few paragraphs from that tribute follow:

"From the way he spoke and wrote about himself, you'd think he was a hopeless bumbler, but the opposite was true. He had a room full of silver that he'd won with a gun. He was earnest about being good at what he did, no matter what it was. And with most things, he was much better than good.

He smiled continually; the smile etched furrows in his face that you could plant corn in. I think he smiled because he knew that we don't get a lot of time on earth, and that it is a damned fine place, despite our efforts to wreck it, and anyone who does not smile simply because he is alive is a fool.

So he wrote about the things that he loved, for nearly three decades, and then, of course, he died. A few weeks later, his friends and family gathered to celebrate his life—he did not want us to mourn his death. It was the most beautiful day of the summer. The crowd ranged from children through his friends of five decades, and there was a piper there, because he loved the wild music of the bagpipe.

At the end of the day, as the long summer evening deepened toward darkness, his friends gave three cheers for his life and what he had meant to them. Then the piper played 'Amazing Grace,' and as the last notes skirled up to the stars, people cried, because they would never see Gene Hill again."

Horatio Bigelow, Mystery Unveiled: from a Yankee's Perspective

> Time, like an ever-rolling stream,
> Bears all its sons away;
> They fly forgotten, as a dream
> Dies at the opening day.
>
> Isaac Watts, 1719

Pictured from left to right are: *Gunnerman*, 1939 (limited to 950 copies); the seldom-seen *Flying Feathers*, 1937; *Gunnerman's Gold*, 1943 (limited to 1000 copies, this being a low-numbered leather variant in its dust jacket); the rare *Scatter-Gun Sketches*, 1922, published by William C. Hazelton. The renowned Derrydale Press, elite publisher of sporting books during the late 1920s to the early1940s, published *Gunnerman*.

Horatio Bigelow was one of the most celebrated sporting writers in the first half of the 20th century. He wrote four books between 1922 and 1943. Unfortunately, not many sportsmen of the current generation are familiar with his prose, although his books are very collectible—seemingly an oxymoron. A possible explanation is that two of his books were produced in limited editions of 1000 or fewer, and two were issued in very small numbers. I am not aware of any reprints. Jim Casada, editor of the 1994 *The Best of Horatio Bigelow*, recently indicated that this anthology is in considerable demand.

Who was this man, Horatio Bigelow? A kind and loving 6-foot 1-inch patrician, he became a highly regarded writer of hunting prose in his day. Until now, his life has been a mystery, and biographical information has been scarce. Is he forgotten? Hardly! After a careful reading of his books and researching local sources of information, I had obtained bits and pieces of his life. Finally, after repeated efforts Googling the author's name on the Internet, I stumbled upon the November, 2008 newsletter issued by the St. Paul's Episcopal Church in Richmond, Virginia, in which was mentioned that Mr. & Mrs. Horatio Bigelow were celebrating a wedding anniversary. Incredibly, this Horatio Bigelow (Rick) turned out to be a grandson of the author. Rick and his wife, Mary Holly, then referred me to Rick's cousin, John M. Hudgins, Jr., the eldest grandson, who lives in Salem, Virginia. Thanks largely to John, this article secures for posterity the missing links in Bigelow's life. Also, I will recite some early sporting experiences of this widely-known scribe of his day that were depicted in his books.

Horatio Bigelow was born January 12, 1877 into a wealthy family in Cambridge, Massachusetts. His father, Albert Smith Bigelow, was a copper magnate who made millions in mine speculations. In the Adirondack Museum in Blue Mountain, New York, there is a large chunk of copper from the Bigelow Mine, located in upstate New York.

In his youth, "Rashe," a child-applied nickname, began his formal shooting education with a couple of instructors on the South Shore (below Boston) around Hingham that were probably chosen by his father. From them he learned gun safety, how to shoot, and then progressed to hunting live shore-birds—sora rail, black-bellied plover, winter and summer yellowlegs, Jack Curlew, Eskimo curlew, robin snipe and "peeps." He got a taste of woodcock and "partridge" (properly, ruffed grouse) followed by ducks, which his W&C Scott, speaking animately in the first person (*Gunnerman*), claimed were his owner's favorite targets. My perception is that Bigelow was more proficient at sustained or swing-through shooting (ducks and geese) as opposed to snap shooting on upland birds. At least one barrel of the Scott was full-choked, so it's no wonder that he seemed to be more successful gunning more distant waterfowl. When partridge and woodcock hunting in eastern Connecticut in the early 1900s, he writes humorously of many misses of the former, not unusual by any standard.

Bigelow attended prestigious Milton Academy—the popular writer Dr. John C. Phillips was a classmate—and graduated Harvard in 1899. He then married Mary (May) Riese, affectionately known as "Wiffie," (like "Biffie") on August 3, 1899. *Gunnerman* is dedicated "to Wiffie, the ever patient listener to these tales," and *Gunnerman's Gold* is dedicated "To M.R.B., the 'home camp' listener to these tales…"

After a brief stint in Seattle working for the Seattle-Tacoma Interurban Railway—his son, Horatio Bigelow, Jr. ("Ray," see below) was born at this time—where he achieved the position of assistant to the chief of construction, his employment search took him back East to a job as superintendent of the Norwich (Connecticut) and the Montville Street (trolley) Railway Companies from about 1901 to approximately 1910. There were two other sons born during this period: John Ripley (Rip) and Samuel (Sam). All three sons are given incidental mention in Bigelow's books. Sam and Ray were avid hunters; Rip was not. There were also two daughters, Nancy Bigelow Hudgins (John's mother) of Washington, D.C. and later McLean, Virginia and Mollie Bigelow Taylor of New Jersey.

From my copy of "Forty Years After," a rare, well-written 13-page chronicle of Bigelow's 40th reunion from Harvard, used as a Christmas greeting to Eugene Connett, publisher of the renown Derrydale Press, I learned that he had two siblings: Albert Francis Bigelow, an attorney, born 10/4/1880 in Brookline, Mass. and another brother who was "Overseer" at Harvard, a member of the Massachusetts Legislature and chairman of the Ways and Means Committee. He was Lieutenant Colonel William DeFord Bigelow ("Duff"), subject of the last chapter in *Gunnerman's Gold*, who died in 1942 at 64. This "Christmas Card" confirmed what I thought previously to be fact: Bigelow lived and worked in New London County, Connecticut for over fifteen years. John Hudgins recalls that his grandfather had a "great time" at his reunion and mentions the gift of champagne received from J. P. Morgan, class of 1889.

In the archives of my mother's family I found an Annual Catalogue of the Norwich Free Academy (NFA), 1916-1917. In it is listed the Lower Middle (sophomore) Class of 1919, in which, under Classical

Course, the name Horatio Bigelow appears. He is not listed among the graduates in the Class of 1919. This was Horatio's first-born son, "Ray." It is clear that he did not complete his secondary education at NFA (my alma mater) because of his family's move to Charleston in 1917. Discovered several years ago, this was my first clue leading to my interest in the Bigelow saga. *Scatter-Gun Sketches*, Bigelow's first book, is filled with references to local families—Abel, Austin, Church, Dennison, Kinne—with whom Horatio bird-hunted in outlying towns surrounding Norwich. Of these companions, Willis Austin and possibly Will Church became life-long correspondents.

On page 88 of *Flying Feathers*, dedicated to his daughter Nancy Bigelow Hudgins, Bigelow wrote in "Just Yesterday": "My job as Superintendent of the Norwich and the Montville Street Railways did not allow much time off..." (This is the only "Yankee" chapter in *Flying Feathers*). The 1901 Norwich City Directory lists Horatio Bigelow residing at 42 Broad Street—a few blocks from NFA—as secretary and superintendent of the Norwich Street Railway Co. and superintendent of the Montville Street Railway Co.

Bigelow lived at 42 Broad Street, Norwich for over 10 years

The 1905 edition lists him as superintendent of the Consolidated Railway Co., 229 Main St, Norwich. By 1912, he is still listed at the same Broad Street address (see photo) but with no occupation. In May of 1910, under Montville News of a local (now defunct) newspaper, appeared the following: "Horatio Bigelow of the Bigelow-Harriman Construction Co. stated yesterday that he hoped to be able to have the big paper mill in Uncasville—part of Montville and now home of the Mohegan Sun Casino—running by Sept. 1."

While superintendent of the Norwich and Montville Street Railways, Bigelow memorialized his bird hunting experiences in Bozrah, Voluntown and Groton, Connecticut—the latter now known as the Submarine Capital of the World—in *Scatter-Gun Sketches* (especially) and *Flying Feathers*. From the very first page of the former tome, it becomes clear that Bigelow is a Boston Brahmin when he refers to his chauffeur, Thompson, as the driver of his "machine" to and from the woodcock and partridge coverts in eastern Connecticut. I went bug-eyed reading about his upland hunts on "Bashan" (Bashon) Hill in Bozrah (see photo) and around the shores of Gardner Lake with Will Church, Willis Austin and Elmer Abel. All are within a few miles of coverts I hunt. On a lunch break, Bigelow failed to lure a brookie with a fishing line from a well on the Abel farm while an old gentleman surreptitiously looked on through a window of a nearby cabin.

Bigelow hunted on the surrounding lands of the Abel Homestead
on Bashon Hill, Bozrah

Embarrassed at being discovered, Bigelow quickly left the scene and rejoined his companions. (Evidentially, a trout placed in the family well kept it clear of falling insects.) There is also some nebulous hearsay that he hunted with my grandfather at our family farm and surrounding coverts here on Raymond Hill in Montville. I was very young at the time, but I recall Gramp telling me about the time, long ago, when he hunted with Mr.—, "who later wrote a book about bird hunting." This happening, along with my upland-focused collection of nearly 400 books, further piqued my interest in Bigelow. My property and its surrounding farms were known as some of the best bird-hunting areas in eastern Connecticut around the turn of the twentieth century.

"Just Yesterday" is a little jewel. In the "fastnesses" (a secure or fortified place, i.e. meager means of transportation) of Voluntown, fifteen miles northeast of Norwich, Bigelow hunted with "Ord" Kinne, who Bigelow claimed was the greatest grouse shot that he had ever seen. While the two were hunting, Kinne shot three of four grouse in the air at the same time, a triple no less on the trickiest of game birds with his Marlin pump. Bigelow wrote that Kinne claimed to have killed nine grouse in ten shots in the cedars surrounding Beach Pond the day before. An expert trap shooter from New York was invited for a two-day holiday to be Kinne's grouse-shooting guest. Kinne shot twenty-five grouse; the guest bagged two.

Bigelow shot the 12 gauge W&C Scott—a Christmas gift from his father when he was fourteen—for about thirty years. It is interesting to note, but not surprising, that its drop at heel was 3⅛ inches, a common dimension—many shotguns had drops in excess of three inches during this era. In a letter to an inquirer who was seeking advice on shooting subjects, he asserted that his friends, Nash Buckingham and Harold Sheldon, were better qualified to make recommendations regarding these matters. In "Hits and Misses" (*Gunnerman*), Bigelow states that all the market hunters used guns with stocks shaped like a "dog's hind leg," and the conviction was that all the shooters of the Golden Age needed to do was bring the gun up and put the bird at the end of the barrels. At some point he adopted the new "religion" (putting one's head down on a straighter stock) and purchased a light 12-gauge double—forsaking his beloved Scott, which he sold eventually—with a 2½-inch drop. He recommended a 12-gauge gun for all shooting to the readers of this chapter. Bigelow also purchased a Remington "automatic," (semiautomatic) presumably for wildfowl gunning.

As to Bigelow's canine hunting companions, it is clear from the reading of his books that he was a setter man through and through, although he did own at least one springer spaniel. This seems contrary to Mr. Casada's Introduction to *The Best of Horatio Bigelow* when he states that Bigelow favored pointers. Magazine articles by Bigelow may have indicated a predilection towards English pointers if the subject was field trials—I have not seen them.

There is no indication that he owned hunting dogs while living in Connecticut. On his many hunting excursions with Will Church in his beloved "Bozry," "Count," Church's setter, was the enabler. After Bigelow's move south, he owned, perhaps among others, English setters Belle, Daisy, Katie and Beau, the latter sired by the national champion, Sport's Peerless Pride.

My impression from his books is that Bigelow headed to the southlands in 1917 for one reason, that being sporting opportunities; finding a job seemed almost secondary. He had experienced the South's exceptional sport by virtue of his memberships in various hunting clubs long before he moved there. However, trouble was brewing with the family fortune.

Three years prior to Bigelow's move south, his father became embroiled in a massive lawsuit against his former business partner involving ownership of the copper mines. The result was a loss of between $2 and $4 million. The lawsuit bogged down for a period of several years, but in the end the $1 million salvaged was placed in a third generation trust. Upon the elder Bigelow's death in 1928, Horatio and his two brothers started to realize income from the estate trust.

In 1917 he acquired a plantation in Charleston, South Carolina where he became a farmer for profit and raised livestock. These ventures were unsuccessful and he lost money. The old W&C Scott was pawned out of necessity. But when his father died, he came into a "strong" inheritance. This prompted his move to Palmyra, Virginia where, in 1934, he purchased Glen Burnie, whose main section was built in 1817 by a nephew of Thomas Jefferson. The sale was facilitated by John (Jack) Hudgins, alias "The Squire," Bigelow's son-in-law who was engaged in real estate at that time. Both were avid quail hunters and spent many memorable days in the field together. After taking advantage of "stimulus" from Roosevelt's "New Deal," the old mansion was transformed to its former glory, along with modern improvements.

Bigelow was chairman of the local Red Cross during World War II, whose purpose was to help rural families with sons serving in the military. Everett Black ("Partner"), a friend and local bird hunter, also hunted quail extensively with Bigelow during this period.

I found it interesting that at some point in Bigelow's life, he became "owner" of four pieces of permanent art—tattoos! John Hudgins recalls that at least one was a duck-hunting scene. Perhaps the others were hunting scenes also.

Bigelow remained at Glen Burnie for fifteen years where he enjoyed living the role of a country squire until his death in December of 1949 at age seventy-one. He was buried just south of Palmyra on Route 15 in the Baptist church graveyard. Mary (Wiffee), who sold Glen Burnie after Horatio's death, lived another twelve years and is buried alongside her husband.

While I would place Bigelow a notch below Nash Buckingham, the *crème de la crème* of the upland/waterfowl purveyors, there is no doubt that he properly belongs to a pantheon of eminent early to mid-twentieth century sporting writers—Havilah Babcock, Corey Ford, Ray Holland, John C. Phillips, Archibald Rutledge, Harold Sheldon, Burton Spiller, Ben Ames Williams and my own favorite writer of dog stories, John Taintor Foote. Although we know almost everything about these well-known writers, with the possible exception of Foote, Bigelow now "joins" this coterie of famous sporting writers, in that his biography is now reasonably complete.

This photo taken of Horatio Bigelow in 1933
at age 56

If Only They Had Lived...

I often wonder what might have been accomplished by two skilled individuals in their particular fields of endeavor had they fulfilled normal life spans. The stories of two important 20th century sporting personalities need to be acknowledged. As important as they were in their time, George Browne, wildlife artist, and Vereen Bell, novelist and writer of bird dog stories, are largely forgotten today, particularly by sportsmen and purveyors of wildlife art and sporting literature.

Several years ago, I discovered the oil paintings of George Browne (1918-1958).

From what little of his work I have seen, he strikes me, and cognoscenti of fine art, as a seldom-rivaled talent in the genre of wildlife painting. A scion of a wealthy family and son of the famous artist, sportsman, explorer, and mountaineer Belmore Browne, he is relatively unknown in art circles today. His paintings are not common, in fact, in a 1988-published monograph, *Mountain Man*, by Robert Bates (Amwell Press), on the life of his father, no incidental mention is made of George's talent.

Because of his short life and limited output, only a few public exhibits exist of his work; all the rest of his estimated 200 oils reside in the hands of private collectors. And they don't come up for sale often. Tom Davis, writing for *Sporting Classics* in the November/December 1993 issue, noted as a byline to his article: "George Browne,"—"the greatest wildlife artist that most people never heard of."

Had not a tragic accident ended his life at age 39, there is a strong possibility that his name would be a household word among sportsmen today. He was that good.

Painting birds—and especially upland birds in the later years of his life after he moved to northwestern Connecticut—was George's admitted forte. Unlike his father's contemporary, Carl Rungius, who was acclaimed for his big game animals with majestic panoramas, he felt a little insecure with his backdrops. That said, George is credited with being the first artist to successfully combine the accurate portrayal of *birds* with an equally detailed landscape that heretofore had been only a suggestion, *à la* Audubon. This was a major leap forward for the genre. My sense is that his backgrounds present an ethereal quality not often seen in later artists' work.

Blind is one eye as a result of an unfortunate childhood accident and possibly dyslexic, Brown overcame many early life adversities, in part due to his mentor father, who encouraged his artistic acumen at a very early age. In fact, Belmore approved George's wish to quit school to pursue an art education.

I viewed my first Browne oil, *Autumn Ruffed Grouse,* in an extensive private collection of A. L. Ripley watercolors and admittedly, it left me with a nondescript perception of the artist's work. But then the owner offered two snapshots of Browne waterfowl paintings that seemed to come alive in my hands.

Sporting Classics released a limited edition print of 500 copies, *Fields of Gold,* in 1993. To my knowledge, no other prints have ever been published. Browne, having done only a little calendar art, disdained illustration.

A joint publishing effort of Wild Wings, Inc. and the *Sporting Heritage Collection* to produce a book on Browne, among others, evidently never materialized. Finally, in a 2004-released book published by Warwick Publishing, Toronto, John Ordeman and Michael Schreiber, tell the story of *George and Belmore Browne, Artists of the North American Wilderness.*

Sam Webb, the famous sportsman, invited Browne and a group of conservation-minded friends to Webb's opulent Adirondack retreat for a meeting and other social pleasures. There, pistol shooting wind-blown balloons on a frozen lake from a porch, a misfire from the pistol of an inexperienced shooter punctured Brown's windpipe and the horrified onlookers watched him slowly die.

Some older members may recall reading in the more popular magazines of the day (late 1930s and early 1940s)—*Collier's, Saturday Evening Post* and *Liberty*—the superb fiction of Vereen Bell, a scion of southern aristocracy. His hunting and fishing articles appeared regularly in *Outdoor Life* and *Field & Stream.*

After graduating from Davidson College in 1932, a short but prolific writing career followed. Serving in World War II as a naval officer, Bell, of Cairo, Georgia was killed during the Second Battle of the Philippine Sea at age thirty-three.

In addition to his fiction and hunting and fishing articles in the above magazines, he wrote three books—all appeared as cheap paperback editions—that were well received, in fact, they achieved best-seller status. Truthfully, I had never heard of Vereen Bell.

In 2000, Wilderness Adventures Press re-published *Brag Dog and Other Stories,* a beautiful hardcopy edition encompassing all his sporting fiction. This originally appeared as a posthumous Armed Services edition. Most of the short stories in *Brag Dog* involve field trialing in the South and on the Canadian prairies. I can describe in one word my reaction to *Brag Dog*—awesome!

Marguerite Kirmse—arguably the greatest dog artist of the last century—was chosen to illustrate the chapter marquees for *Brag Dog.* Known for her illustrations in *Lassie Come Home* (who, as a child doesn't remember this tearjerker) and two Derrydale monographs, *Marguerite Kirmse's Dogs* and *Dogs in the Field,* she also illustrated many of Rudyard Kipling's novels.

Probably Bell's greatest claim to fame was his novel *Swamp Water.* Set in the Okefenokee Swamp, this widely popular novel was a best seller in 1941 and made him a wealthy man. Darryl Zanuck produced a movie of this thrilling adventure.

Vereen Bell's prodigious ability as a writer has been obscured by time. That he would have become one of the great sporting scribes of twentieth century is almost not conjectural. Had he lived to maturity and continued to write in his chosen field of endeavor, I believe he would be mentioned in the same breath as the great sporting writers of the 20th century, Buckingham, Babcock, Spiller, Sheldon, etc. His accurate recording of the Negro dialect was perceptive, but it was his ability to spin a yarn that kept me glued to the fiction of this talented writer of yesteryear.

Consummate Lab Lover

Robert F. Jones was a popular writer of upland prose who caught my attention. In one of his last books, *The Hunter in My Heart*, Jones' essays—many of which appeared in his "The Dawn Patrol" column of *Shooting Sportsman* magazine—cover many subjects related to bird hunting.

In a short essay also entitled "The Hunter in My Heart," Jones pledged not to shoot woodcock, his favorite game bird, because of his love for this species—its physical appearance, habits, and its declining numbers. When this piece first appeared in magazine form, the reader response was quite negative, as I recall. Those responding wouldn't be willing to make the sacrifice. I suspect the Jones has relented from his pledge somewhat, not because of the readership's criticism, but because of the instinctive hunter in his heart—the itch to pull the trigger on a flushed bird he has sworn off.

I know exactly where Jones is coming from. It has something to do with age and a lifetime of killing.

Declining numbers of the American woodcock are well-accompanied by a slower beating drum year after year. I, like Jones, considered shooting less (or not at all) at this grand game bird from time to time. My thoughts: Just work the dogs and fire blanks when the birds flush or hunt some other wild bird instead, like grouse. Wrong! Since grouse have virtually vanished from my coverts and practically so throughout my state, I will reluctantly look to pen-raised pheasants as my principle pursuit of flying game and take reasonable numbers of woodcock and the occasional grouse in and out of state—mostly the latter. That seems reasonable.

Jones prefers hunting with Labrador retrievers even though he appears to favor upland birds over waterfowl. He asserts that the non-pointing breeds offer more challenge when game is near, that is, the location of the flush is not as precise as with a pointing dog. (How about a *point* thirty-feet away from the bird?—that can be maddening!) He admits that the opportunities are less with flushing breeds but claims his two Labs flush to the gun, offering the opportunity for going away shots. Nice; I've never heard of that.

Jones is pessimistic about the future of wild bird hunting as a result of the human population explosion, expressed in "Through the Glass, Darkly"—

"The enclosure of common lands (i.e. the posting of America) compelled us through the last decades of the second millennium to rely more on 'shooting preserves' to find our sport. Most of these private, club-like game parks are pleasant enough places, where we can talk the talk with our fellow sportsmen, work our dogs on abundant game birds, shoot clays or pheasants or quail till our shoulders ache and our hearts are content (or least until our checkbooks squeal for mercy and we howl for another single-malt Scotch, please no ice). But believe me pardner, it ain't the same as shooting wild."

Amen!

For Christmas, I received Jones' latest novel, *The Run to Gitchee Gummee*, a riveting story about a sensational canoe trip (actually two) down the Firesteel River to the "Shining Big Sea Water," Longfellow's Lake Superior in *Hiawatha*. Yup, there's sex, violence, and conjured images of the Korean War but plenty of fishing and hunting. The language is a bit salty, but I'm sure most readers can handle it.

I happened to be reading the editor's page in *Shooting Sportsman* and learned that Jones died of pancreatic cancer in December of 2002.

I believe he was only in his late 60s. Ironically, his much-loved Jack Russell terrier, Roz, died of the same disease several months earlier.

Jones was one of the fine sporting writers of the twentieth century whose legacy will have a lasting impact on upland hunters.

The Mysterious Death of Edmund W. Davis

Edmund Walstein Davis was born of wealth and privilege in 1853 in Providence, Rhode Island. His grandfather, a licensed preacher, discovered "Pain Killer," and his father improved the successful marketing of the product the world over. It was such an effective painkiller that heathens worshipped the very bottle it came in. Money, wealth and empowerment allowed Edmund Davis to pursue a sporting life of leisure. He hunted in all states and Canada for big and small game in the late nineteenth century. Besides his accomplishment of being one of only two men who caught *two* giant Atlantic salmon weighing 50 pounds or more, he is remembered by sportsmen for his *Salmon Fishing on the Grand Cascapedia* (1904) and *Woodcock Shooting* (1908). They tell the stories of a man who fished for salmon on the Grand Cascapedia in Quebec Province and shot woodcock in New Brunswick. Davis states in *Woodcock Shooting* that his dog, Lady Kate, was the "first English setter to enter the covers of New Brunswick and convince the natives of the superiority of this breed."

The original edition of both books was limited to 100 copies and both are highly sought after by bibliophiles. Another 100 copies of *Salmon Fishing* were also issued in 1904. Both titles were republished in recent years in tasteful limited editions. Value: I would estimate $10,000 or more for the original pair in fine condition.

Davis died at his Red Camp on the Grand Cascapedia June 20, 1908, and for ninety-three years following his death, the sporting world—those interested in the Davis saga—had been led to believe that he simply died from an accidental gunshot wound. As discovered in an article, "Tragedy at Red Camp" by John Mundt, first appearing in the Spring/Summer 2001 issue of The Angler's Club Bulletin, there is much more to the story.

In the late 1990s a bookseller friend presented for my examination an as-issued and pristine copy of the 1908 edition of *Woodcock Shooting*. I had heard from some uncertain source that there are no signed copies extant. If memory serves accurately, Davis signed this particular copy, but I cannot swear to it. If true, this would put the release date of this book in a window encompassing about five and one-half months prior to his death in June of 1908.

Davis inherited family wealth—his only sibling died in infancy—in his twenties, and from what I have read about Davis, he never had to work—and perhaps didn't for all intents and purposes—although his firm, the Davis-Lawrence Company of New York City, continued in the business of medicine. If all his energy involved salmon fishing and hunting, I suppose we sportsmen should be envious. Somehow I have reservations, not because of what he did but because his enormous wealth bought everything in his life. He, along with other wealthy Americans, was able to buy expensive salmon leases on the Grand Cascapedia. Hunting in New Brunswick, he sent a companion ahead to purchase leases. It's unfair to speculate that he was not philanthropic. Did his wealth allow him to expel other energy into helping others, or did he just play? It's difficult to judge a man without knowing something more about his life.

In spite of Davis' immense wealth, I find him to be especially perceptive of his physical surroundings, not that these two attributes need be mutually exclusive. His lyrical style is uncommon to sporting writers of that period, and his tranquil poetry makes for pleasant reading. Davis begins "My Autumn Shooting of 1905" (that he doesn't want to end) with:

> Autumn, I love thy bower,
> With faded garlands drest;
> How sweet alone to linger there,
> When tempests ride the midnight air,
> To snatch from mirth a fleeting hour,
> The Sabbath of the breast

The following refers to the woodcock:

> When I arise and see the day I sigh for thee;
> When the light rises high and the dew is gone,
> And noon lies heavy on flower and tree,
> And weary day turns to his rest,
> Lingering like an unloved guest,
>   I sigh for thee!

The partridge loves the fruitful fells   (upland thicket)
The plover loves the mountains;
The woodcock loves the lonely dells;
The soaring hern the fountains;   (heron)
Through lofty groves the cushat roves, (European pigeon)
The path of man to shun it
The hazel bush o'erhangs the thrush;
The spreading thorn the linnet.   (European songbird)

Are these passages indicative of a man preoccupied with materialism attributable to wealth? My answer would be—no.

But the purpose of this writing is to contemplate the circumstances of Davis' death, as Mr. Mundt, the "Investigator," has so carefully researched. I can add practically nothing to his facts, rather speculation—for nothing can be proven—that he has already presented. And the reason I do this is because I admire the man who so eloquently wrote about the "sport of kings" and hunted the mythic bird.

The obituaries appearing in a Providence newspaper and the *New York Times* and printed in "Tragedy at Red Camp" offer different details relative to Davis' death. In the former, his son, Steuart Davis, who was present when his father died, asserted that while at Red Camp, the elder Davis was sitting on the porch "when a flock of game birds flew by. Hastening to pick off some of the birds Mr. Davis stooped, seized his shotgun, which was lying at his feet and as he raised it accidentally caused its discharge." Shot in the head, Mr. Davis fell dead. Two questions arise: Why was Davis shooting "game birds" in June? He doesn't strike me as a man who would shoot game out of season (it's possible that flying game was legal in June). Could "game birds" have been crows and misquoted by the newspaper reporter? Secondly, he was an accomplished wingshooter, and retrieving his shotgun in such a careless manner seems unlikely. Was Steuart's story that he gave to this newspaper a fabrication—and why?

The *New York Times* version differs from the foregoing.

"My father was examining a new gun, and we were arranging for a canoe trip into the forest. We don't know exactly how the accident happened. He was looking into the muzzle when the trigger, which was imperfectly caught, was released. The gun exploded and the shot was driven into my father's head. He died instantly."

One has to wonder if this awkward explanation was in Steuart's words, or paraphrased by the reporter. Now there are two different accountings of Davis' death, both relayed to the newspapers by Steuart Davis. Both indicate that he died accidentally by his own hand. Once again, it is inconceivable that Davis could be so outlandishly reckless with a gun.

Mr. Mundt interviewed members of several long-time area families. While all information given was hearsay, that is, passed down through generations, the consensus was that Steuart shot Edmund Davis. In one case, an accident; the other two involved clay pigeon shooting. Steuart dropped the gun, which discharged and killed his father. In another widely believed version, Steuart was walking behind his father while crow shooting when he accidentally shot his father in the head. A third account has Davis dead in a rocking chair at Red Camp with a shotgun on his lap. This doesn't sound like an accident.

A prevalent opinion among residents and those connected with the camp was that father and son did not get along and were constantly arguing. There had been a violent quarrel the night before he died.

There may have been a motive for the younger Davis to kill his father. Mrs. Edmund Davis also fished for salmon and frequently joined her husband on the river. She always signed in her catch "Mrs. Davis"—her given name was Maria—in the camp scorebook. Curiously, there are entries for one "Marie" on two occasions in June. The Davis obituaries further noted that his estranged wife had moved abroad and that there were "family differences."

Mr. Mundt then speculates that there may have been a romantic relationship between Davis and Marie. If this were true, it could have been possible for the family wealth to pass to the prospective wife of Edmund Davis and not Steuart. Who was Marie? A lover? Did Steuart discover his father's liaison?

Another theory: Some were of the opinion that Davis committed suicide.

As I was reading this fascinating account of intrigue, the thought came to me as to why an investigation was never pursued. Why didn't someone call the Mounties? A river guide stated to Mr. Mundt that there was no law authority in those days. Telephone communication was non-existent in the hinterlands—fast-forward a few decades and maybe there would have been a different outcome. Were any other guests present at Red Camp other than Steuart? Evidently it was Steuart's word alone as to the circumstances surrounding his father's death.

On page seventy-three of *Woodcock Shooting*, Davis speaks of one day retiring from the sporting life with pleasant memories:

> When all the world is old lad,
> And all the trees are brown,
> And all the sport is stale lad,
> And all the wheels run down,
> Creep home and take your place there
> The spent and maimed among.
> God grant you find one face there
> You loved when all was young.

Ironically, Edmund Davis never came home, except in death.

The Uncertainties of Travel

As a rule, I do not make it a practice to read and collect books on the subject of fishing. I dearly love to fish for trout, but in the last few years, conflicting venues seemed to rear their ugly heads in the spring of the year. It is not a question of which pleasures I enjoy most. Spring is busy for me, but unfortunately, most priorities are work related, here on the retired farm.

Any reasonably complete collection of sporting books begs for a focal point or narrow niche, be it trout fishing, salmon fishing, waterfowl, big game, etc. To have a little of each is okay and even desirable, but the collection will probably never be more than an incomplete configuration of various subjects. My thing is upland hunting and its related sub-topics, such as bird dogs, double shotguns, upland books, and upland sporting art.

Carrying a compressed focus to an extreme, for example, some collectors try to amass all of Isaac Walton's *The Complete Angler*, which was first published in the 1600s. According to Judith Bowman, a leading sporting bookseller, at least five hundred varying editions have been published since then, and she offered that it is the third-most reproduced book following *Pilgrim's Progress* and the *Holy Bible*.

For many years, I thought that the only remote association with Walton in my library was a rare forty-three page lampoon entitled *The Uncertainties of Travel – A Plain Statement by a Certain Traveller*, attributed to Dr. George A. Bethune, privately printed in 1880. Bethune (Harvard 1831) was an M.D. who I presumed to be the first American editor of Walton's *The Complete Angler*. Subsequently, I discovered that the Walton connection was with the Rev. Dr. George W. Bethune, who also amassed a large and amazing collection of fishing books. Anyway, my rare book, a non-fishing parody, was dedicated to the gentlemen of the Somerset Club of Boston, of which Bethune (George A.) evidently was a fellow member.

The author, a well-to-do resident of Boston (or its environs), wrote this humorous chronicle of his summer journey ending with a woodcock hunt on Long Island, the prime reason for my coveting this book. It had been previously listed by a well-known New York City bookseller (it may be the same book). However, I must admit that some of my interest in this dog-accompanied excursion via train and boat was the "getting to" his objective and his short overnight stay in New London, Connecticut, located just a few miles down-river from my home.

Bethune left Boston in July of 1878 via the Boston & Providence Railroad on a New London-bound train, accompanied by his English setter, to which he never referred by name. After having some interesting experiences in the Whaling City, Bethune chartered a sloop to Long Island, New York for $10, which he felt was a little steep. The twenty-eight miles to the intended port—the reader presumes on the eastern end of the island—took sixteen hours in very calm seas. The shooting coverts were just a few miles inland and were familiar to Bethune, as he had hunted the same area several years before.

I conjure an image of this gentleman hunting the Long Island coverts, meticulously dressed, with a tie of course, sweating profusely and cussing in the fully-leafed underbrush, with temperatures in the ninety-degree range. It is not surprising that after a morning's hunt he was determined to enjoy a "surf-bath" a few miles distant. He had the beach to himself and was able to swim *"puris naturalibus."*

As it happened, he found sparse numbers of woodcock in the few days he hunted and postulated, 125 years ago, that the bird was in trouble numerically. If the numbers of these birds continue to decline at the present rate, he predicted, the woodcock will soon go the way of the dodo and "be in demand for Barnum." Further, he states that the late change in the law (New York) extending the "close" season to September was a mistake as the bird is "sick" in the molting month and should not be shot. (I surmise that Bethune meant extending the *open* season through September.)

It's interesting that he chose to hunt Long Island's migratory woodcock, but maybe even back then it was considered a jumping off place to Cape May, New Jersey, a big-time staging area in the bird's southerly migration route. But read on.

It seems that Bethune had a dual motive for going to Long Island—to attend a meeting (one presumes annual meeting) in New York City of the proprietors of the newly formed Manhattan Beach Railroad, of which he supposedly was a shareholder. Most likely, he concluded there was nothing wrong with mixing a little business and pleasure. When he arrived at the other end of the island, after much inconvenience based on a comedy of misinformation in making connections, as described in detail in this book, he found the meeting had been postponed until the following week! One is reminded that Mr. Bell's invention that we take for granted today had not yet come upon the scene.

The Williams-McCorrison Connection

"I would rather be sad in Maine than happy anywhere else."

E. B. White

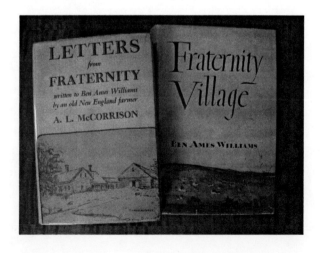

The displaced Southerner, Ben Ames Williams, famous novelist of the early 20th Century, needs no introduction. Perhaps his most well-known sporting book, *The Happy End,* was published by the Derrydale Press in 1939. Williams speaks to me eloquently in his mythical *Fraternity Village,* which contains short hunting and fishing stories rooted in the state of Maine. He understood the connection between dog and man, which is so poignantly dramatized in his short story, "Old Tantrybogus," about an English setter. This first appeared in a book called *Thrifty Stock and Other Stories* in 1923. If you own and love a hunting dog and haven't read it, I almost feel sorry for you. Williams sets the stage for this heart-wrenching tale with the following:

"A dog does not live as long as a man and this natural law is the fount of many tears. If boy and puppy might grow to manhood and doghood together, and together grow old, and so in due course die, full many a heartache might be avoided. But the world is not so ordered, and dogs will die and men will weep for them so long as there are dogs and men."

Over the years I have read several short stories and novels about bird dogs. In "Old Tantrybogus," Williams captured the essence of the bond between dog and man better than any other writer, and a few darn good ones come to mind—*Algonquin* by Dion Henderson, *Pocono Shot* and *Dumb Bell of Brookfield* by John Taintor Foote, *Old Red, a* juvenile story by James Kjelgaard and the recent novel, *Jenny Willow* (a beautiful story destined to become a classic), by the contemporary sporting writer, Mike Gaddis. Evans asserted in his introduction to Williams' "Old Tantrybogus" in *The Bird Dog Book*—"My God, how he knew a bird dog." This strong statement, coming from Evans makes me shudder and become misty-eyed. Over the long years, my many bird dogs have given me the same emotional perception of the passion and particularly the sorrow about which Williams speaks.

Hardscrabble

A.L. McCorrison is hardly a household word, even among collectors of hunting and fishing prose, in fact he never actually wrote a book. Back in the 1920s he befriended Williams, the immensely popular novelist and sporting writer from the Chestnut Hill section of Boston, when the latter drove into the driveway of McCorrison's Searsmont, Maine farm, "Hardscrabble." Fraternity Village is the fictional name given to Searsmont in Williams' writings. In motoring through Searsmont a few years ago, I was amazed to see that the "Fraternity Village General Store" had taken on William's fictional name. I recognized McCorrison's mid-nineteenth century farmhouse, "Hardscrabble" (above), from the dust jacket of *Letters from Fraternity*. Both seemed unchanged in 70 or so years.

Ben Williams and Bert McCorrison became lifelong friends and steadfast hunting and fishing partners. It was during this period that Williams recognized the talents of this simple but perceptive New England farmer. That McCorrison did not worship material pleasures is a gross understatement. His world, his life, his *raison d'être*, consisted of the everyday occurrences that most of us matter-of-factly accept as concomitants to our daily existence. His talent was recording on paper, in the form of letters, what he saw and experienced in his little world. More than that, his God-given gift was transforming life's simple realities into sustaining pleasures.

The recipient of these letters from Fraternity was, of course, Williams, who had them published, unedited, in 1930. McCorrison was Chet McAusland woven into Williams' short stories; Old Tantrybogus (Tantry), previously known as "Job" in this tale, was McAusland's setter. In real life, he was actually a composite of setters that McCorrison owned during his life. The Williams/McCorrison friendship was so penetrating that the latter bequeathed his farm to Williams, "lock, stock, and barrel." Upon Williams' death, the property passed to Ben Ames Williams, Jr., head of the Trust Division of the then First National Bank of Boston. A heart-wrenching eulogy, "Chet McAusland of Fraternity," can be found in Williams' *Fraternity Village*.

Sadly, at least from my observation, Williams' heirs—or perhaps some other successor to the property—sold at least part of the land to developers, and the once tranquil scene has been compromised somewhat, in my opinion, by a fairly substantial backland housing development.

Unfortunately, this little book, especially in its dust jacket, is rarer than hens' teeth, possibly because of a limited run and/or because it went the way of the dinosaur due to its fragile binding.

Letters from Fraternity personifies my grandfather to a tee. How could McCorrison and my mentor be so much alike without being the same person? These frugal New England farmers each lived and worked the same land all their lives, rejoicing in the same simple pleasures and hardly ever traveled more than a few miles from home during their long lives. They didn't need to see the world; they had their dreamland all around them.

Letters and "Old Tantrybogus" helped me refocus on some of life's cherished values that have become important to me, in particular, the man-dog relationship and life's simple pleasures.

Visions of New England Upland Sport

Aiden Lassell Ripley, *Woodcock Cover*, Limited Edition Print

As a life-long New Englander and upland hunter, a heritage of which I am justly proud, I have no responsibility to verbally defend my passion to others. However, my *joie de vivre* is best explained to non-practitioners by visions of my pastime through the images of A. Lassell Ripley and Ogden M. Pleissner, the *ne plus ultra* duo of sporting artists that dominated this genre in the early to mid-20th century. Memories of days afield in New England come alive as a result of the talented men behind the brushes of these two members elected to the National Academy of Design.

Aiden Lassell Ripley (1896-1969) was a premier illustrator of books, oil and watercolor painter of sporting scenes, urban artist, and etcher. Although several before him painted upland scenes, namely A.B. Frost, Edmund Osthaus, John M. Tracy, Percival Rosseau, to name a few, I would classify Ripley as the first painter and etcher of field sport tending to concentrate mostly on upland hunting.

His art was published in two posthumous volumes. In *Paintings*, his versatility becomes readily apparent in the many non-sporting paintings of urban subjects in and around the Boston area. His numerous etchings, manifested in *Sporting Etchings*—forty appear in this monograph—add credence to the many mediums in which he successfully worked. Etchings, not to be confused with commercially produced prints—photographic reproductions of paintings or drawings—represent personal endeavors by artists that are reproduced on a one-by-one painstaking process for a very limited edition. Only nine of his paintings were published as signed, limited edition (but unnumbered) prints—technically known as color-offset lithographs. They are not commonly available in the secondary market and are prized by purveyors of upland art. The best of these, in my opinion, is *Woodcock Cover,* which, together with a Ripley etching on either side, reposes over my living room sofa.

Ripley matured in a circle of famous Boston artists—who no doubt influenced his style—such as renowned etcher Frank W. Benson, impressionist William Merritt Chase, and the eminent portraitist, John Singer Sargent. Interestingly, Ripley's earlier watercolors appear to be executed in a more impressionistic style than his later paintings.

With one of my hunting partners, Ken Dugas, I had the opportunity of viewing what probably is the premier Ripley collection of original art in the world several years ago in the home and business of a private collector, and it's right in my back yard, so to speak! I cannot begin to convey my ebullience as I viewed this extensive collection.

Although he loved trout fishing around his Lexington, Massachusetts home and salmon fishing on the Northwest Miramichi in New Brunswick, his images portraying these subjects are not often seen, at least from my limited perspective.

I find it strange that Ripley disclosed to his friend, Guido Perera, who wrote the Introduction to *Sporting Etchings*, that he could bag more grouse in the absence of a highly trained grouse dog. This may have been true in Ripley's experience and understandable back in the days of plentiful grouse populations but only if one gauges success solely by the number of birds brought to bag. To prove his point, Ripley and Perera moved twenty-two grouse on a dogless hunt in coverts just twenty miles southwest of Boston, but they only shot one!

I consider my English setters the glue that pulls all the joys of upland bird hunting together. I have often said that if I couldn't hunt over dogs trained by my hand, the sport would be far less appealing to me. Watching a pointing dog hunt the uplands is the focus of the chase. In my mind, a less than perfect dog is preferable to no dog—

anytime. Obviously, an out-of-control canine is an abomination that should best be left in the home kennel. Someone said that Ripley's hunting dogs—English pointers—were not the most highly trained animals.

Ogden M. Pleissner watercolor (untitled)
Courtesy Mrs. Ruth Blakney

Ogden Minton Pleissner (1905-1983) first and foremost considered himself a landscape artist who liked the sporting life. Born in Brooklyn, New York, summers were spent in Wyoming where he was given the opportunity to sketch, hunt, and fish.

A commissioned artist during World War II, some of his war paintings hang at West Point, the Pentagon, and the Air Force Academy. In the non-sporting art world, he is not considered avant-garde because he added nothing to art history that had not already been done by his predecessors, such as the exalted Winslow Homer. This is the reason why he is not better known outside the sporting genre. But in the latter endeavor, along with Ripley, he is considered one of the great sporting artists of the twentieth century.

Professionally prolific, his legacy was 2500 large oils, watercolors, and more numerous smaller paintings. He supervised the production of thirty prints and eight drypoints (five salmon) in small editions, the latter being quite rare.

While taking a class of study in Cape Breton, Nova Scotia, he was introduced to salmon fishing on the Margaree River and was smitten for life. It is in this subject matter that Pleissner is probably best known. In fact, he produced eleven salmon prints compared to nine trout, eight upland and three waterfowl. Perhaps his most famous print is *Blue Boat on the Saint Anne,* the original version of which resides in the Shelburne Museum just south of Burlington, Vermont. Signed limited edition (but not numbered) prints—300 were published—of *Blue Boat* will bring $5,000 or more.

Elected Academician in the prestigious National Academy in 1940, I think of Pleissner as a Vermont artist—he lived in Pawlet and Manchester for more than thirty-five years—who was probably at his best painting on the great salmon waters of the Maritime Provinces. Perhaps more secondarily acclaimed, his New England upland art ranks right along with those of his contemporary, Lassell Ripley. All my life I coveted a copy—270 were produced—of *Hillside Orchard-Grouse Shooting,* but never got around to owning it until just recently. Others I treasure are *October Snow* and *Quail Hunters,* a southern scene with vibrant fall colors.

The one book published posthumously in 1984, *The Art of Ogden Pleissner* by Peter Berg, was very well done in trade, limited, and deluxe limited editions.

Invited to dine out at an area retirement home a few months ago by a woman who was a long-lost pre-teen acquaintance, my wife and I followed up the delicious meal with a tour of our gracious host's apartment. I sensed inexplicable exhilaration as we entered the living room, for there, centered above the sofa, was one of the most beautiful upland grouse hunting scenes that I have ever seen—two pointing dogs and a lone hunter painted in the unmistakable Vermont countryside. My mind was in a whirl. I could not believe what I was seeing. A first blush glance identified it as a Ripley, or was it a Pleissner? It turned out to be a half-sheet Pleissner watercolor with gorgeous fall colors of sugar maples contrasted with dark green of a spaced copse of white pines with leafless apple trees in the distance. As I regained composure, I told my friend that it was an expensive painting in today's market. To some limited extent, she was aware of its value but was pleasantly surprised when a subsequent appraisal indicated a price above even my liberal estimate. Purchased by a family member back in the 1950s at Drew Holl's Crossroads of Sport in New York City for an estimated $500, this untitled gem is apparently unknown in art and literature (illustration) circles. It will forever endure in my mind as the quintessence, the perfect embodiment, of New England upland gunning.

William Schaldach's Vermont

William Schaldach, Derrydale aquatint
Woodcock

When I leave town on a sporting vacation, there is always an extra supplication given to the Highest Power for His cooperation in sending reasonable weather, which realistically has always been controlled by the law of averages. My destination was a little hamlet—Morgan, Vermont, about ten miles south of the Canadian border.

Whenever I contemplate bird hunting or trout fishing in Vermont, William Schaldach immediately comes to mind. In my thinking, Schaldach and Vermont are interchangeable. When I think of one, I think of the other. Although born and raised in Indiana, much of his writing and art speak of and to the Green Mountain state, where he lived the sporting life for many years. His classic writings of trout fishing, woodcock and grouse shooting grace the libraries of sporting enthusiasts the world over, including mine. His hand colored—by the artist—Derrydale aquatint, "Woodcock," hangs prominently in my dining room.

When I arrived in Morgan for a bit of trout fishing, I was told that winter had just ended a few days ago—May 26! But, on a positive vein, no rain, other than a few sprinkles and cloudy skies, was forecast for the next several days—good fishing conditions. We would try for landlocked salmon on the Clyde, native trout on the Black, Willoughby, and Missisquoi Rivers. Just what exactly is a native trout up there I really never found out. Some say rainbows, some insist it's a brookie. Either way, the truth is that most, if not all, are stocked fish.

I think of Bill Schaldach principally in terms of his etchings of salmon and trout, woodcock and grouse, the dual aristocrats of fish and game. But he also wrote (and illustrated) some pretty darn good books such as *Coverts & Casts, Currents & Eddies, Upland Gunning* and *The Wind on Your Cheek*, among others. The Schaldach touch, as Arnold Gingrich called it, is "the difference between the days spent out-of-doors by the sensitive artist and the unthinking clod." Schaldach, compared with other writers of yesteryear, seemed to be more in touch with his surroundings...

"We had a sharp frost last night. The hilly pasture that rises abruptly from the back of the house has taken on a pearly cast. Goldenrod skeletons and clumps of sweet fern, faded New England asters, hardhack and bracken are woven decoratively throughout the acres of frosty meadow grasses to form a gigantic Persian rug."

The Clyde River, running its famous waters through Newport and into Lake Memphremagog, yielded several pounds of salmon to my guide and me—all 6-7" smolts! No one was taking any big fish that we heard of. We hit a couple of nice hatches on the Missisquoi, just below the old power mill and almost always in viewing distance of the still-snow-covered Jay Peak. Mostly browns rose to the Hendricksons and Adamses. We caught nothing big, just nice fighting fish in the 10" to 12" range. A dozen or so were caught and released in the pool below the mill. I wanted to keep a few for the pan, but my guide,

Dave Smith (a transplanted Vermonter from the mid-West), said that he had not killed a fish in several years and evidently prided himself because of it. Talk about intimidation! Next time I think I'll fish with his son Francis, the other half of the guiding team known as Northeast Kingdom Outfitters. He may allow me to keep a few fish!

The Northeast Kingdom (where Morgan is located) is really a different world, desolate and lonely in the winter, little traveled by tourists in the summer. Its beauty is unsurpassed year round in the New England states, in my opinion. But for skiing, too bad there's not much else to do besides huntin' and fishin' in the shadows of covered bridges.

It is not unusual for older sportsmen to lose interest in their sport as the bones get tired. Many just retain the memories and go on to different pursuits. Schaldach not only walked away from the uplands and streams on which he had spent a lifetime, but he seemed to have severed all connection from the writing and the art as well. He moved to Tubac, Arizona where he became interested in the archaeology of the Southwest Indians.

Letter to a Sportsman/Writer

Mr. Tom Davis
200 Arrowhead Drive
Green Bay, WI 54301

Dear Tom,

I especially cherish the March/April issue of *Sporting Classics* because of your well-done feature article on A.L. Ripley. Repeat readings are the norm for fear that I may have missed something previously unknown to me. I connect to many sporting artists, but I've always favored Ripley above all others, with Ogden Pleissner rated a very close second. Thank you so much for being such a fine contributor to the upland sporting life.

I may have mentioned to you in our conversation awhile back— you called me regarding the feature article I wrote for *Double Gun Journal*—that I had the pleasure of viewing a private collection of Ripley paintings in West Hartford, Connecticut several years ago. There must have been twenty to thirty major works at this collector's home. I called John Culler back in the days when you guys at *Sporting Classics* were spitting out art books like a swimmer in salt water and suggested that the sporting art publishing world needed to fill a vacuum—a fine monograph on Ripley—and I knew where there was a whole bunch of his paintings all under one roof, well actually two—his business was also chock-full. Yeah, a couple books have been done, but they said too little about the man. That's where you would come into the picture.

Maybe this is a dumb question, but who would be willing to publish such a book—presuming that you would be the author? Knowing what I do about the stuff you write, you've just got to be a big fan of Ripley. I just have that feeling.

Your mention of Ripley being a member of the prestigious National Academy—an admirable accomplishment for a sporting artist—has always been a bit confusing to me. While Pleissner's publisher most always used "N.A." after his name on prints, evidently Ripley did not, although occasionally one notes "A.N.A." after his name, which I presume designates Associate of National Academy, presumably a lesser honor.

As a collector of limited edition and rare sporting books, your reference to Ripley's fishing club struck a covetous note. In 1958, J.C. Greenway wrote a little history of *The Laurel Brook Club*, privately printed, limited to 150 copies, and illustrated by none other than Aiden Lassell Ripley. I've seen this rare gem a time or two at sporting book auctions where it'll probably fetch $400 - $500. I don't own it, but it would really make a nice addition to my modest collection of Ripley stuff.

My copy of *Tranquillity Revisited* is a prized possession, and while you write that this is the only Derrydale "dedicated" to Ripley's art, there were four other Derrydales illustrated by Ripley, namely: *John Tobias, Sportsman; Jing* (that wonderful dog story); *Falling Leaves*, and *The One-Eyed Poacher of Privilege*. Admittedly, the color plates in *Tranquillity Revisited* surpass by far the other Ripley-illustrated Derrydale books.

On another subject, your "Gundogs" column was interesting as usual. Dogs are my life too, sort of. You may remember I called you, too late, several years ago looking for a pup from one of your litters. A biddable Chief setter—I heard that Mike Seminatore's famous Chief line has just about petered out—owns me and although fast approaching ten, she still runs like an English pointer. Age has compressed her range a little—she's still remarkably quick—so that she is ideal for woodcock and grouse here in New England. But I like my dogs "out there," not boot-lickers. My two regrets are that I never ran her in field trials and that I had her spayed.

My youngster, Molly, is of Grouse Ridge breeding, but I'm far more than a "couple of handshakes away from the Queen! What a sweetheart (Molly, not necessarily the Queen). [Readers of this letter need to know that Davis' column talks of a canine advisor to Princess Margaret who inquired of Davis whether the English setter pup with Grouse Ridge breeding she received as a gift was worth training. One of the perks of the job, writes the tongue-in-cheek Davis, was that he was "just a "couple of handshakes away from the Queen."]

You mention in "Gundogs" your inclusion on the design team for I. Rizzini over/unders. From the few I've seen, this firm makes fine guns. Several years ago I custom-ordered a F.lli Rizzini 20-gauge side-by-side game gun from New England Arms and have closely followed the development of high-end Italian guns. My opinion is that a couple of Italy's best makers attain perfection regardless of the number of man-hours it takes to achieve that standard and in most cases for less money than the finest English names, but that may be splitting hairs now in several instances. As far as Italian production guns are concerned, it's not even a race. They are way ahead of the competition.

Thanks for reading my ramblings. What I really started out to convey is my congratulations on the great job you are doing. Keep up the good work!

The Dogs

Liberty's Last Day

The third of October was not a particularly unusual day in the life of this writer—other than perhaps worrying about what part of the budget would take a hit when state income taxes make their deductible presence in the paycheck on the morrow—except for the fact that I made the decision to end the life of my old and suffering English setter of eleven plus years.

Liberty, born on the Fourth of July, was a faithful canine and a good field performer until premature old age made its inexorable assault, to the extent that I had not hunted with him in the past few years, other than an occasional and brief foray into the back 40 in pursuit of our mutual evanescent friends, John and Mary Woodcock. Liberty, a Ryman, was my second bird dog.

Daylight started to fade when Bess, my five-year-old Old Hemlock setter, and I made a practice run looking for native birds. And we found a few as is most often the case if spring rains have been reasonably spare.

It soon became apparent that Liberty had followed us when I heard his distressful bark in yonder dell. Not to be left out, he wanted to be part of the excitement. But his hindquarters were gone, and with eyes and ears failing, his still-good nose seemed to be the only connection to insouciant bird hunting years. How he dragged himself one-fourth mile over rocks and rills I will never know, but it was obvious he couldn't get back to the house without help from his mentor.

After the long trip back with him in my arms, I made the inevitable judgment to do what had to be done. But he seemed to be somewhat better the next day, aspirin having eased the pain somewhat...

My mind went back in time when Lib came home to live with us. We motored to the DeCoverly Kennels, Tunkhannock, Pennsylvania where Ken Alexander was in the process of revitalizing the famed Ryman strain of English setters. I remember him presenting my wife and me with a slide show of his project. He had a kennel full of setters and high aspirations. Several puppies were available. We chose a seven-week-old pup, soon-to-be a heavily ticked tri-color with no patches. I ran into Ken a few years back at the annual Vintage Cup at the Orvis Shooting Grounds in Sandanona, New York. We chatted several minutes about the Ryman line and hunting dogs in general. He did not seem to recall our initial daylong visit. Even though I admire the Ryman and Old Hemlock strains, my preference over the years gradually evolved into favoring a more modest sized and faster handling setter.

After being with us a few years, Lib decided to go scouting. Where he went I do not know. He pretty much had the run of the place, as I never kept him kenneled much of the time when I was out and about. After much searching and calling for a few days, I came to the conclusion that he had been "dognapped"—I had dreamed his bird hunting prowess had spread far and wide— or, with some shame on my part, ran off chasing deer. After a week or so I was messing around with something near his kennel and looked up to see Lib standing there, wagging his tail and looking at me as if to say, "where's my dinner?" O joy of joys! He looked weary and gaunt, like he hadn't had a square meal since he left home a week earlier. Should I lavish him with praise or scold him? I did the former with much celebration, as the latter option would have proved meaningless...

Long-time dog owners know the agony of indecision. I rationalized that he'd be better tomorrow. Besides, what right did I have to take a life, notwithstanding anthropomorphic judgment?

Sunday was miserable weather wise, and Lib had regressed. When he begged to be held, Julie, my aspiring veterinarian daughter, administered the OD of sodium pentothal as I cradled him in my arms. His life slowly drifted away and he was at peace. I laid him to rest besides Troubles in the first orchard, the warm, soft rain mixing with tears and turbulence of a still questioning mind. Rest easy Pal...

Second Wind

Last week, I wrote the following email to my hunting buddies, Greg and Ken:

"I suspect that Blaze is knocking at death's door. Although she still eats and drinks, she can hardly stand and is disoriented. She seems to have lost partial use of her hind legs. For the first time in a few days I let her go at three p.m. and she didn't come back. I put on my electronic earmuffs (to better hear her bell) and heard a faint ringing in the Stony Lot. I found her there, bedded down for the night. I led her back to her kennel, but she couldn't follow, so I had to carry her and lift her into the kennel run. She ate heartily and then just stood, trembling, not knowing what to do. I don't think she remembers how to "nose" her door open to enter the doghouse. Just three months shy of fifteen, my sadness is comforted by recalling the profound joy of all the great bird-hunting years she gave me."

Ken called a few days after returning home from Key West. He told me about the problems that he was having with Maggie, Blaze's littermate. Ironically (or perhaps not), Maggie was experiencing the same symptoms of old age as Blaze. We compared notes. She'd soiled her quarters as did Blaze, and her hind legs were giving out. Both setters seemed to be digressing exactly the same way. What should we do? We both agreed that a visit to our respective vets would be pointless. Both, most likely, would confirm what we already know: They would advise that the time has probably come, and that the "humane" deed would be to put the dogs down. My thoughts harkened back to Ben Ames Williams' fictional *Old Tantrybogus* and how the old dog's life ended. Tantry had suffered in old age and on his last hunt he pointed a woodcock:

"And of a sudden, without thought or plan but on the unconsidered impulse of the moment, Chet dropped his gun till the muzzle was just behind Old Tandry's head. At the roar of it a woodcock rose on shrilling wings—rose and flew swiftly up the run with never a charge of shot pursuing. Chet had not even seen it go. The man was on his knees, cradling the old dog in his arms, crying out as though Tantry still could hear: 'Tantry! Tantry! Why did I have to go and—I'm a murderer, Tantry! Plain murderer! That's what I am, old dog. He sat back on his heels, laid the white body down and folded his arms across his face, as a boy does, weeping. In the still crisp air a sound seemed still ringing—the sound of a dog's bark—the bark of Old Tantrybogus, yet strangely different too. Stronger, richer, with a new and youthful timbre in its tones; like the bark of a young strong dog setting forth on an eternal hunt with a well-loved master through alder runs where woodcock were as thick as autumn leaves."

Ken and I agreed that when Maggie and Blaze are ready to go to dog Heaven, we would take each to the vet for the "shot" that accommodates this necessity. What we would not do is leave the remains. Both would be taken home for burial, rather than discarded in an unfeeling and callous manner—into a dumpster. But, for both Ken and me, that time has not yet come.

We concurred that genes have a lot to do with their longevity. Ken also owned Maggie's mother, Trix, who lived to be fifteen. Too bad this line (Chief) could not have been perpetuated, as neither Maggie nor Blaze had pups.

As the days shorten and the juices start to flow in anticipation of the upcoming hunting season in out-of-state venues, I ponder what should be done. If I determine that Blaze's attentive needs will be a problem for my schoolteacher spouse, I will be taxed to make a decision, a judgment that most likely will be deferred until a week or so prior to my departure. Possibly fate will be kind with a pronounced change in her condition—for better or for worse.

She remained in her doghouse for several days, exiting only to drink and eat, for which she had no loss of desire. At other times, she couldn't be coaxed to exit her run for a bit of exercise. I tied her house door open so she no longer has to enter with her nose. Compounding her obvious problems, she hears very little and a cataract has completely blinded one eye. Yeah, she does look to be fifteen.

Yesterday morning, slamming the rear garage door shut on the way out, I made the short walk to the dog kennels. Jing immediately started to bark as is customary. Blaze heard the ruckus, came out of her doghouse and stood at the kennel gate jumping up and down anxiously waiting to leave. Once opened, she jumped down, ran across the barnyard and down the lane. I heard her bell tinkling for a few hundred feet, and I went about my chores thanking God for the miraculous change. Ten minutes later she returned, went immediately to her kennel, jumped up the eighteen-inches to the kennel floor, took a long drink and retired. No relapse is evident; in fact, she seems a little more active with each passing day. Go figure.

And so, we will take each day as it comes, one at a time. It just may be that God will favor her, and I will be able to leave home in peace and then later on take her on a few short pheasant hunts at the club. *

*Note: Autumn Blaze, born December 3, 1991, died November 18, 2006, two weeks and a day shy of fifteen. My wish for a final hunt with her went unfulfilled.

My Gundogs

Percival Rosseau, *Partners*, etching 1932

My journey with gundogs began in my late twenties after my wife and I moved out of our one and only apartment in the suburbs and built our life-long home on ancestral lands adjacent to my family's early eighteenth century homestead. Keeping a hunting dog now became possible. When I was growing up, my father—with mother's help—raised prize-winning roses. I can see him now, red-faced and cussing at a neighbor's English setter running slipshod through the rose beds with no abandon. Little did I know that setters would be my life's joy in a few years. The neighbor, a newspaper publisher and a very highly respected gentleman, would become a friend and occasional hunting partner in the distant future. Unlike the many breeds of gundogs owned by noted writer Ray P. Holland and memorialized in his 1929 book, *My Gun Dogs*, I have always owned only English setters.

It has been pretty much accepted that breed-related superiority—read ability—is nonsense. What makes a superior gundog is an individual matter, that is to say, within breeds there are good and not-so-good performers. That said, I prefer to hunt with English setters, pointing specialists of the uplands, because of their grace, style—in my mind the most important attributes—and conformation. Setters are traditional, eager to please, affectionate, and because of their longer coats, able to withstand the rigors of cold weather and downright inhospitable offerings of dense, often impassable, New England bird coverts. I'm a one-breed owner because I'm not a waterfowl hunter or rabbit chaser. I have no desire to own a generalist or, as they are known today, the versatile breeds, popular as they are. If waterfowl hunting was among my pursuits, along with upland birds, I would probably own a Lab or golden retriever—but that's only if I couldn't own more than one breed for each specialty.

My first setter pup, "Chief," was a mistake, that is, I was not knowledgeable in the ways of keeping a gundog. I knew nothing about breeding and the necessity of emulating a mother's propinquity in the early days of separation. When a pup came along via an ad in the local newspaper, I jumped at the opportunity. Chief cost me $35 and remained with me for a whole week, until his incessant nocturnal barking forced me to return him to the breeder. I made a big mistake in doing so and obviously will never know how he turned out. That experience was a hard-learned lesson.

Troubles (5/71-12/79) was purchased in Chester, Conn. He brought to bag more birds per season than any of my setters. An on-and-off retriever, he was a meat dog through and through. Without counting all my journal entries, I'd estimate that I shot 210 woodcock and grouse (mostly the former) over him in his seven seasons, with a smattering of pheasants. Native game was plentiful, and most birds were taken within a walking-mile radius of my home. Although I can't seem to picture him in my mind, he taught me a lot about birds and bird hunting in my formative years.

Liberty, a Ryman setter whelped on the Fourth of July 1980, was retrieved by auto from DeCoverly Gun Dog Kennels in Tunkhannock, Pennsylvania. A tricolor, he possessed good looks and was picture-perfect. He found and pointed oodles of woodcock and grouse. He loved the hunt but was not particularly biddable, was hardheaded, didn't hunt to the gun or consistently retrieve. Once he started a deer and disappeared for a week. I hunted with him for ten seasons. About 230 woodcock (mostly), grouse and many pheasants fell to the gun behind Liberty.

Old Hemlock Best (7/86-12/98) was purchased from the Muehlbauers (owners of the brood bitch, Old Hemlock Fairie), at George and Kay Evans' home, Old Hemlock, in Bruceton Mills, WV. Sire was Evans' personal gundog, Old Hemlock Quest. I loved "Bess" because she was so beautiful and affectionate. A liver and white Belton, she was a good hunter and fair retriever, especially in her early years. She positioned her tail below 180 degrees when pointing. I found her to be short on speed and quickness, attributes that I so much desire in a setter, although other grouse and woodcock hunters may demand a slower and closer working dog as their ideal. Like all my gundogs, Bess had free reign of my property when I was outside tending to property chores. With blindness taking its toll, she wandered off one evening and was killed by a hit-and-run truck driver in front of a neighbor's house.

Autumn Blaze (12/91 - /- will soon be fifteen. Out of famous Chief ancestry, she was my smallest setter. I did not hunt her this past season because of old age (hearing and eyesight impaired), preferring to spend time with the new pup. Blaze was very quick and agile, an awesome natural backer and a moderate ranger. She was a pleasure to watch in the field. When young, she was a fantastic retriever but lost it after a couple of seasons, probably as a result of being clawed by a wounded cock pheasant. At that point, I should have hired a professional trainer to cure the problem. Blaze was somewhat aloof and didn't possess the pleasing personality or conformation of earlier and later-owned setters. She was all business and a top-notch woodcock and grouse dog. If there were birds around, she would find them. My only regret is that I never introduced her to the field-trial world. I think she would have been a winner. Her sibling, owned by Ken Dugas, is still alive, and that says a lot for the genes they carry.

Molly (7/30/98-10/24/03), scion of great-name field trial ancestry—ten lines to Grouse Ridge breeding in five generations—caused me much anguish when kidney failure took her to dog heaven at five years of age. Molly did it all, and the pain is still evident as I reflect on her short but productive life. It's strange how you forget dog countenances and mannerisms over the years, even with photos readily available. I try to remember, yet still cannot recollect, the little nuances that caused me to love her. Some would claim she had one small weakness. Her tail tip tended to "sickle" somewhat on long-held points. As a hunter and not a field-trialer, this never bothered me. She had a fantastic nose and was a splendid retriever.

Going Long Jingo, whelped 2/13/04 is my current superstar. His breeding is Grouse Ridge—paternal grandsire is Grouse Ridge Reroy—and Lloyd Murray's Long Gone Setters line of Stark, New Hampshire. Paternal grand dam is Long Gone Agnes. Mr. Jing, (as I have come to call him) is now four years-old, weighs fifty pounds and already has had a lot of experience on woodcock in four seasons afield. He retrieves well—fetches his food dish when commanded or when he's hungry—and was steady to wing and shot as a result of intense practice with a blank pistol on returning woodcock migrations. I took him off this regimen when I determined that the potential for lost birds was too great. I remember shooting at a woodcock which, if hit, would have landed in a fast flowing stream. A delayed retrieve would have been impossible. After pointing a pheasant he will break point and circle to cut off a potential escape. Then he will point again at a different angle. He also does this on woodcock and grouse. For sure, this is gene related. I believe he may be the best overall performer of any of my previous setters. His conformation is super—looks just like Robert Abbett's *English Setter* (setter head) oil painting. Color is all white with black—minimal tan—spotting. He carries a one o'clock, poker-straight tail, which, on occasion, tends to "flag" if birds are not close. We're working to correct this. Extremely biddable, Mr. Jing is a moderate ranger.

Jing

In assessing the successes of my setters in terms of birds bagged, one must consider game availability in light of the times. For instance, in Troubles' second season when he was not fully trained and tended to range too far, I shot twelve grouse over him. I stopped hunting grouse locally several years ago because birds were scarce, but my dogs of later times were of superior breeding, in my opinion, and had better training—this amateur trainer has learned a lot over the years! Doubtless, if game were not so scarce today compared to earlier years, my later-generation bird dogs would have been more creditable bird finders.

The disparity of dog lives and human lives is unfortunate. If you get ten good seasons from your dog, you're lucky. Hunting seasons are short. Most hunters work at least five days per week, so that leaves seven or eight Saturdays at most per hunting season to hunt with your partner on wild birds. But we all have obligations having to do with wives and kids, as more and more time is demanded for sports, Boy Scouts, etc. The result is far too few days spent in the fields and woods. I am blessed in retirement in that I am able to spend quality time with my dogs virtually every day on my land and surrounding coverts. Just to watch Mr. Jing run around always looking for something to find or point is spending quality time and an immense source of satisfaction and joy.

We have all heard stories of how people have become attached to their dogs, in many cases a substitute for the lack of human love because of a deceased spouse, for example. When the dog passes, one often hears, "I will never own another dog because of the heartbreak." We all know that the attachment and love is real without "substitution." And when the time comes for a dog to go, it is a heart-rending experience, especially if death is accidental or premature. Molly was a prime example.

Writer Corey Ford knew the anguish of loss when his setter was accidentally shot to death by a deer hunter. In "Just a Dog," Ford's emotion is so poignantly captured when he wrote an open letter to the careless hunter through Ray Holland's column in *Field & Stream.*

".......Just a dog, Mr. Coggins. Just a little English setter I have hunted with for quite a few years. Just a little female setter who was very proud and stanch on point, and who always held her head high, and whose eyes had the brown of October in them. We had hunted a lot of alder thickets and apple orchards together, the little setter and I. She knew me and I knew her, and we liked to hunt together. We had hunted woodcock this fall, and grouse, and in just another week we were planning to go down to Carolina together and look for quail. But yesterday morning she ran down in the fields in front of my house, and you saw her flick in the bushes, and you shot her.

You shot her through the back, you said, and broke her spine. She crawled out of the bushes and across the field towards you, dragging her hind legs. She was coming to you to help her. She was a gentle pup, and nobody had ever hurt her, and she could not understand. She began hauling herself toward you, and looking at you with her brown eyes, and you put a second bullet through her head. You were a sportsman for that.

I know you didn't mean it Mr. Coggins. You felt sorry afterwards. You told me that it really spoiled your deer hunting the rest of the day. It spoiled my bird hunting the rest of a lifetime.

......I hope that the next time you raise a rifle to your shoulder you will see her over the sights, dragging herself toward you across the field, with blood running from her mouth and down her white chest. I hope you will see her eyes......."

Ramblings

I spent a good part of October up north bird hunting. In early September of 2003, my young setter, Molly, was diagnosed with terminal kidney failure, probably as a result of Lyme disease. The vets don't know for sure. She hunted valiantly in Vermont, but was not able to do the Maine trip. Midway through the latter, I called home and reluctantly agreed with my wife that it was time for her to leave us. I had hugged her goodbye and told her to be a good dog before I went away. She was.

Private moments in Maine were tearful, and when the appointed time came back home, we paused in the field from afar, and I mumbled a few words as Molly's life peacefully drifted away in the arms of loved ones. We were just a few yards from where she made the incredible retrieve up and over river ramparts and through swirling waters exactly one year before. The vet placed her in a box and my wife and granddaughter buried her under the Twenty-Ounce apple tree in the first orchard.

I've partnered with many English setters in my time, and all lived reasonably long dog lives. Molly, just five-years-old and loaded with Grouse Ridge ancestry, was a big part of my reason for living. Her passing caused me great pain and extinguished my usual hunting frenzy for the season. How I ever pulled myself together to follow through with the Maine trip, I will never know. Now, almost two years later, I still grieve for her.

Obviously, life goes on, and I'm thankful that twelve-year-old Blaze, still quick and reasonably fast, carried the ball in northern climes, having hunted virtually all day, every day.

Oh yeah, they'll be another one. Blaze—of Chief ancestry—will only be able to carry on for another year or two. With Tim Brennan's help—who else?—and connections, I zeroed in on the bloodlines and mating that we thought would best serve my needs in terms of breeding and timing. (Tim Brennan is *the* dog man at Snake Meadow Club.) An interesting coincidence developed. Lloyd Murray, a well-known breeder of English setters, accepted a bitch for stud service to his 4X champion male, Nixon, at his Long Gone Kennels in the far reaches of northern New Hampshire. Tim knew Lloyd's grandfather many years ago; hence the dialog between the two on my behalf, which resulted in my "pick" of the litter. Tim told me that the owner of the female belonged to a guy that lived near the casino (Mohegan Sun, Uncasville, Connecticut). Turns out the owner, Jeff, lives not ten minutes from me and is brother to our own club member, Dave Clark. Talk about a small world!

Shortly thereafter, I learned that Jeff's Samantha, alias "Sam" developed a uterine infection and had to be spayed. Back to square one? Nope, not exactly. I touched base with the owner of another in-season bitch with the right genes in Central Vermont that was also bred to Lloyd's male, Nixon. I still retained the "pick."

My hunting partner, Greg, and I headed for Plainfield, Vermont in late March of 2003 to exercise my "pick." Turns out that I leaned toward a male which happened to be the runt of the litter; not a female that I desired. I went with my choice in terms of head confirmation, the absence of patches, and color—white. I realized that coloration and other features can change in a seven-week-old pup, and that the little ticking and spotting visible would become more pronounced in time. Much to my surprise, Greg also purchased a good-sized black-masked female. Paternal grandsire of this litter is Grouse Ridge Reroy, a well-known field trial winner from the Grouse Ridge line. I'm not sure we expected to be returning with two pups, but the return trip was without "incident."

North Country flushes for both Maine and Vermont were comparable to 2002. In seven days of actual hunting (it rained or snowed two days), my human and canine partners moved ninety-five woodcock and forty-two grouse. It's been said that seeing is believing. We didn't see but heard several woodcock flushes, which obviously did not afford shots. You expect this from grouse but from woodcock? They just don't seem to sit still anymore; under-dog-nose flushes are not as common as in past years. We also witnessed flushed birds hitting the ground and running to more protective cover. The average kill was an even two woodcock per day per hunter. Forget about the King of the Uplands!

My Blue Hat

Setter Head, oil painting by Robert Abbett

My new Snake Meadow Club hat is a favorite, you know, just like the venerable old style headgear that was available in blue, green or maroon with the oval club logo encased in gold trim. There probably aren't too many of the originals left. Reposing in my closet is an original unworn green version, but it's not intended for wear. It seems too big for my head, and I dislike its blocky design. When sitting atop my crown, vanity tells me that my head looks like a pearl enveloped in an oyster shell. Besides, it may be valuable some day. (Some guys think everything is collectible.)

There seems to be no shortage of baseball-style "reproductions" around these days at the club, like the above blue likeness I bought at Sears—made-up hats in whatever color using the inceptive logo patch attached. For a buck, Stan Ward will sell you an original stick-on, heat-applied oval, if you must have one. I've even seen several members wearing traditional camouflage hats with the old patch. Whatever turns you on!

Funny thing about hats. You wear them a few years and then they should be retired because of a combination of spattered paint, sweat, blood and maybe from some incident of frustration, throwing it on the ground and stomping on it a few times. I've seen some pretty sad cases. Some folks become very possessive of their long-worn chapeaus and are hesitant to part company with such old friends. Once, when hunting in New Brunswick years ago, a guide showed us the home of his nephew. Inside, lined up on shelves in every room, were baseball-style hats, hundreds of them. Again, whatever turns you on!

Anyway, my blue facsimile turned up missing in early spring. Four-month-old Jing, my English setter water dog specialist, was the likely culprit. He takes all my stuff and my wife's outdoor slippers, chews them a bit and hides them under the shrubbery or in the woods behind the house. I really don't mind though; he's a terrific retriever. He ran off with a recently-killed mammoth mole "stolen" from my lawn trap—my side lawn looked like a glacier had rolled over the place—and hid it under the rhododendrons along the west wall. No problem with that. I looked for my sorely-missed Snake Meadow Club hat for the better part of two weeks with no success and chalked it up to a loss. The hard-learned lesson is simple; hang it up when you're through with it.

The dogs and I take three-mile strolls about every other day—helps toughen all three of us—along old logging roads and public utility owned blacktop. After Jing flushed the sometimes-present wild turkey, Blaze pointed near the woodcock singing ground with Jing sort of backing her. As the northerly woodcock migrations had ended several weeks before, I suspected what Blaze had found—a "little russet fella'," who must have decided to hang around to raise a family. Sure enough, the woodcock matron's feigned, fluttering rise with deeply depressed tail and dangling feet attracted my attention. She put down not more than twenty feet away. Faking a wing injury, she had tried to draw me away, a ruse I'd seen many times over the years. If a second flush had been attempted, the same scenario would have played out. Her short and feeble flight seemed to suggest, "I'm easy; come get me, but leave my babies alone." Instinctively looking down by my feet I spied two chicks, each about the size of a half-dollar camouflaged in the dead leaves and other debris. Fearful of stepping on unseen fluffy black and buff brood mates, I gingerly backed off. In the meantime, Blaze, having moved a few feet at the flush, stood at my command "whoa." But where was Jing?

Seems he had tired of this silly little game and was up in the woodcock singing ground running around joyfully with my blue club hat! Seeing that we were about a quarter-mile from my house, I can't explain how my hat got there. Maybe I had inadvertently dropped it and then forgot about it on a previous jaunt after stopping on a break to remove the soiled, sweat-permeated crown protector to better wipe my brow. Give it back, he would not! Proud as the pet but now unfettered peacock running loose over the adjacent hills just over the town line in Bozrah as of late, Jing ran all the way home with his prize, finally dropped it on the rear patio and then went off looking for something else to steal.

Jing's First Grouse Find

Author's note. The following e-mail was written to Lloyd Murray, breeder of Long Gone setters and Doug Lilley, owner of the Central Vermont brood bitch. Lloyd's stud dog, Long Gone Nixon, progeny of Grouse Ridge Reroy and Long Gone Agnes, was bred to Lilley Hill Miss Lilley at Lloyd's kennels at Stark, New Hampshire. Jing, a Friday the thirteenth puppy, was whelped at Plainfield, Vermont.

Nov. 3, 2004
Hi Lloyd and Doug,

First of all, Doug, I would again like to thank you for making our visit an enjoyable one last March 28 at your Vermont farm. Your countryside sure is beautiful. The trip home with the two pups was uneventful with only a few "accidents," as I recall, but we were well prepared for the expected.

I hunted in Maine eight days this year and wanted to keep you abreast of Jing's progress.

I think he did yeoman service for being only eight-months-old (whelped Feb. 13, 2004). Of course, I had my old Chief setter, Blaze, along with Jing's sibling, Molly II, the latter belonging to my hunting partner, Greg Teifert. Blaze did well for her thirteen years. She and Katy, Greg's eight-year-old setter bitch, found many of our twenty-nine birds bagged, including three grouse on this five-day hunt. (They found a lot of our misses, too!)

First off, Jing, being the runt of the litter, now weighs, I would estimate, forty-seven to forty-eight pounds. Molly, his littermate, which Greg purchased from Doug and who was bigger at six weeks, must weigh about twenty-five pounds soaking wet! You never know. Of course, both have not yet matured physically. Jing is fast and a moderate ranger, just what I like—not a boot licker or a horizon buster. I got lucky with this pup!

Jing put it all together up north, after having done really well on stocked pheasants here in Connecticut. He retrieves fairly well on wild birds, has a super-sensitive nose, and again, is fast and birdy. We shot (or shot at) several woodcock over him. One particular find was spectacular.

There were three of us this day—former Maine guide and long-time friend Fred Westerberg, Greg, and I—hunting the Stow Meadows, a huge intervale cover on the New Hampshire-Maine border. We came upon a large fairly open area along the Cold River with a thick clump of raspberries in the middle, about fifteen feet in diameter. Jing slid into a point when he reached it. We surrounded the weeds with a pincer movement. I was down in a hole and wasn't in a position to shoot. Greg was off to the right restraining the other pup. After having had much time to prepare, Fred walked in slowly to flush the bird. Jing, the puppy, remained steady for what seemed like an eternity. No bird. After making our presence more noisily known with loud stomping and thrashing, this tightly holding woodcock finally decided to exit in a noisy flush. It presented a nice straightaway opportunity for Fred. But wait a minute—that was a.....grouse! We couldn't believe that Fred blew the shot. You gotta know Fred though; he admits to not being that great a shot. Nice dog work and I was beaming-proud of the puppy for holding that grouse for such a long time until we kicked it out.

There's more shooting to be done in Connecticut this year, as early to mid-November is prime time for late-migrating woodcock. Also, we'll be shooting pheasants at Snake Meadow until the end of December, or maybe into January. I suspect that by the end of next season or sooner I'll have a thoroughly trained puppy, fully on his way to being steady to wing and shot. By the way, Jing has no patches, just moderately sized ticking, mostly black but some tan on his face and front legs, a real handsome boy. Looks just like his daddy without the eye patch.

There is one developing concern, which I don't know whether to worry about or ignore. Sometimes, but not always, Jing flags on point with pheasants. I tried feathering his tail and other far-fetched schemes, but nothing seems to help so far. It may be uncertainty on points, but maybe I've got to keep "whoa" to a minimum and let him work out the scent on his own time. He's probably too young for me to be concerned at this time.

Best regards,
Paul Chase

Miraculous Escape

Looking down on a flock of goldeneyes from the dam

Sunday, January 27 was a day to long remember. I almost lost my dog to a cold and icy death.

"Hey Paul, my wife and I will be leaving on a cruise for ten days next week. Bill's watching Katie; can you babysit Molly?" Of course I agreed to his request because Greg is my friend and hunting partner. Molly, his English setter, is a sibling of my Mr. Jing. Both were purchased together as six-week-old puppies from Plainfield, Vermont.

The last time Greg left Molly with me she decided to play hide and seek when I was running the two dogs on my acreage. No problem;

she was just "hiding" for awhile and soon rejoined us. During that brief interim of concern, which seemed much longer at the time, I tried to imagine what it would be like to lose a friend's dog on my watch.

Placing my Dogtra around Molly's neck, we started out on our every-other-day run on this particular Sunday, a great day to be alive. The shadows were starting to lengthen as we headed through grown-up pasture starting to look more like pole-timber. The dogs were well under control as we passed through the Woodcock Singing Ground and into the cover from which I had cut this year's supply of mixed hardwoods, a promising grouse cover if I ever saw one. Then the dogs became more anxious for a find as they started to stretch out.

Continuing through the heavy cover, I depended more and more on my whistle to keep the two big-running dogs within occasional eyesight. Crossing through the bar-way where the woods open up to saw-timber, the dogs rushed down the hill, continued along the water-filled woods road and proceeded up over the next rise. "Whoa!" I shouted when the duo disappeared over the ridge to the right leading to Beaver Dam. I forged ahead. After a tap on the transmitter, Molly, followed by Jing, appeared on the main path before the stream crosses over the rip rap-bottomed road. We exited the northern boundary of my property and headed toward the gated blacktop road to Stony Brook Reservoir—open only to infrequently-used service vehicles—belonging to the Norwich Department of Public Utilities and the occasional walker. Their employees know me as the adjacent landowner who is seen frequently walking his dog(s) even though, technically, trespassers are not allowed.

Down, down, down we went toward the earthen dam at the bottom of the access road where the blacktop ends and where walkers cross the eastern boundary of the waterway. The dogs continued coursing back and forth on both sides of the road, keeping in touch perfectly. Just before we reached the bottom of the hill, I heard and then saw the flush of a resident flock of goldeneyes from the reservoir beyond the ice to my left. When I reached the bottom, Molly heeled to my call, and we started across the dam. But where was Jing? My eyes searched the area; I called, I whistled. No Jing. Then I heard a bark. Where? Again, a bark. I tried to focus on the sound that seemed to be coming from out in the reservoir.

Suddenly I heard splashing out on the open water. I located the sound and then, to my horror (Jing was thrashing around in the potable water supply!), saw him desperately trying to get a foothold on the ice about fifty yards from shore. I watched my helpless dog for a few seconds, realized what was happening, and then panicked in fear of his life. Gingerly at first, but with no second thoughts about falling through the ice myself, I gradually worked my way out over the smooth surface, conscious of crackling sounds below and around me, my eyes peeled straight ahead watching Jing's futile attempts to lift himself up on solid ice.

I could see Jing's self-rescue wasn't going to happen, as his struggle began to lessen from exhaustion. When within ten feet, I bellied over the black and thinning ice to lower the center of gravity and to spread my weight, stuck out my arm and met Jing's desperate outstretched paw in my palm. Would the ice hold our weight? Luckily, it did. Jing whined a little but with a dual effort, my dog was back on the ice and nonchalantly headed toward shore on his own like nothing had happened, I an emotional and physical wreck, looking up, moist-eyed, thanking the Maker. Our reunion would have to wait for solid ground, as I carefully followed Jing to the rip rap base of the dam.

Thinking back on this incident, I was extremely fortunate to escape with my life, let alone Jing's. Over the years, dogs belonging to my friends under similar circumstances weren't so lucky. What started out as a concern for being responsible for my friend's Molly could have ended up with lives lost, caused by my usually-under-control Jing.

The Birds

Woodcock Melancholy

Aiden Lassell Ripley, *Woodcock Shooting*, etching

We had been duly warned. Dismal, dismal, dismal, echoed the words of the redoubtable Greg Sepik of the U.S. Fish and Wildlife Service's Region Five in Calais, Maine. He was referring to the 1996 woodcock availability and what hunters could expect.

In the *Bangor Daily News*, sporting writer/artist Tom Hennessey painted a similar picture for this species and other game. Both blamed the bird's reduced numbers on dry weather, wet weather, and cold weather.

Generally, inclement conditions up and down the Atlantic Flyway exacerbated the long-term downward trend—two and one-half percent per year since 1968—of this grand game bird that is rapidly becoming the pointing dog owner's choice for the ultimate experience in upland gunning.

Throughout much of the breeding range, the unusually cold and wet spring raised havoc with family planning. Throw in the summer drought that occurred over much of the Northeast, and starvation became a factor. And then, to complete the triple whammy, the "Sunny South" experienced record cold and snowfall.

Indeed, there is talk of a reduced limit for 1997 and/or a shorter season, but I believe the USF&WS will defer its decision until after 1998 when all states are mandated to participate in the Harvest Information Program (HIP). All hunters who harvest this migratory species will be required to participate in order for the feds to gather more information about the bird's numbers.

There is so much about this bird that has been left to speculation. Many authorities have stated that no data exists to suggest that hunting has a meaningful effect on woodcock numbers. But until the feds learn how many birds are killed each year, the effect of hunting on populations will continue to be a guessing game.

No doubt, far and away the biggest factor in the bird's long-term downward trend is the spiraling disappearance of suitable habitat. The double-barrel action of backhoe and bulldozer is the American woodcock's and other wildlife's greatest threat. Politically, it is obviously farcical to fight development.

One action that we can take as individual landowners is to manage the land. I have not heard of a convincing argument as to why Snake Meadow Club should not have a Stewardship Incentive Plan on at least a portion of its property, and this has been my sermon for years in *Snake Meadow Happenings*. If we, as sportsmen, don't do it, who the hell else will take charge—P.E.T.A. or Friends of Animals?

Ministrations aside, I cannot recall in recent years of a more "doom and gloom" prophecy. Having taken it seriously, I expected little success on my bird hunting journeys in northern New England this past October.

Just south of Quebec Province in the Northeast Kingdom of Vermont, I found grouse in numbers that I had not seen in years, although my guide said that they were not as plentiful as last year based on mental notations made of reduced drumming during spring trout fishing. I was early for woodcock as we appeared to be getting into native populations only, not flight birds. They were small, indicating delayed reproduction because of the cold, wet spring. So far, there were no surprises.

Then came the Maine hunt, where we consider two good days of a three-day trip as being successful. I have to say that we had three excellent days with forty-five woodcock moved. My shooting was a bit sub-par, unlike my experience in Vermont where I couldn't miss. But, Greg, my hunting partner, atoned for my one for three shooting average with near-perfect precision. We could always count on action no matter where we went. The Intervale Cover at Stow (on the New Hampshire border) was particularly impressive; no big concentrations but always a bird or two no matter where we went.

So, I guess, in our experience anyway, the dire forecast really had no effect on the situation as we found it. At least a few hunters, in their published comments, said they weren't going to shoot, as they would be satisfied just to watch their dogs work the covers. Admirable. I respect these folks for their sacrifice.

Think about the migration for a moment. Unlike migratory waterfowl, woodcock pretty much follow individual instincts when heading for southern climes. You're fortunate when you "hit" multiple birds or "flights." Other times, you can't buy a bird when weather conditions are not favorable, such as a long and unusually warm spell. I'm reminded of Hal Sheldon's "Ghost Birds" in *Tranquility Revisited*, first published in 1940. What you typically get is a trickle throughout the season, absent any severe weather conditions, and that's ideal.

In my youth, I recall my grandfather telling about the mass concentration of woodcock that appeared in the barnyard one cold and moonlight October night. He had gone out to the barn in the late evening to retrieve a broken harness that needed to be repaired. Birds were everywhere—in the hundreds. One suspects that a "blow" up north caused these birds to migrate en masse.

The long-term downward trend is not a measurable annual phenomenon from the individual hunter's perspective. In my experience, annual differences in birds moved are more of a function on how you hit the flights. I did not get into any large concentrations this year, but I did miss one by a few hours here in Connecticut. Chalk (woodcock droppings) was extant in profusion over a large area. Instead of the normal splash (1.5 inches or so in diameter) here and there, the mingled effect was several chalkings within the diameter of a large cow flop spread over several square yards. I can only imagine what that covert might have been like had I been there a day of two earlier. I have never seen anything like this in my forty years of hunting.

Tame Grouse

Occasionally, one encounters a tale about a tame grouse in the midst of a civilized world. No, I'm not talking about far-northern birds that have had no contact with man and have a reactive sense of jumping up on the nearest tree branch for a better look at this strange interloper. In such places, these uneducated denizens often times are potshot with .22 rifles. Farther south—virtually all the U.S.—you're lucky to catch a glimpse of this wild, fleeting King of the Uplands. Many times, you might be aware of the bird's departing presence by a distant muffle of wings, or a nearer, unseen flush evidenced by an intimidating and heart wrenching roar amidst a few falling leaves.

A "tame" grouse, one that is rather immune to man's presence for some unknown reason, is a rare phenomenon. I first witnessed this strange occurrence on the morning of May 28, 1994. The harsh winter had kept me from timely wood cutting chores, and I was still using the chain saw on this late date. That a grouse was even in the immediate area, with all my noise making, was, in itself, unusual.

After refueling, and in preparation for a last go at a twenty-four inch, seventy-five-year-old red oak, the strutting bird, twenty feet distant, appeared in a cleared area that I planned to convert into a woodcock singing ground. He took no particular notice of me, as I stood frozen in my tracks with mouth agape. This was no fairer-sexed biddy trying to lure me from her brood. It was definitely of male persuasion.

He jumped up on one of my carefully constructed environmental brush piles and then did a slow tightrope act back and forth across the top of a stacked cord of wood, all at a measured twelve feet from this observer. Finally, he disappeared behind another woodpile and showed no particular concern as I intercepted his path when he emerged. I kept prodding him to come to me by making silly little sounds, much the same as when calling a puppy. I traversed a parallel course for several feet as my friend casually pecked at whatever was on the ground, only occasionally glancing up to make sure that I wasn't taking undue liberties. In the interest of a possible future liaison, I backed off carefully and watched him slowly disappear into the adjoining wild apple thicket.

The next Saturday—a June gem—found me starting the Herculean task of hand-splitting five cords of mixed hardwoods—mostly hickory. He must have been watching me all along because when I cut the tractor engine at the second stop, Mr. Grouse came running down the woods road toward me as if responding to an invitation from a newly found mate. I sat on the back of my 1950s vintage U-haul, watching in amazement the antics of this seemingly crazed critter. He wanted to come to hand so badly but would stop about thirty inches from my dangling feet.

The swinging maul biting against hard bitternut hickory seemed to bore him, and he hunkered down in the brush awaiting my next attention-getting break. He stayed with me all morning, and as I drove off with a load of wood, he followed the Kubota diesel for a minute or so.

Armed with a 35mm camera and a little birdseed, I was ready for him on June 11th. He was at my side after ten minutes of splitting, anxious to resume our friendship. He didn't particularly relish the birdseed, as he was more interested in pecking my outstretched fingers. He communicated with clucking and faint cooing and seemed to enjoy posing for pictures. He flitted from log to log as I split, always keeping within three or four feet, until I stopped. Then he would almost come to hand.

The fourth Saturday of our tryst had this doting partridge in my lap as I sat against a woodpile. Is he convinced that I'm a she? Am I dealing with a retarded "ruff," a pariah amongst a dwindling few? Or does he have an uncanny sense that my releasing of herbaceous growth will benefit his lot? How about a defective gene—the one that controls fear? The answer is probably none of the foregoing. The Ruffed Grouse Society told me in all likelihood that Mr. Grouse was an unusually aggressive male just doing his thing—protecting his territory!

Beware of Promises!

When I attended the Vintage Cup double gun championships at
Orvis Sandanona in September 2004, I stopped at the table of Tobique
Valley Outfitters, Riley Brook, New Brunswick and had an amiable
chat with Dan Pichette, who is one of their guides. He told a good
story of plentiful birds in his delightful Canadian accent. Would I like
to put my name in the bowl and possibly win a three-day hunting trip,
aye? Why not! My luck at winning anything is practically nil, but
what was there to lose?

Later that day, I ran into—almost literally doing the rounds in his
golf cart—Ray Poudrier, president of the Order of Edwardian Gunners,
aka the Vintagers, who had hunted with this New Brunswick outfitter
in 2003. His praise of the experience was superlative, notwithstanding
his suggestion that we bring our own dogs. No problem; we would do
that anyway. Just maybe I would book a hunting trip with this outfit
even if I weren't the lucky winner. The costs seemed reasonable. Imagine
my surprise when I received a call from Dan early the following week
informing me that I was the lucky winner! Arrangements were made
during the next several days and my hunting partner, Greg, arranged to
make the sojourn with me in mid-October.

I recalled receiving a letter dated in 1985 from New Brunswick
guide Fred Webb in response to my inquiry regarding a bird-hunting
trip in that province, where he ran a guide service. Currently a
professional big game guide haunting the Northwest Territories and the
newly formed Nunavut Territory in Canada, Webb jogged my memory
of that letter recently when I read a colorful chapter he wrote for the
recently published book *Beyond Hill Country – Gene Hill Remembered.*
(Amwell Press)

His priceless response (unedited) follows:

Dear Sir:

I am sorry I cannot help you as we have discontinued our bird
shooting as of several years ago because of many changes in the
area.
When I started the business we had a virtually untouched area,
birds were numerous and coverts undisturbed. Since that time

a few things have changed. Now, everyone with an empty camp, and some of them heads to match, thinks they are bird-shooting guides. Every good cover has been plowed up, posted, or taken up by some rural slum in the form of camps or trailers. It is over with.

Grouse continue to be fairly plentiful in deep woods, always subject to their ups and downs of course. The woodcock have steadily declined. The only reason kill figures have perhaps increased is because a thousand times more people are killing them, and biologists always base their guesses on the count of dead critters rather than make any attempt to census live ones. The woodcock shooting should be very sharply curtailed over <u>all</u> of its range before it is extinct. Naturally, many other reasons than hunters have affected the bird, but for goddam sure when the whole modern world and its problems are against it, then a twelve month open season somewhere along its route is too much.

Anyway, sorry I can't help you except to warn you to be <u>very</u> cautious before believing anyone in New Brunswick or Maine telling you about wonderful woodcock hunting nowadays; they just might be bullshitting you.

Sincerely,
Fred Webb

Mr. Webb is decisively clear on the positions he takes. I suspect there are many truths in his letter, but he is flat-out wrong in that he fails to mention singing counts, which are taken annually in order to determine breeding populations. There is, in fact, a census of "live critters." In his defense, annual singing counts may not have commenced when he wrote this letter. Also of note is that an awareness of the decline in numbers prompted the Feds later that year to decrease the daily limit from five to three birds (in the states at least) and to reduce the length of the hunting season in all states to thirty days. The Canadian authorities, however, have not reduced their daily bag limit of eight birds and their woodcock season of two and one-half months, which is extremely liberal. If the U.S. statistics prove that woodcock are steadily declining, why haven't the Canadian authorities curtailed its shooting as Mr. Webb suggests?

My forthcoming adventure in New Brunswick is eagerly anticipated. However, I think this trip is more about grouse than woodcock, the latter having experienced a long and steady decline in numbers, as pontificated—I should say predicted—by Mr. Webb way back in 1985.

Winter Woodcock

Jing

A late December conversation with a hunting friend went something like this: Hey Ken, Mr. Jing (my setter) and I are seeing several woodcock every day on the managed section of my property. Care to come along to watch? (Ken's setter, Maggie, who just turned fifteen, couldn't oblige as her bird finding days ended this past fall.) He jumped at the opportunity, although he may have doubted my incredulous claim. "Sure, how's Friday, December 29 at one o'clock?" We agreed on the time and made a date.

Every hunter knows that woodcock from New England and the Maritime Provinces move to the Gulf States for the winter months. After the first or a series of hard frosts and favorable winds their individual migratory instincts cause them to move south via the Eastern Flyway. Their departure usually occurs in October through November, depending on weather conditions. They arrive back at their birthing grounds as early as mid-February into March.

The thirty-day hunting season for woodcock ended on November 18, so our planned excursion was for the benefit of our curiosity—and Jing's further training. He likes to "hunt" woodcock in the off-season; in fact, he was largely bird-trained on the returning migrants in late February and March of the past two years. He'll be three in a few months.

After the season ended, I didn't think too much about why I continued to see four or five birds every time Jing and I went out. It had remained warm with no snow, and only one or two frosts had whitened the early morning landscape. Then I started to question the physical ability of these small birds to continue their late journey south, arrive at their destination—and then turn around and head north for the breeding season. I suspected that one day very soon they would come to their senses and "hit the road." That was a few weeks before Christmas.

Several times after that realization, Jing and I continued to find birds in or near wet areas, sometimes almost literally in puddles of water, accompanied by the myriad telltale presence of chalk—everywhere. I was almost certain that I was seeing the same birds, as there always seemed to be four or five on every outing. But our search was casual, and never was there any attempt to cover every nook and cranny of this ten-acre covert in order to determine how many birds were actually in residence. I resolved to do this with Ken on the 29th.

"Management" of this small portion of my fields and woodlands consists of winter and spring cutting of firewood to feed my warm air wood furnace. The annual heating requirement is only five or so cords, but I have been selectively harvesting (not clear cutting) the same quantity in this covert for several years. What was once a mixture of pole and saw timber now consists of open areas with an ever-increasing understory of mixed vegetation—grape vines, body-abusing multiflora rose, and the baneful bittersweet. Fortunately, the hardwoods—mostly hickory—are regenerating and in time will provide some shade and, hopefully, reasonable control of the nasty oriental intruder. In all probability, a few herbicide applications may be necessary in the future. But for now the whole area is reasonably open, which bodes well for relatively easy gunning the few times I hunt it in early November.

After viewing a recent addition to my modest sporting art collection and exchanging a sporting book or two, Ken and I started out in the cool stillness of the early sun-emblazoned afternoon. As usual, Mr. Jing was frothing at the bit in his kennel, surmising that another day in the field was about to begin. We had hunted "real time" pheasants at the club a few days before and "pretend" woodcock just yesterday. His enthusiasm abounds!

Arriving at my recently acclaimed covert, Jing went about his business under good control, and I was sure he would jack up any moment. However, he showed us nothing but keen interest and good form in his methodical search. "The birds have left," I almost said out loud to Ken. But then of a sudden Jing made game and displayed a breathtaking point, his body crouched, head level, tail high, as in an Osthaus painting. Breathlessly, we watched the drama unfold. The ground to Jing's front was open with no cover afforded any living being. Standing in our tracks, I searched for the beaded eye. "There," I pointed, and Ken followed my extended hand to a point four feet in front of Jing's nose. As we walked forward, she (the woodcock) rose up on extended legs and then, as the encroaching pressure mounted, leaped into the air, back over steady-to-wing-Jing's up-stretched head. Ken's imaginary double followed its course, and I heard him exclaim, "Dead bird."

And so it continued that afternoon just three days before New Year's. We moved nine different birds for ten points. Two other finds warrant mention. Jing pointed a bird that was located over the ubiquitous New England stonewall. Not satisfied with his positioning, he ran along the wall several feet and then placed his front paws atop the wall and pointed again into the next woodlot. The woodcock rose on the other side, and again I heard Ken say, "Dead bird." Later, working in an open saw-timbered area filled with giant tulip poplar, a highly unlikely resting spot for the evanescent feathered recluse, Mr. Jing pointed not far from a very slight water flow a few yards distant. Sure enough, another longbill lifted in front of two gawking and unbelieving Nimrods. "Gotcha," uttered Ken. Again and again and again, we found the migrants around wet areas.

So what's happening here? Is what we are witnessing a result of El Niño or changing weather patterns due to global warming? Can it be explained simply by extended warm, quasi-Indian summer-like conditions, an infrequent or one-time occurrence in southern New England? Even in the Rangeley Lakes area of northwestern Maine, long-time residents cannot remember when the lake was not frozen by January 1. Do the birds have a clue? Do their innate biological clocks not sense that a higher probability of severe weather conditions later on could limit their southern journey—read imperil their very existence—by procrastinating into early winter? Have they decided to remain in coverts composed of spring holes that never freeze and "stick it out" like their brethren, the American robin and Canada goose?

In all probability, what I have been seeing for the past several weeks is a trickle of different birds that are "here today and gone tomorrow." The extreme warm weather and lack of major fronts occurring so late in the year and into the next has simply delayed normal migratory patterns, and I suspect that my covert will be devoid of woodcock activity soon. In the meantime, during the next few weeks, Jing and I will monitor the continued presence—or absence—of Harold Sheldon's "ghost birds," keeping special watch on my covert, especially during the full of the Wolf Moon beginning on January third.

The Guns

Success Story

Some years ago, a few shotgun fanciers and I paid a visit to Tony Galazan's gun shop, a converted garage in New Britain. He always seemed to advertise nice guns, and he was close by, maybe an hour or so away. Tony could always be found in the vicinity of Jim Austin's New England Arms' table at the Hartford Gun Shows in Glastonbury and always seemed like a nice young kid hanging on Austin's coattails.

In due time it became evident that he was a knowledgeable purveyor of classic double guns and could be counted on always having a fine display of high-grade smoothbores. Soon it was common gossip in the gun trade that Tony had allegedly faked the missing Czar Nicholas A1 Special that had fooled all the experts. Tony was sued and wound up in court, but no proof of his indiscretions was ever forthcoming. One thing was proven by this little prank; his machining and gunsmithing abilities are first rate.

Several years later Tony surprised gundom by resurrecting the famed Ainsley Fox, "The Finest Gun in the World," the by-line in the ads state (just like the original Fox). Another by-line has been added: "The finest craftsmanship in the world." The pundits said it couldn't be done, but he succeeded in recreating a domestically produced double where others had failed. What an accomplishment—and most observers believe that it's a finer gun than the original! But this was just the beginning.

Over the last decade of the twentieth century, Tony assembled a U.S. team of trained foreign-born gunsmiths, an administrative staff, and a beautiful factory and showroom (by appointment only) in his on-going effort to produce a domestically produced dynasty of fine guns. The factory encompasses several acres and contains the latest in CNC machinery and other equipment.

Preceding Tony's efforts, Tom Skeuse brought back the famed Parker from about 1984 to 1988, but it was produced in Japan. This is an amazing story in itself. Suffice it to say that when the contract with Winchester's Olin-Kodensha plant was due to expire because of a change in plant production mandates (from guns to auto parts), Skeuse couldn't produce the Parker elsewhere without escalating costs.

After resurrecting the Fox, did Tony rest easy? Not by a long shot. His firm, the Connecticut Shotgun Manufacturing Company, is now fabricating the custom built Winchester Model 21 Grand American with prices starting at around $50,000. Although the Model 21 is not my cup of tea in the annals of best lightweight and finely balanced upland scatterguns, it has established a niche of followers in the shotgun world, strength of action being its major forte.

The *piece de resistance* is the A. Galazan-produced sidelock superposed, which, although at first blush appears to be almost a dead ringer for the exquisite Boss O/U, is newly designed, not a copy of the Boss. Prices start at $38,000 *sans* engraving. Not lacking in modesty, Tony claims it's the finest sidelock in the world. He may be correct. What makes me proud is the engraving on the barrels, "New Britain, Connecticut, USA," not someplace in Great Britain or Italy.

I must admit that the few sidelocks I have seen from photographs carry rather bizarre engraving, but that is no reflection of the gun's quality. Being custom made, you can order the most conservative English rose and scroll, the latter being reflected in CSMC's 2006 calendar with an exquisitely fine, Winston Churchill-engraved, case-colored A. Galazan sidelock.

Galazan realized that only a few of the most fortunate world-class purveyors of fine shotguns could afford such a firearm. Recently I saw the first ad in *Shooting Sportsman* magazine announcing the RBL, the long-rumored and much more modestly priced side-by-side game gun that will appeal to hunters. Options are numerous, the most expensive of which is exhibition wood at an extra $700. No-cost standard options include a choice of single trigger (a modified Model 21) or double triggers, straight or pistol grip, and a choice of two lengths of pull. The price of the RBL (round body boxlock) is just $2799 with standard options. If you pay up front, he takes off $300! This gun is a machine made 20-gauge boxlock, as you would expect, but this is a class act according to those who have examined it. I suspect that the machining is as good—or better—than that employed by the world's finest shotgun makers. As with any endeavor Tony undertakes, most likely time will prove this latest entry to be an extremely high value—a straight-out production gun mimicking a hand-made firearm. I had the opportunity to have a factory tour recently and was particularly impressed by the laser machine that produced perfect stock and forearm checkering for the RBL. I asked how one could tell the difference between hand checkering and machine made checkering. The plant manager responded, "Our laser checkering is too perfect."

Is this the end of the chronology? Hardly. Announced in December of 2005 under the ownership of Remington Arms, Parker's last domestic producer, a very limited number of 28-gauge AAHE Grade Parkers will be produced by CSMC starting at $49,000. Will there be other gauges and grades? Based on the provenance and technological acumen of CSMC, and especially high demand for Parkers, my answer would have to be in the affirmative. An exciting new chapter in the production of "the old reliable" is about to be written.

A few years ago I asked Tony what were his criteria for being a top maker today, aside from obvious superior quality. His singular requirement without blinking a gunmaker's eyelash: the ability to improve mechanics and be innovative. In other words, what is a maker doing different (and presumably better)? I think this attribute describes Connecticut Shotgun Manufacturing Co. to a tee, especially as reflected by the superb A. Galazan sidelocks and, of course, the new RBL.

I wished Tony luck with his Fox project several years ago—little did I know what the future would bring. He made it big time, and then some!

For Woodcock and Other Things: Ordering a Best Gun

After several years of collecting, shooting, admiring, and coveting that which I could not afford, I decided, in June of 1987, to order a custom-made shotgun primarily for woodcock, but not so specialized as to preclude its use on other upland species. I love older double barrel

101

shotguns, for they seem to exude a mystical aura from insouciant times when game was plentiful. Yet, I felt that this "mystique" had been built into the price of certain "best" guns making them unaffordable and more expensive than their intrinsic worth. Parkers, for example, are excellent guns, but their collectible status and price escalation has put them in a class of "best," which, arguably, they are not.

I like petite guns and toyed with ordering a 28 gauge. I shoot reasonably well, but hunting pheasant at the local gun club would be a secondary use. In my estimation, going-away ringnecks require more than a 28 for consistent and clean kills. So the 20 would be the gauge of choice, as it can handle an ounce of sixes quite efficiently. I considered the 16 gauge for its versatility, but again, it lacked the petiteness and lighter weight that I so much desire when making half-day forays into upland coverts.

Best overall quality would be, far and away, the most important consideration—without giving a king's ransom. For all intents and purposes, this ruled out the sidelock action, which the trade has always priced much higher than boxlocks. Aphoristically, the increased labor required for the production of sidelocks does not justify the higher cost of several thousand dollars over boxlocks. Welcome to the real world. I could get a lesser-quality sidelock for the same price (or less—much less in some instances) as a best-quality boxlock, but that would not be consistent with my foremost objective—the very highest level of craftsmanship. A best gun is not only judged by exterior fit and finish. The presence of interior quality is what sometimes separates the really top makers from just good producers of fine doubles, in my estimation. Some would opine, "out of sight, out of mind," as it were. My gun would have to be made like the proverbial Swiss watch inside.

There would be an emphasis on utility over collectability. As much as we all like to see our toys rampantly appreciate in value, that honor, as least for the present (1999), must be reserved for the best London sidelocks. This brought me to another consideration—should my gun be handcrafted in England? After all, the production of fine doubles was brought to a zenith in that country between the two world wars, and several fine guns are still being made. Most are very expensive, however, and since I had a limited budget I decided not to go that route, even though I am basically an Anglophile with deep English roots.

I have an open mind when it comes to engraving. Traditional English rose and scroll is always tasteful. I do not particularly care for heavy scroll, gold inlay, or the very broad brush approach to game scene engraving, especially as is frequently seen on high-grade Italian sidelocks, but these biases are simply a matter of personal preference.

Over the years, I established a relationship with New England Arms, located at Kittery Point, Maine. I had purchase two sideplate Lefevers from the company and paid fair prices for these guns. The showroom, at the tip of Kittery Point, is a masterpiece of cherry cabinetry containing a wide array of world-class shotguns offering ample choices—a veritable treasure trove of the world's best—, which should not fail to galvanize the most discriminating or stolid buyer. New England Arms would be my agent. David Trevallion, formerly of Purdey's and renowned for his stock work, suggested some minute changes to stock dimensions. Game and skeet shooting over the years had pretty much established proper stock requirements, but I agreed with David as to a bit more length and slightly less drop at heel (14⅜ x 2¼). Malfeasance on my part took the form of rendering a little 20-gauge EE Grade Syracuse Lefever as earnest money, but that is another story.

After a brief dalliance with various Spanish sidelocks such as AYA, Arrieta, and others (most of which I consider best buys), the Val Trompia (Trompia Valley) artisans of northern Italy caught my critical eye as being the quintessence of quality. My gun would be made by F.lli (abbreviation for brothers) Rizzini of Magno. The Rizzini firm, which originally consisted of five siblings, has been fabricating very high quality side-by-sides since the mid-1970s. (Prior to that, they produced medium quality production guns, i.e. A & F Rizzini, Zoli Rizzini.) Unlike many prestigious makers, especially of years past, F.lli Rizzini boxlocks are equal in quality to their sidelocks. Approximately twenty sidelocks and boxlocks are handmade annually. If I were hard pressed to single out the one outstanding visual attribute of Rizzini doubles, it would have to be extreme high quality of metal work.

I examined a few of this maker's specimens at New England Arms before making a final decision. I detached the finely-struck barrels noting the almost invisible line indicating chopperlump (demibloc) barrel joining. I examined the water table and knuckle pin configuration. I liked the scalloped line of the action back joining the stock wood. I removed the inspection plate, which exposed the cocking levers and tumblers of the lock mechanisms. All parts were meticulously stone polished to a glass-like finish. Most screw heads would not be visible were it not for their slots, which were so narrow one wonders how turnscrew heads could be sized down and still impart the necessary torque to turn the screws. I was impressed with total precision and refinement—the cachet of a best gun.

All wood examined was highly figured Circassian walnut. Some years ago the Rizzini firm purchased one whole twenty-five-year-old Circassian walnut tree that had been growing in Yugoslavia for $16,000. Some stocks will be better than others, of course, but you generally get what you pay for. Exceptional wood is very expensive, even in the raw state. Rizzini has a reputation for providing very high quality wood.

Best Rizzini sidelocks (Model R-1) and boxlocks (Model R-2) have several patented enhancements that are masterpieces of mechanical precision. The single most distinguishing mechanical characteristic is the ejector system developed in 1976. It allows the barrels to be opened and closed with virtually no effort. Knowledgeable gun buffs would compare this system with Holland and Holland and Lebeau-Courally. The Lebeau is more complex. Since it uses a coil spring, resistance increases as the barrels are closed to the breech. One would encounter more resistance in cocking the H&H in that one must overcome a fairly resistant dead zone based on the way that system works. Rizzini utilizes double leaf springs, the result being less effort as cocking reaches completion.

The famous Rizzini single trigger must be considered one of the few fine mono-triggers available today. This patented mechanism, activated by recoil, is strong, clean, efficient, and dependable. It is frequently seen on Rizzini doubles. That being said, however, I opted for double triggers. There are definite occasions for shooting the tighter barrel first. The best single trigger made cannot compete with the instant selectivity of two triggers, notably so when wearing shooting gloves. The front trigger would be articulated—standard on Rizzini guns. Pulls would be normal—about three pounds for the right barrel, a bit more for the left. Absolutely pristine and crisp is the way that I would describe Rizzini boxlock trigger pulls, which are usually a basic weakness of this action type lacking intercepting safety sears. Typical boxlock pulls tend to be heavy because of the safety factor. Not so with the R-2 because of the 90-degree angle between sear tail and bent in tumbler. Together with Rizzini's faultless interior finishing, this enhancement invites comparison with Holland-type trigger pulls, the H&H sidelock being the most copied in the world.

My personal preference was for a light game gun. I gave New England Arms just a bit of leeway regarding weight—between five and one-half and five and three-quarter pounds. Although my ramblings in the coverts are shorter than they used to be, a four to five hour hunt is common. I would definitely feel an extra half pound after such a stint. I agree that car-hopping from covert to covert might allow a heaver gun with less wispiness. Contrary to popular opinion, I have found that there are many opportunities for woodcock that require a swing-though method of leading. It is not all snap shooting (poke shooting is more descriptive). Because of this and because the gun would be used on other upland species, I chose 27-inch barrels. In fact, I pondered ordering 28-inch tubes. My reasoning was to impart a little more stability and follow-though into a light game gun by employing longer than traditional 25 or 26-inch barrels that are frequently seen on guns used in the thickets.

I deliberated over choke requirements at length with New England Arms. The final specification was loose improved cylinder (about .003 -.004) in the right barrel and improved cylinder in the left (about .010). Rizzini barrels are made from high quality UM6 steel; they are not chrome lined. Barrels are absolute perfection, inside and out.

Other than two previously owned straight stocked Browning Superposed Superlights, most of my game guns have been configured with semi-pistol (sometimes called half of ball grip) stocks. The ball grips of my Prussian Dalys were standard fare and make for comfortable shooting guns. I own a 20-gauge Parker with the classic mismatch (according to some) of pistol grip and splinter forend. Poor hands-in-line arrangement notwithstanding, I like the feel of the gun, especially after David Trevallion removed four ounces from the #1 Parker buttstock. But in the interest of slimness, sleekness, and classic lines, I decided to order a traditional straight stock and splinter forend. Rizzini configures a semi-beavertail forend that is quite nice, however.

Protection to the checkered butt would be provided by fine scroll-engraved heel and toe plates, which would complement the engraving on the action.

Boxlocks are somewhat limited as to the amount of engraving surface. Fine English scroll would be my preference with 100% coverage. I wanted a game scene on the floorplate done in the banknote style. I scoured my sporting art books for something acceptable and appropriate. Had Marco Nobili's *Fucili D'Autore* been available back in 1987, I would have chosen the English setter head that appears on page 286 of this fine publication—with the addition of a retrieved woodcock in its mouth. "Victorian" is the way I would describe a print of *Hanging Woodcock* done by H.M. Clay in 1861, which appears in Robert Elman's *The Great American Shooting Prints*. It appealed to me and I chose this.

Having established other details regarding pitch and castoff, gold oval with initials, and other engraving particulars, the gun was ordered June 5, 1987. I waited, anxiously, for eighteen months and one day before taking delivery December 6, 1988. I opened the full leather, billiard cloth-lined Nizzoli case to reveal the object of this discussion and my reason for living for the past year and a half. The effect of the fine but deeply cut scroll engraving was reminiscent of early Premier Grade Churchills. Needless to say, I was not disappointed—and that understates my total elation. After just looking at this five-pound nine-ounce beauty for several days, but long before the 1989 hunting season, I did extensive pattern testing with factory-loaded Winchester AA No. 9 skeet loads. The final results revealed forty-one percent for the right barrel, fifty two percent for the left—right on the money.

Looking back on the project, I would make no changes, although at present the 28 gauge is seeing increased popularity, as are longer barrels. These preferences run in cycles.

Of course, there will be others. Back to the discussion about a nifty little 28—on page 532 of Nobili's seminal monograph is a magnificent Luciano Bosis boxlock.....

A Mystery Solved

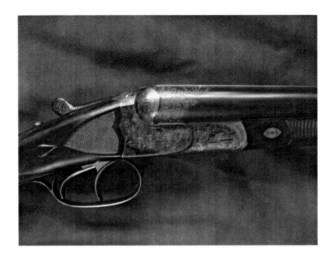

Some of you know that I have a fetish for fine guns—not that I can afford them! It's possible to spend six figures for a new twin-tubed English or Italian shotgun, even those of pre-owned persuasion! Likewise, a name-brand antique bamboo stick for fishing purists will command several thousand dollars. Does it catch any more fish; does an exquisite scattergun kill any cleaner? Probably not. Nevertheless, the feel and balance of a handcrafted piece is pure delight for serious bird hunters and fly fishers. Are there alternatives to paying a king's ransom for the best?

The Prussian-made Charles Daly brand of side-by-side shotguns imported from Germany during the last quarter of the nineteenth century to about the mid-1930s were about as good as guns get. Much information recently came to light about the mysterious "Prussian" Dalys, in particular, the post-Lindner-made Dalys. Handmade in Suhl, many of the higher grades of Prussian persuasion, according to noted gun writer Don Zutz, were as good as anything the British were making at this time and should be considered premium artifacts.

Generally speaking, German engraving and other aesthetics are not in keeping with American tastes. Even the German aristocracy preferred English guns with their traditional scroll-engraved patterns as opposed to heavy chiseled oak leafed-surrounded hunting scenes, sling swivels, and horn trigger guards common to high-grade German guns.

Imported by the well-known New York firm of Shoverling, Daly and Gales, design features and intrinsic quality of these fine imports were outstanding, in addition to being engraved to suit American preferences. But it is the flowing lines, mechanics, and highest quality of fit and finish— not just the engraving—that enamored Americans to these beautiful guns. Most had interceptors, a safety feature not normally seen on Anson & Deely boxlocks.

Gun purists acknowledge that the very best of the Prussian Dalys were made by Heinrich August Lindner and are stamped H A L just forward of the barrel flats. Unfortunately, not much is known about the man and his gun production. Although Suhl was not bombed during World War II, very few, if any, records exist, perhaps partially accounted for by the wartime collection of paper.

As was common in the trade, Lindner depended on outworkers for various functions such as actioners, barrel makers, and stock makers. Evidentially he retired during World War I or soon thereafter but continued to be the contact person for the New York importer until his death in 1933.

Who else besides HAL is credited with making Daly guns? There were probably more than a few—Sauer for one—but much information remains to come to light. After the First World War, according to Hans Pflingsten in an article appearing in *The Double Gun & Single Shot Journal,* production passed to Schilling, Triebel and (H. A.) Lindner, the latter reportedly only involved with export relations with the N.Y. Daly firm. Thereafter, from the early 1920s until the early to middle 1930s —the end of the Prussian Daly era—Daly guns were evidently produced by August Schüler, unknown until now. They are of very high quality also.

By way of comparison to a well-known American boxlock, in 1904 a #375 Diamond Quality, the most ornate Daly gun produced at that time, sold for $375. The highest grade Parker, an AAH Grade, sold for $425. Hype and Parker mystique (I won't get into why) command out-of-sight prices for "the old reliable." Currently, Dalys are still reasonable; that's of course, if you can find one. Quite possibly the reason for this is too few guns available, mandating relatively few collectors—

unlike Parkers. The price for an extremely rare Daly Diamond Quality or Regent Diamond Quality gun in 28 gauge assuredly would be an obvious exception.

A few years ago, a well-known gun dealer sent my friend Bill Shipman three Daly guns for possible purchase—a 16-gauge Diamond, a 20 gauge of Empire Quality and a 28 gauge of Superior Quality. As I personally favor these Prussian-made guns, Bill wanted my opinion. He had already received a professional appraisal as to the worth of the three specimens. The 28 was the first Daly in this gauge that I had even seen. It was very petite, probably made for a distaff shooter. To make a long story short, something was wrong, or at least suspect, with all three. At an average price of about ten grand apiece, I needed to be more convinced that they hadn't been messed with. The most honest of the three, the 16-gauge Diamond, had seen a lot of use and was loose of action, unusual for a Prussian Daly. Bill's and my opinion and that of the professional gunsmith, Abe Chaber, was that the trio was overpriced. What a shame, as these rarities come up for sale far too infrequently.

A 20-gauge Schüler-made Diamond Grade has become one of my favorite upland game guns in recent years for my northern forays chasing grouse and woodcock (along with a custom-made R-2 F.lli Rizzini). Weighing exactly five and one-half pounds with 28-inch barrels, it's one of my choice toys. Abe Chaber took a look at this gun at the Orvis Sandanona shooting grounds a few years back and quickly pronounced that it should be relegated to a bank vault. Retaining virtually all its vivid case colors, it's really too nice to shoot but, what the heck, that's what guns are for and it fits me like a dream.

On a whim, I entered a mint condition Empire Grade—presumably another Schüler-made gun—at the *Concours d'Elegance* of Fine Guns at The Vintage Cup held at the Orvis Sandanona shooting grounds in Millbrook, N.Y. in 2001. This mid-grade 12 gauge six and one-half pound piece with 28-inch barrels, made in 1930, fetched the Gold Medal in the Classic European Boxlock category. Quality and maker's reputation notwithstanding, competing with the world's best speaks volumes about the superb condition and aesthetics of this Empire Grade gun. I always wondered who laid claim (very silently) to its making. Now I know.

Clubbing at the Club

"…like a baseball bunt on a high fastball."

Three Snake Meadow Club members, Attorney Carl Anderson, club Secretary George Calkins, and I, along with George's guest, Gil Roberts, witnessed a bizarre occurrence at the Annual Hunt & Banquet held November 30 at the club grounds. With its 262 acres located in the towns of Plainfield and Killingly, Snake Meadow is one of Connecticut's premier sportsman's clubs, bird hunting and trout fishing being its forte. It enjoys a small membership that rarely reaches 100.

The Annual Hunt and Banquet is a very special event that is known throughout eastern Connecticut for its overabundance of stocked pheasant. Bag limits—and diets—are frequently overlooked on this exclusive occasion. The mid-day meal is a gastronomical delight, and that's reason enough for most hunting to occur during the morning. However, several stalwart souls indulge in the bird-hunting matinee on leftovers.

And so it was that the foursome, after savoring the delicious and filling feast, found itself working Area #3 with Blaze, my English setter. Carl and I were the gunners, George and Gil, the observers. The classy little setter, of the all-but-disappeared Chief strain, established a staunch point, but the gunners and observers failed to locate the supposed pheasant, even in the sparse ground cover.

Finally, after much looking and stomping and of doubting my dog's veracity, I spied the glint of the bird's eye in dying grass that you wouldn't think capable of concealing a toad, never mind a pheasant.

Relieved that Blaze was not false pointing old scent (this was the third hunt of the day in Area #3), I kicked out the bird, a hen pheasant. Carl, my equestrian friend, got off two straightaway shots with his vintage 20-gauge DHE Parker double, but the bird failed to drop. It appeared to have been hit however, as evidenced by its short 125-foot flight.

As Blaze approached the bird's landing spot, the panicky hen quickly re-flushed in a low line of flight, headed back in our direction and was upon us before a meat-saving shot could be contemplated by either of the slow-thinking Nimrods. Judged by its speed, it did not appear that this bird had taken any shot on the previous flush.

With absolutely no forethought or hesitation, I raised the little 20-gauge Diamond Grade Prussian-made Charles Daly over my head—as in club—and with a quick downward thrust, intercepted the hen's flight with a sharp blow to the head, whereupon she fell dead at my feet with nary a twitch.

Cheering and laughter erupted from my observing friends. Still unbelieving, I hesitated, but soon I too celebrated the uniqueness of what had just occurred. In truth, my unspoken concern was for the condition of the thin-walled barrels of the five and one-half pound Daly, a premium artifact, which took the hit about ten inches from the muzzle. A superficial glance showed no damage. Not wanting to dampen the mirth of the moment, I deferred a thorough examination to the privacy afforded me later in the day. Fortunately, the long-awaited inspection proved my cherished Daly to be without compromise—not a scratch.

Reflecting on the incident, it was not so much the force of my blow that killed the pheasant as it was estimating the speed and straight-line flight of the bird and its subsequent collision with my barrels. As described later by my friends: "What we saw was a quick but short downward thrust like a baseball bunt on a high fastball." Gil recalls "seeing the hen with swept-back wings in a diving fashion with the sun reflecting off a very sharp beak."

I saved the cost of a cartridge, but it could have been an expensive clubbing!

Entrepreneur Par Excellence

Last year, it was my good fortune to have attended an exhibit at the Wadsworth Athenaeum in Hartford, Connecticut honoring American business tycoon, Col. Samuel Colt. At the time, I thought that his legacy as an entrepreneur in the firearms manufacturing field was unsurpassed, this on top of notables Oliver Winchester, Eliphalet Remington, Dan Wesson, Dan LeFever and John Browning.

There is another name that many purveyors of firearms take for granted in this modern age of technology, one whose accomplishments are far-reaching, whose philanthropy will make possible the finest display of domestic firearms in the soon-to-be-opened National Firearms Museum. He is William Batterman Ruger, an American legend.* A staunch supporter of the NRA and the Second Amendment, Ruger and his company, Sturm, Ruger & Co., Inc. of Southport, Connecticut revolutionized firearms manufacture by perfecting the metallurgical process of investment casting, a less expensive method of producing receivers and other parts, compared to traditional and more labor-intensive forgings.

With more than 2000 employees and production facilities in Newport, New Hampshire and four other locations, Ruger is the largest firearms manufacturer in the U.S. with about 20% of the market. Recently, soft gun sales have been offset somewhat by the production and sale of titanium golf heads to the Callaway Golf Company.

I wish I had owned the company's stock—symbol RGR on the Big Board—over the years, but in the past year or so the stock has hovered in the eighteen-nineteen dollar range, probably more as a result of the perception of the future restriction of firearms sales than other factors.

There's no question that Ruger makes quality firearms at affordable prices—rifles, pistols, and shotguns. Ruger felt that America needed a good over and under shotgun, and with the demise of Remington's model 32 and 3200, the Ruger Red Label, made in 12, 20 and 28 gauge, was conceived to embody the great mechanical features, such as interceptors, and modern design of some of the world's finest stack-barrel shotguns. My only criticism is that it's a bit heavy for my taste as a *hunting* arm, even in its upland configuration.

The side-by-side 12-gauge Gold Label, made in both straight grip and pistol grip, is more adapted to upland hunting, primarily because of its lighter six and one-half pounds. Of Bill Ruger's own design and with a price tag of about $2050, this scattergun is within reach of most serious bird hunters. Inspired by the famous Dickson Round Action, which was a personal favorite of Ruger, this shotgun adds versatility to this affordable family of guns. My personal thought is that Ruger has broken tradition from shotguns on the heavy side to an extremely light 12 gauge. Weight-wise, I wonder what's in store for the sure-to-come 20 gauge or possibly a 28? Put each a tad under six pounds and I probably will own the 20.

Bill Ruger was a self-made man, having amassed his wealth by virtue of an intense interest in the mechanics of firearms and good old-fashioned business acumen. He was a collector of paintings, sculpture, sport and vintage autos, books, and firearms.

Of a familiar note was his unflagging support of the Second Amendment and his uncompromising stand on not giving concessions to gun prohibitionists, a somewhat divisive position even among NRA members, or, more accurately, why some refuse to support the NRA. Quoting Ruger:

"A constant problem the industry has is that you can't compromise with prohibitionists. Every time you concede an inch, it's a wasted concession...These people are not interested in rational discourse on how society can best control violent criminals. They simply hate guns, and a complete elimination of these inanimate objects is their actual goal...I think what is often lost sight of today is that the Constitution is there to protect the citizen from the government...This (the Bill of Rights) gave the document that force which it still has today, and people who talk about doodling with this thing or making it say what they want it to say are the very ones we should regard as dangerous and wrong to listen to...These people can't leave well enough alone, and they can't enjoy a beautiful thing without trying to spoil or tinker with it."

Note: Bill Ruger, Sr. passed away July 6, 2002

The Hunts

Intervale Incident

We had experienced cool, star-streaked nights and crisp autumn days in eastern Connecticut. More of the same was anticipated for more northern climes, particularly western Maine, where we were headed for a three-day hunt with Maine Guide Fred Westerberg. Fred had become more than a guide over the twenty years—with just a few annual lapses because of foul weather—that we had hunted with him. He was a friend and humorous confidant; that was almost as important a reason for going as the birds. In other words, Fred also provided the entertainment!

We like overnight stays in Bridgton—a throwback in time— at Grady's West Shore Motel on Route 302, where we—the dogs especially—always enjoy a short, before-breakfast walk down the hill to the shores of Highland Lake. On top of the hill just after the town's main street is Tom's Homestead, venue for outstanding dinners and a fabulous Victorian atmosphere. On the east side of town the popular Black Horse Tavern offers fine ambience and cuisine, which we appreciate after a tiring—but always exhilarating—day in the field.

Stow, Maine is an itty-bitty place on Route 113. A walk-in eatery at a three-way junction—Stow Corner Store—serves homemade pastry made on premises, light meals, etc. Just about every other passing vehicle stops there, so I surmise that it must be the proverbial gold mine. Oh yes, there is the Stow Town Hall up the road and the Stow Baptist Church across the way. That's about it.

We surmised that because the weather seemed proper for flighting woodcock, we would realize ample opportunities and ample bags. The Intervale, running through Stow Meadows, is a huge covert that usually produces lively action, depending on how you hit the flights. As it turned out, we hunted the alders surrounding the meadows for two of the three days, the Brownfield Covert being the choice for the odd day. Serpentine meanderings of the Cold River pose minimal inconvenience for fording farmers and hunters requiring access to rich bottomlands, surrounding alder runs, and promiscuous patches of raspberry and other vegetation—as long as accessing vehicles are equipped with four-wheel drive!

We filled our game bags by lunch break, partly in an again-found patch of cover that had been off limits but recently regained. Suddenly a northwesterly wind picked up, hopefully not an ominous sign of future events. Ironically, Fred first noticed a loss of power in his pickup throughout the morning, and when we attempted to depart at mid-afternoon, his cantankerous pickup's engine decided not to turn over. Nearest help, he figured, was Wayne McAllister, a Yankee farmer of these parts whose farm was up on the ridge over in Chatham, New Hampshire. Wayne is a patron of Fred's canoe rental shop that also carries archery equipment.

Dick Curriden, my hunting partner, and I cleaned our day's bag—which included a snipe—in the river, each of us silently praying to all known gods that we would not have to suffer the deleterious effects of spending the night in the field without adequate provisions—at least we would have our birds to eat, which we could prepare on the Coleman cook stove. I began to visualize where we would sleep. Two of us could repose in the capped truck body. The unlucky one—yours truly of course, being the shortest by an inch or so—would have to be content sleeping in the cramped cab. The dogs would have to stay outside the truck in their kennels.

Before long, Wayne and Fred returned in a silage truck and attempted to jump the battery, but it wasn't meant to be. We waited another anguishing half-hour until Wayne returned with his big four-wheel drive Allis Chalmers. Well, by golly, he yanked Fred's Dodge Ram with the three of us, three bewildered bird dogs, and all our equipment across the river and back up the hill to his farm with nary a growl.

We enjoyed hot coffee and tea in the ambience of Wayne's Federal farmhouse—a real unspoiled classic—awaiting the return of Wayne Jr., who was bow-hunting moose up on the ridge, to transport us back to "civilization." He soon returned, without success as I recall, and we had to listen to Fred's stories all the way back to his shop, located across the highway from the celebrated Fryeburg Fairgrounds. Far worst things could have happened!

A few Interesting Places and Hunts

Finally, in late October of 1997, after having just about given up on serious New England grouse shooting, I struck the mother lode in northeastern Vermont, about 10 miles south of Quebec Province near Lake Memphremagog. I only shot a few, but my guide Dave Smith did quite well over one of my setters, who did a fantastic job on the drummers. Who's guiding whom here? We moved twenty-three grouse in one covert and had an estimated twenty-five productives on the three-day hunt. Connecting on these avian tricksters with at least some degree of consistency is quite another matter!

I find it interesting that the northern New England states allow a daily bag of four birds, which I believe is only realistically applicable to native groundswatters who ride the roads at dusk with shotguns at ready in the family chariot. The biddies are drawn to the gravel, which aids in digestion. Bird dog men, though, don't seem to attain the limit often, if at all; it's too challenging, even when you find birds.

Several years ago, I discovered an out-of-the-way country inn in the Northeast Kingdom of Vermont. Coventry, a little town located a few miles south of Newport, held the secret for my favorite reason for heading north in the first place—well almost. Heermansmith (double "e" intended) Farm & Inn, a vintage 1830-1840 era Georgian farmhouse turned country inn, quaintly sits in an idyllic setting, surrounded by rolling hills, farm land, and fronted by a picturesque trout stream. It's the epitome of rural Vermont. It was, for many years, "the Northeast Kingdom's best-kept secret." I enjoyed some pretty good trout fishing under the covered bridge the spring before last, and then some kid torched it the following Halloween. (Fortunately, it has since been restored.) Premier hosts Jack and Louise Smith were the quintessence of homely hospitality.

The fine cuisine at Heermansmith was an Epicurean's delight, definitely Four-Star. Responsible for this sterling reputation was

Chef Jon Fletcher, a mainstay at the inn for the last few years. When requested, he would prepare a hunter's bag of woodcock better than I've ever tasted, especially when preceded by a fruit-crushed Southern Comfort old-fashioned!

Jack Smith's ancestors occupied the farm during its early years and had imbued Jack with a sense of "home" when he returned from the business world after retirement. Sadly, Louise passed in 1999, leaving Jack, who is now in his 80s, with the burden of running the inn. He did just that for a few years. When the inn closed, patrons who had traveled great distances to partake of consummate table fare were sorely disappointed. Hunters, trout fishermen, snowmobilers, skiers, travelers, and locals dining out for the evening, loved the relaxed atmosphere and unpretentious ambiance. I stayed at the inn several years either alone, with my wife, or with a hunting partner, but I haven't returned to the Northeast Kingdom since it closed. I miss it.

Following Louise's death in early October of 1999, Jack honored our reservation and arranged for us to stay at the Village House Inn a few miles down the road in Albany, another one-horse town. Our able hostess was Kate Fletcher (formerly married to Jon, majordomo at Heermansmith), who provided us with fine cuisine and accommodations. I recall one summer my wife and I vacationed a few days in the Northeast Kingdom. We invited our guide of several years, Dave Smith (no relation to Jack), co-owner of Northeast Kingdom Outfitters, and his wife Rose, to join us for an evening meal at the Village House Inn. Kate was the charming hostess and all enjoyed an exquisite meal. The last I knew, it too had closed.

Notwithstanding a change in venue from Coventry to Albany, forced by Louise's death and the subsequent occupation of Heermansmith Inn by Jack Smith's grieving family, the bird hunting that year was superlative. Woodcock and grouse were plentiful, and we had good success. Lots of birds kept dogs and hunters on the *qui vive* with few dull lapses.

One of our more interesting Vermont experiences was being frisked by Bubba, a Vermont game warden. Greg, my hunting partner, and I were eating lunch in the field when Bubba appeared with "GAME WARDEN" emblazoned over the side of his pickup. We must have done something wrong because before we knew what was happening he had us leaning against the truck body with upheld arms, undergoing a bodily search. Noticing that Dave, our guide, was snickering, we quickly suspected a set-up. Seems that Dave and Bubba were friends and hunt waterfowl together on occasion. There was still fun to come. With literally several thousand dollars worth of scatterguns reposing on the dog kennels—Greg's Arrietta and my F.lli Rizzini—Bubba wouldn't be intimidated by our tongue-in-cheek even swap offer for his Ruger Red Label. Said jovial Bubba in all seriousness, "I like my Ruga." (No discourtesy to Red Labels, as they are highly respected production shotguns.)

Dropping down a few latitudes into western Maine, where occasionally we come across a civilized hunter—no complaints regarding the lack thereof in the Green Mountain state—with a bird dog, we found birds consistently. Woodcock, that is. We even managed to shoot a few grouse as a bonus. After the hunt, I reminded my Moosehead Lake, Greenville, Maine hunting partner and correspondent that there are fairly good numbers of ruffed grouse in his state, contrary to his sense that there are not. Also porcupines.

My setter's bell was silent for too long no more than fifteen feet away, where I suspected no bird was hanging out. Blaze finally came about, and I chalked it up to another incident of unexplained behavior. All of a sudden she began to choke, wheeze, and violently shake her head. We spent the next fifteen minutes removing more than fifty porky quills from her bloody mouth and throat. This could have been really serious but amazingly, within a matter of a few minutes, she resumed her bird searching just as if nothing had happened. Hopefully she learned a lesson.

The next day we dined at noon on the fruits of the past few days' labor in Roy's cover, aside the North Fryeburg covered bridge. This cover is openly different, that is, past its regenerated prime but still holding a few birds. Boy, did we suck up those grilled 'cock—ummm.

So all's well that ends well in the Pine Tree State, and with that the annual wild bird hunting excursions came to a close for the season. If one attributes success to birds brought to bag, then I can say that between my hunting partner and my Vermont/Maine guides, more often than not we bagged limits of woodcock in six days of gunning, in addition to several drummers—but nowhere near bag limits on the King of the Uplands.

Last Hunt of the Season

Saturday, November 28 was the last hunt of the year for my setters and me, at least on wild birds. The weather was almost like Indian summer—technically about the first two weeks in November—but with sporadic fair weather clouds. My back acreage had been the target of too many hunts—a small covert can only take a few poundings during the short season—but was convenient in that I had other plans to occupy my alternative pleasures—called work—for the better part of the day. I reasoned that warm temperatures would provide the straggling migratory male woodcock cortege with an excuse to be lazy and stay put (typical of males of all species?). No such luck.

A copious "fall" of 'cock had not materialized in the past few days, notwithstanding the recent northeasterly "blow." I would be content to have my dogs dink around in the aftermath of what had been a successful but average gunning season in terms of starts and kills—average bag for me is about twenty to thirty woodcock, ten to eighteen club-shot pheasant, and a handful of grouse. In other ways, it had been of season of memories, as is every year I'm alive, ambulatory, able to take nourishment, and perceive delight in God's creation.

My dogs and I proceeded directly to the area where woodcock were the most likely to be found—a former hickory grove where I used to shoot squirrels as a kid, but since selectively cut and turning brushy with wild rose and regenerating hardwoods. Point! And then a back, or was it another point? The dogs were standing their bird head to head with about six feet separating their noses. I spotted the sitting bird in a little open area just as his nerves caused him to move a bit. The cornered 'cock, not wishing to prolong the ambience of the moment for my sake, lifted straight up, and I swung the little 20-gauge Prussian Daly up through and beyond his anticipated path of flight and slapped the front trigger as he—he turned out to be she—struggled to catch up with my barrels, or so it seemed. Miss this opportunity Chase, and your --- is grass, as it were.

Alas, the shot was true, and the object of my hunt tumbled to earth. Blaze, casting a furtive glance at her bracemate, and not with a great deal of alacrity, retrieved to hand, all the while wondering why this smelly apparition couldn't be left where it landed.

The field dressing ritual complete with my trusty and long-used Puma Bird Hunter, we headed up the lane for home as the dogs continued to course the covert. From a distance in the north came the familiar flutter of grouse wings. The sound grew louder, and the King of the Uplands materialized, heading straight for my head. My mind jammed. Don't shoot! I had worked too long and hard getting a few birds to live in this habitat; it was off-limits for grouse shooting. In disappointment, the age-old instinct prevailed, and as I did a 180, dropped the barrels below the fleeting target—as in a skeet station one high house—and touched the front trigger. Even though I had taken no grouse from this covert, I wish I had missed as I watched this cock bird abruptly tumble out of flight. Bess pointed dead and Blaze briefly honored, but the fluttering death throes in the dry leaves caught her attention. The undefined scent of grouse filled her brain as she connected this new bird with that strange and alluring redolence that she occasionally encountered in this first season of her puppyhood. She wanted to taste every feather in spite of my insistent "fetch." But she did, and I was glad for her new experience with this grand bird.

Bittersweet was my reaction as I examined, with thumping heart and tearful countenance, this beautiful, brown phase, mature cock partridge with six and one-half inch tail feathers, a trophy to be prized as much as any whitetail. Would he have sired more birds the following spring had he lived? Will other males be attracted to my covert? Despite my misgivings, its taking was the crowning glory to another gunning season. Who could ask for more?

North Country Musings

The dogs were a bit fearful at first

Greg and I were only a little disappointed when reflecting on our annual journey north in October of 2005. With three English setter companions, my Mr. Jing, and Greg's Katie and Molly, we moved sixty-five woodcock and fourteen grouse for a total of seventy-nine birds. That sounds pretty good on the surface, but we hunted five and one-half days—three days in New Brunswick and two and one-half days in mid-central Maine. Looking at the combined numbers from a more meaningful perspective, we averaged 11.82 woodcock flushes and 2.55 grouse flushes per day—not especially good compared with recent trips, particularly regarding the latter. Just a few years ago it was not unusual to move more than 100 woodcock in Maine and Vermont in six days. When we "hit" the flights in some past years, we experienced that in just three days of shooting.

We had read about what to expect—cold, wet springs would be the cause of low brood production. I think the pundits nailed the reason right on the head. We bagged exactly one third—twenty-six—of the birds flushed. That's the good news. Anytime you can average one bird shot to three birds moved, you've done well, in my opinion.

Notwithstanding the relatively bearish statistics, we had some interesting, enjoyable, and downright laughable experiences. On the last day of hunting in New Brunswick our guide of the day and co-owner of Tobique Valley Outfitters of Riley Brook, Dave McClure, proposed a tour of an island in the Tobique River, presumably not bird-hunted in recent times. Preparations were made the previous day—food prepared for the noon meal and the motorized bateau moved downriver and secured at its landing.

The dogs were a bit fearful at first but soon became accustomed to the water and the short trip up-river to the island's destination point.

Interesting? Through some good work, we did find a few grouse and woodcock on the island. Point! Mr. Jing's first encounter produced a woodcock that flushed between my feet when I stepped over a small rotted log. I was so taken by surprise that it left me flat on my butt—and red faced!

Enjoyable? Just before I collected a grouse and a pair of woodcock, Dave left us to prepare the mid-day meal. What a glorious collation it was—a few munchies to start, followed by scrumptious pan-fried grouse (always delicious) and exquisite woodcock, which had been marinated overnight in a not-too-secret sauce of Dave's making. Chunks of the dark meat were wrapped in bacon with a small piece of onion and tomato and then slowly pan-fried over a kindled fire. Dave had completely succeeded in removing the livery flavor of the crepuscular bogsuckers (sorry Mr. Evans) and replaced it with a piquancy that was delectable, nothing quite like I've ever had.

Laughable? One gentleman staying at the lodge made it known that he never missed a woodcock. He was a personable chap who was evidentially well traveled and had been on many bird-hunting trips in the course of his life, but we still had to question his incredulous claim. Could he be that good? As he was a regular guest at the lodge, I questioned Dave as to the veracity. "Yup, it's true, I've never seen him miss," Dave said, "But he waits out at the edge of an open field until the dog points in the tangled alders, and the handler flushes the bird out toward 'Mr. Never Miss.'"

In addition to Dave, I can't say enough about the guiding team that was assigned to us—Dan Pichette and "Uncle" Mikey. But what can the best guides do if the migrants are holding up north? Cold, wet springs presumably had kept the grouse population in check. As has been said many times, woodcock encounters are a matter of timing. I never saw such great cover.

Dropping down to Milo, Maine, and our unusually comfortable summer cottage on Schoodic Lake, we had good success with woodcock north of Lagrange the first two days, attaining just one woodcock shy of a dual limit. On the second day of the hunt, there were two incidents—one coincidental and one amusing—that atoned for Saturday, a day that was virtually dry in terms of sightings.

We had just begun to hunt a cutover area where we had success the day before. In the distance we heard a vehicle approaching slowly over the main logging trail. We were in the boonies where there's virtually no traffic. An extended cab, diesel pickup with dogs loaded aboard pulled up behind our Jeep as if its occupants were about to hunt "our" covert. The driver got out, shook hands with Greg, who then introduced me to—none other than Dave Marshall, a well known Rhode Island area dog trainer, who we knew hunted and trained dogs in the coverts in and around Lagrange. We killed an hour with pleasant conversation, Dave sharing the whereabouts of some coverts south of Milo, which unfortunately proved to be completely devoid of birds on day three but showed future promise. Again, I think it was a *matter of timing*. One of Dave's tongue-in-cheek pronouncements was that he thought the woodcock migrations skipped over the state of Maine this year, as he was not finding many opportunities. When I saw Dave again, however, he said woodcock were everywhere a week later.

Heading toward Lagrange on the second Maine day, we became confused trying to interpret my out-of-date Maine topographical atlas. Approaching civilization, we came upon a mail truck. "Is this … Road?" Greg asked the mail lady inside the familiar USPS vehicle. Ironically, she didn't know and had no clue how to read the topo map Greg offered her. But she seemed interested and asked what we were hunting. "Grouse and woodcock," said Greg.

"Do you mean paaaartridge?"

"Yes, that's the bird," Greg responded.

She pronounced the first syllable in partridge somewhere between paar (as in Jack Paar) and pear (as in fruit). Then, while still sitting in the driver's seat, this ingenuous postal matron drew her fists up under her armpits and flapped her elbows continually to imitate a flushing grouse in an attempt to visually demonstrate the bird we were hunting. We laughed all the way back to Schoodic. Turned out we weren't lost and were exactly where we were supposed to be.

No doubt that we saw fewer birds on our northern journey this year. A week and a half after returning, I went to a local covert in Connecticut to see if I could find any longbills. I didn't expect much action, but inside an hour Mr. Jing found fifteen of the migrants, the most I'd ever seen in this twenty-acre tract. Go figure. Although we're told every year (from singing ground counts and wingbees) that woodcock numbers are declining, a lot certainly seems to depend on how you hit the flights. Relative bird scarcity being what it is, timing is *everything*.

To the End of the Earth

Last September 23rd, my shooting friend, Dick Curriden, and I departed from his palatial log home overlooking Moosehead Lake in Greenville, Maine on a motor trip that would take us through Quebec and ultimately to a remote hunting camp located some 100 miles south of James Bay, Ontario. We had planned this trip for over a year and were jubilant over the prospect of forty-grouse flushes per day, as was claimed by the ads to be a possibility. The long distance seemed a reasonable trade-off in order to experience what had not been seen in our bailiwick for several decades.

After crossing the border near Jackman, we enjoyed our first foreign repast at the Benedict Arnold Inn, named after the infamous Revolutionary War hero/traitor—I was born in Norwich, Connecticut, General Arnold's hometown—and seemed indicative of good things to come. After an overnight stay in Central Quebec, we motored the next day under lowery skies to our next sleepover in North Bay, Ontario, a quaint New England-like town where we acquired hunting licenses.

Dick arranged with two Mississippi friends—one a Connecticut expatriate—to rendezvous in Cochrane, Ontario, homebase for the famed Polar Express excursion train. Our guide, Robert, met us at the depot where we exchanged introductions and pleasantries before heading northeast over some pretty rough roads. The sighting of our first ever spruce grouse along the way seemed a good omen.

We reached the end of the trail some two hours later. All baggage, dogs, guns, personal provisions for the next five days, were loaded into Robert's boat and ferried up the river to his camp. Notwithstanding a little light rain, so far so good.

The dawn of the next day was shrouded with clouds and drizzle. We shook off the gloom with youth's optimism (we're not young!) and started up the trail, eagerly awaiting copious numbers of grouse flushes. Maybe I could manage a double, perhaps even a lucky triple (with my double!). Was the one case of ammo I brought enough?

Soon we had a point. The grouse, hard-pressed by Blaze, my English setter, hopped up onto a low-lying tree limb and stared at the funny looking creatures in pursuit. The subsequent pincer movement forced its flight, which was followed by three clean ignominious misses. The rain continued, and we saw no more grouse that day.

Those of you who are familiar with grouse habits know that wet conditions force them to remain "holed" up in the evergreens, and there isn't much opportunity for action. We found a few woodcock the next day, this being the northern-most latitude for longbills. The rain continued.

To abbreviate this tale of woe, the inclement weather endured through Wednesday, at which point we all had enough. Besides, the forecast was for more of the same for the next few days. Dick will often betray his inclination not to hunt in the rain with his oft quoted and haughty "I don't own any rain gear." Just maybe this had something to do with our less than exuberant desire to hold out a bit longer, although it was never solely his idea to "hang it up."

Dick McClure, who writes "North of the Border" in *Gun Dog* magazine, wrote recently in "The Missing Flight" that grouse and other game were scarce (at least in the more easterly and southerly portions of Ontario), and that the usual woodcock flights never came. Relieved wallets and empty game bags were somewhat overlooked after reading his consoling words. In addition, we enjoyed Robert's company as we shared well-prepared meals in his modest galley. He's a fine cook and conversationalist.

The journey home was rather uneventful except for a one-car, driver-incurred fender bender, rather hood bender, suffered by Dick's

Dakota southeast of Cochrane. Let's just say that you need to allow more time to stop on a rain-slicked gravel highway!

On a positive note, we came upon a most beautiful scene just west of the Quebec town of LaPatrie before crossing the border at Coburn-Gore, Maine. This little town sits in a deep valley, and as we approached it from the west, I thought it to be just about the prettiest and most alluring place that I had even seen. Could the encompassing hills be the venue for a future hunt?

Trending into Maine: A Young Bird Dog Comes of Age

I dream about bright, starlit, milk-streaked heavens, with Orion, the equatorial hunter, wistfully foreboding pleasant and rewarding shooting holidays. I see flight birds in my dreams—woodcock moving in their fall-long peregrinations under full Hunter and Beaver Moons, instinctively seeking southern climes...

A cold blast of early October snow in northern New England produced a reasonably good "fall" of 'cock. Hunting with my friend George in the Northeast Kingdom of Vermont, we captured the tail end of this good shooting. But the scourge of mass woodcock flights became the norm over the next several days: mild weather returned and southerly winds prevailed—conditions that produce, at best, the proverbial "trickle" of birds. A week later, Greg, my Maine hunting partner, and I were somewhat apprehensive as we headed for the Pine Tree State. We would require good dog work, carefully selected coverts and perseverance over the next four days. I'd best be in reasonable physical condition or muscle spasms would do me in.

We wrestle with the question of the timing of our out-of-state hunts every year. You can never predict the weather, but it seems that *later* is better, all other factors being equal. The leaves are down and possibly the birds are "jitterier" about being so far north, even in the mild weather of an Indian summer. They'll be moving, no doubt, regardless of extreme weather fronts. Earlier may be okay because of the advantage of encountering always-present native birds, but you will have difficulty seeing the flushes through the leaf canopy. Regardless of when we go, there will always be the excitement of watching the dogs course the familiar and newly-found lowlands that attract woodcock.

127

Given the proper breeding, training an upland pointing dog on "the little russet feller" will save you time and perhaps money in achieving the goal of a finished bird dog.

Our canine enablers on this hunt were: Molly, a medium-going, three-year-old Grouse Ridge blooded, tri-color English setter; Blaze, a soon-to-be ten-year-old tri-color setter from the all-but-disappeared Chief breeding and Greg's Kate, Molly's five-year-old dam—three eager to please females.

I should not forget to mention our hard-working flusher, covert-busting and humorous guide of many years, the redoubtable—as in awe inspiring—Fred Westerberg. Working out of Fryeburg, Maine, Fred and his wife, Prudy, operate the very successful Saco River Canoe and Kayak, one of the largest canoe rental outfitters in New England. Dry summers are a boon to this business, and this year had been no exception.

The question for us was: would the lack of rainfall keep us close to wet areas and watercourses? Baked upland feeding grounds are not conducive for attracting woodcock because of the probing nature of their feeding. On the other hand, the higher up, hardwood ridges would produce the best grouse shooting. We stayed in the lowlands.

The plan was to hunt the Intervale Covert near the New Hampshire border where the flights are usually consistent, the South Arm Covert (South Arm is a small town at the base of Lower Richardson Lake that could be hit or miss based on past experience), the coverts in the general vicinity of Andover, and numerous other smaller hot spots. We decided to forego the beautiful Schoolteacher Covert (right out of a Ripley painting) in West Bethel, which is probably the most traditional of our favored choices, but not productive in the past few years

On this trip I had occasion to solidify an opinion that I have held for many years—you'll find more birds with a wider ranging pointing dog than you will with a close worker. Molly is a young bitch who knows her stuff, while Blaze, arguably the best setter that I have owned, is an older matron who has slowed down somewhat in the last two years. Consequently, their divergent ranges seem to complement each other. Both have great olfactory senses. We hunted them as a brace much of the four days. Guess who found more birds?—the moderate ranger, Molly.

William Harnden Foster, famed author of *New England Grouse Shooting,* wrote a paper that was read before the New England Game Conference in 1930 entitled *Birds Dogs in New England,* in which he extolled the virtues of wider rangers. In fact, he mostly used English pointers, the traditional big running quail dog of the South. It's only my opinion, but I believe Foster was correct. The medium to wide pointing dog, with an adjusted range of no more than about fifty yards or so in close New England coverts, must be well trained—and well bred—to stand birds up to several minutes and be steady until the gunner arrives. Grouse don't always cooperate, but this is just what the doctor ordered for woodcock. The excitement of observing a fast, snappy pointing dog is one of the great joys of upland hunting.

Additionally, I believe a wider ranging pointing dog should defy tradition and wear a beeper rather than a bell in brushy areas. I have consumed far too much time looking for a belled dog on point than I care to remember. The beeper solves this problem in big northern New England coverts as this technology allows the hunter to make a beeline for the action without hesitation. Foster didn't have the advantage of this technology. That said, there is nothing more frustrating in the field than a poorly trained and out-of-control pointing dog that continually bumps birds and favors the hunter with its presence only once in a while, if at all. As a result, the inexperienced hunter will often insist on a bootlicker in order to provide the opportunity for shots.

Unlike many bird hunters who favor grouse, I prefer the consistency of hunting woodcock when working with a young dog. I get lucky with grouse once in a while, but held points that produce shootable situations are few and far between, at least where we hunt. Given a choice, I'll take woodcock and hope for the opportunity to bag old ruff on occasion. No apologies to author Ted Nelson Lundrigan, who has expressed quite the opposite preference in his book, *Hunting the Sun.* No question, though; most consider grouse the King of the Uplands.

Woodcock hunters have been bombarded continuously with disquieting predictions of declining woodcock numbers. This doom and gloom is based on spring singing ground surveys and wing surveys indicative of brood success. Our Maine hunting experiences over the past seventeen years have <u>not</u> confirmed the published findings of the pundits. Because singing ground locations change over time, could it be that this survey is no longer completely accurate? Could it be that our dogs are that much better and we, as handlers and shooters, are more proficient? Hardly. In fact, at the very worst, the number of sightings has remained fairly constant over the past several years on our hunting forays into western Maine. This past season was the exception and beyond our expectations.

There were several notable and memorable highlights on this hunt. Molly and I worked hard during the spring and summer months with retrieving various bucks and dummies. She was force-broke the previous year, but was unproven on wild bird retrieving. Realizing that some dogs don't like the taste of woodcock, I was elated when she performed many of the retrieves, some in water and one beyond the farther bank of fast-running water. Her swimming experience up until now had been limited to occasional fun and games.

Many pointing dogs do not retrieve. This is the downside to many an English setter and English pointer whose forebears were exposed to the southern field trial circuit. Undoubtedly, this is the result of a genetic throwback where points and steadiness on quail are the crowning glory and constitute the end of the game. Birds are not shot, and retrieving is not taught, in fact, it is discouraged as being detrimental to wing and shot steadiness. Some believe that "pointing dead" accomplishes the same end result as retrieving. A good case against this argument is the inability to bring game to bag that has been shot over water.

Swimming across the Cold River after a bird that I downed with the left barrel of my 20 bore, Prussian-made Diamond Grade Daly, Molly's hindquarters got stuck under a partially submerged fallen tree. We all stood aghast watching her front legs paddle furiously to free herself in the swift current. Just as a very wet Fred arrived to the rescue, Molly broke loose, continued to the far shore and clambered up the near vertical embankment in search of the fallen woodcock. She found the bird quickly, joyfully retrieved it back down the steep bank and into the swirling waters again, fearlessly paddling the twenty to twenty-five feet across the deep water into the waiting hands of her tearful but elated master. This is the stuff that I thought only the retriever breeds could pull off.

Hunting along the Ellis River on day three, I missed a bird that back-doored Molly's point at river's edge. It appeared to be a clean miss. On the way back forty-five minutes later, I thought it strange that she headed directly for me, for I had not whistled her in. She had a mission—to deliver to hand a very dead but still warm woodcock.

Last year Molly proved herself to be a fast and stylish finder with a "long" nose, steady as a rock on point, a natural backer like Blaze and Katie, and now, an enthusiastic retriever. There is one small fault that will improve, hopefully, with experience—false pointing. Woodcock splash (chalk) emits a strong scent, even when a bird is no longer present. All of my dogs over the years have done it. In her defense, there were some occasions when false pointing was suspected. Because of her excellent scenting ability, we eventually found birds hanging out along the fringes several yards distant. Always trust your dog.

On many occasions, we had three dogs down at the same time. It's probably not a good practice, especially in dense cover, but it was not unmanageable. All dogs are fantastic backers and handle easily. Two immobile setters with tails high honoring the point dog is a delight to behold. Fred's German shorthair, Kara, is also a good finder, backer and retriever. No, we didn't put four dogs down together!

In our four days of shooting, we moved ninety-five woodcock and ten grouse. Greg got lucky and nailed one of the latter, after what we presume was a point on a skittish bird that flew his way. We achieved daily limits on woodcock, with even old Fred—he's my age—participating in the shooting. Had we concentrated on grouse, I'm afraid we would have been disappointed, not necessarily in terms of game bagged, but because of lesser opportunities afforded young Molly.

Fred's field lunches are the best. On these trips, the *tour de force* in our guide's culinary repertoire is a noon meal of sautéed woodcock breasts on the last day of the hunt. Yum. (Notwithstanding Fred's considerable talent, we're still searching for another recipe.) During the preceding days of the hunt, hamburgers and other hot-cooked meals are a welcome change from the usual sandwiches. Lunch hour is a time to relax, shoot the breeze, recap our experiences and tell tall stories (mostly Fred's).

On arriving at my home in Connecticut, and after resting a gaunt and weary Molly for a few days, I took her on a gun-less stroll to my own managed woodcock covert. "One of 'my' birds," I thought, as she skidded into a stylish point. I trampled the mostly open area around her, but no bird came out. I feared a false point and commanded her to "get ahead."

She only rolled her eyes. Just as I started to make another pass around her, all hell broke loose in a god-awful tangle of multiflora rose, greenbrier, and bittersweet, barely ten feet to her left. You guessed it—old ruff himself!

Windmills and Bird Dog Days

Our journey to the Pine Tree State in October was an Interesting experience. Fully armed, we felt like Cervantes' Don Quixote ready to take on myriad windmills that loomed on the eastern landscape just south of Danforth on Route 169 in northern Maine. With thirty-some-odd extant and one-fourth mile apart, another eighteen or more of the whirligigs were on the horizon (no pun intended). "Let's get 'em," I said to Sancho, nay, Greg, but they weren't in the mood to fight as their props stood silent, unmoving, not yet operational as transmission lines were in the construction stage. G.E., the brainchild of this remote project, brought visual proof of changing times to come.

We left early Sunday, Oct. 19 and guided by a trustworthy GPS, our destination was Wilderness Escape Outfitters near the New Brunswick border. Having missed my usual Sunday a.m. church venue, I surmised coincidence when the GPS put us smack dab at the entrance to Belinda's Redemption Center. Wait a minute; I did not feel I was here to be redeemed; we had other plans! Besides, salvation aside, the sign in front of the establishment said "closed Sundays." Smarten up, Chase, this is a recycle center, a junkyard. Phew! Blame the miscalculation to a programming error, or whatever.

Anyway, we hunted north of Danforth for two days, rain curtailing by a day the first leg of our week-long hunt. Accommodations and cuisine were all first class and highly recommended. Unfortunately, woodcock flights of any consequence had not yet materialized.

Political observations pre-November 4 in the North Country were not surprising. We never saw an Obama/Biden advertisement; had to go to the cities/larger towns to see them. The explanation by my Democrat friends was that "they're just one-issue, gun-totin', redneck conservatives."

Randy, the lodge owner, pronounced that "you'll never see posted land" up here. If "no hunting" signs do appear the property was probably purchased by city folk, i.e. those who live south of Bangor. Expect the cabin or cottage to be torched forthwith by "natives."

Randy dosen't like the idea of windmills so close to the vast acreage that he owns, particularly his waterfront property. Noise would be offensive to his vacationing summer guests seeking solitude and relaxation. (We learned later that noise is really not a big factor.) The unsightly machines on the horizon would not be appreciated, but he was quick to add, however, that most of the townspeople were in favor of the project because real estate taxes will be reduced.

Dropping down southwest for the usual three-day stay at our familiar cottage at Scoodic Lake in Milo on rainy Wednesday, we experienced seasonally mild weather and good success. Pounding the covers consistently with our setters, hydration and relief became the usual order. In contemplating the excitement of the day, don't ever do what I did—put your skivvies on backwards!

After having achieved limits on woodcock for two days running, our traditional hunt with dogs usually ended by leaving the canines in the Jeep to pursue the wily grouse by employing stealth, silence and pincer movements in areas where grouse were known to be feeding on thorn apples (cockspur hawthorn). Sometimes it worked; most of the time we were outwitted.

Once, when arriving back at the Jeep late in the day, I felt the call to nature. Breaking my double gun, I, well, you know. It was just at that moment when an eruption took place not ten feet in front of me. (Of course, the setters had been kenneled.) A straightaway, open-field shot on the upland king was the result—a gimme—if I hadn't been preoccupied!

I keep telling myself that the results of any bird hunting excursion are not important and that just being in the beautiful Maine woods and watching the graceful setters work regenerating farm land is what it's all about. That said, you do like to see some proof of your adventure, to say nothing of the culinary qualities of properly prepared woodcock. Unlike previous years, accurate sighting counts were not kept, but the four and one-half days produced twenty-five birds bagged—five grouse and twenty woodcock. Cost of the trip? About $70 per bird! Our tally represented a thirty-three percent reduction (although we hunted one day less) from the previous year's New Brunswick/Milo hunt.

The Land

"Progress?"

Those who contemplate the beauty of the earth find
reserves of strength that will endure as long as life lasts
Rachel Carlson

I love rambling farm walls as they meander over unfettered rolling
hills and vibrant green, rye-planted sward of early spring connecting
timeless eighteenth century dwellings and farms, the quiet of back roads
less traveled, and the simplicity of ingenuous people toiling the land
who possess a strong Puritan work ethic. You can still see bountiful
countryside and witness faithful stewards of the land, only now you
have to look beyond the confinement of where the majority of us live.

Sometimes it's hard to picture in my mind's far recesses a place I
used to know over the distant hill from my acres, a serene meadow
strewn with Jersey cattle with a little trout stream running through
it. Change comes in many forms, but I cannot agree that all of it
is beneficial, not necessarily in economic terms but as to the void of
tranquil space that so many of us now visually seek.

The "meadow" of which I speak is the Wal-Mart/Big Y complex
in Norwich. Mr. Van Winkle (Rip) would be aghast at a journey to
the present. Many other farms I loved in my youth are gone, replaced
with housing developments and strip malls. Yes, vestiges remain.
Stonewalls provide evidence of earlier times, that is, those that haven't
been stripped from the land and sold off to developers of Fairfield
County mansions.

You can argue that the destruction of open space is the result of
a growing population that requires ever-increasing housing, schools,

education funding (usually the most expensive municipal budget line item), consumer goods, and services. But urban sprawl is the archenemy of what philosophers began to call "quality of life" issues in the last quarter or so of the twentieth century. Until our town fathers get the drift on how to stop this scourge—much of what we call "progress" is better described as destruction—the process will continue, in deference to presumed economic well-being.

Some towns—mostly those with more wealth—recognize the pitfalls of over-development and are taking steps to stop rampant eradication of our natural resources. As land becomes available for sale from private sources, open-space purchases (with the help of state and federal funds) become options for our municipal fathers and its citizenry. Taking land out of the one-time development cycle is effectively one way to limit urban sprawl. If towns have a greater requirement for workers based on planned industrial and service growth, housing construction can only be made available within the parameters established by zoning regulations. In many cases, urban sprawl is the only remedy to satisfy a burgeoning population. Ideally, housing availability should dictate how many industrial/service jobs a town can support, not vice-versa. Secondly, is it too far-fetched to close the doors of a town to new residents? Controlled shrinkage? Maybe not...

Everyone has heard of Youngstown, Ohio, once a steel-making hub. Its population is vastly reduced from what it once was. Whole sections of the city have given way to abandoned nothingness. Bucking conventional wisdom, the mayor has a plan—after removing the debris from abandoned properties—to recreate green space amidst large-plot neighborhoods. Because of population shrinkage, he envisions far fewer roads to maintain, as well as savings on other infrastructure expenses. Admittedly, this situation is the result of a failed economic infrastructure, an isolated happening. The plan may succeed, but that's another story.

As a life-long hunter of native haunts, I am particularly sensitive to the elimination of field and forest at an alarming pace. Unless towns possess the will (budgetary acumen) to purchase land—preferable because it's permanent (I think)—and/or private citizens possess the resolve to preserve the land with or without gifts to land trusts for the visual quality-of-life enhancement for posterity, then we are doomed to a disfigured landscape that appeals to no one except shortsighted municipalities that are unwilling—most are unable—to prioritize the real needs of its citizens. If the people care, then let them be heard.

Recently, while thumbing through *My New England*, a collection of essays written in 1972 by Frank Woolner, a well-known sporting personality several decades ago, the pages flipped to an essay entitled "Elegy for a Ruffed Grouse." One recalls Woolner for a couple of other reasons. He also wrote *Timberdoodle!* and *Grouse and Grouse Shooting*. These "how to" titles were very popular back in the 1970s; in fact, I believe the former title was recently reprinted under a different name. Woolner was also an avid salt-water fisherman, and at one time he was editor of *Salt Water Fishing* magazine. I admire Woolner as a writer—never mind that he hunted upland species with a sawed-off semi-auto 12 gauge. That borders on sacrilege! Incidentally, Woolner's brother, who worked for the Massachusetts Department of Environmental Protection (or whatever they call it in Massachusetts), was the gentlemen responsible for the proliferation of blaze orange clothing that is required in practically all states today when hunting upland game.

Anyway, "Elegy" is really not about hunting or fishing per se—or grouse either for that matter. It's about the destruction of wildlife and the greed of man, all in the name of "progress," spelled d e v e l o p m e n t.

It is almost a daily occurrence to read about hunters being maligned, but how many times do we see animals "ground into roadbeds" or wasted in the gutters of civilization? How many thousands of deer? Where is the outrage? Woolner writes –

"While do-gooders argue about game hogs who take more than their fair share of trout, great industrial complexes gobble up complete trout streams and reduce them to trickly seeps of oily pollution. There are laws against the plucking of certain wildflowers, but none to curb the developer who bulldozes an entire hillside, burns its trees and buries its life-giving streams. Those who fight the trend find themselves an unpopular minority. Progress is a strange word, and it doesn't mean a step forward for the multitudes. Too often, progress means power for the few at the expense of natural resources, which enrich the many. Hunters are (simply) pikers in the rape of wild things. All of us, whether hunters, nature lovers, or simply citizens who delight in a balanced wilderness, will lose. We fight for the same things, but we are thwarted by a civilization which seems to regard all wild creatures as expendable."

In reading Woolner's essay, I focused on a local situation in Lisbon (Connecticut), the proposed Lisbon Landing, replete with Home Depot and whatever other big-name discounters come to mind. I've not seen much environmental objection in the newspapers, other than from one local resident whose tranquility would be profoundly disrupted by incessant traffic. Everyone seems to be in favor of it.

Traveling west on I-395 and looking south in the vicinity of Exit 84 where this shopping mall is contemplated, one encounters a broad, undulating expanse of recently abandoned farmland that serves as welcome relief to the hustle and bustle of coming and going. It is a small portion of eastern Connecticut worth preserving. But the green sward is gone now, no corn was reaped and no rye grass grows. It just lies fallow like a tempter's snare, silent and sullen, overcome with weeds and awaiting the desecrators' plunder. Ah, but the feckless farmer who owns it has profit on his brain, and one can only presume that the sale of development rights to the state of Connecticut was not a viable alternative, for whatever reason. Funny thing; I thought all farmers loved the land.

Lisbon citizenry should wake up and realize that this is a terrible price to pay for convenience and a few dollars saved on purchases. I'm not sure that it will reduce real estate taxes at all. In fact, taxes will probably increase in time, given that workers will move into town, raise families, and put pressure on the educational resources of the community.

Lisbon should take pride for retaining its rural character and not be cajoled into thinking that the approval of this project by the townspeople will remove the stigma "not progressive." Evidently, though, it's a "done deal," and the people have spoken.

In his book *Hunting the Whole Way Home,* author Sydney Lea decries the loss of habitat to subdivisions, etc. "I pledged I'd never inhabit ground I couldn't pee on in broad daylight." I like that.

Mary Walton, known to some of her political antagonists as the CAVE* of Griswold (the town immediately north of Lisbon), where were you?—fighting the environmental battles in your own town?

*<u>C</u>itizens <u>A</u>gainst <u>V</u>irtually <u>E</u>verything

Disappearing Habitat

In my late teens, now a memory of distant decades, Saturdays were special. I'd gobble down breakfast, grab the gun—no dog in those days—and head north out the back door and through the barnyard. The small family farms of the neighbors were in the process or had been retired, and the regeneration of secondary growth had reached moderate stages. The end was approaching for superb upland hunting. Grouse and woodcock were abundant. Even without the aid of a dog, I knew where every grouse lived and where woodcock could be found on sunny knolls in copses of birch and other young hardwoods. (There is little speckled alder in the eastern part of Connecticut.) Bagging a few woodcock and maybe a grouse in a morning's hunt was the rule rather than the exception. Several years later I trained my first English setter, Troubles, and was on my way to more abundant bags.

Just recently, after having abandoned these coverts many years ago in deference to out-of-state venues and canned club sport with pheasants galore to fill the void, I took Jing on that still-familiar journey of youth's years. I could not believe the change that had occurred. The regenerating fields that I remember were now grown up to pole and saw timber. The only openings of consequence were woods roads made by recreational vehicles, and on the slopes erosion had taken place. The little sunlight that came through these sparse openings allowed minimal amounts of the invasive Japanese barberry (*Berberis*) to grow. There was no wildlife in these barren coverts except deer, evidenced by myriad deer stands. The youths that ride these roads in their four-wheelers probably would not know a grouse from a grackle.

The foregoing is a familiar story over much of Connecticut. The farms are gone, many lost to residential and commercial development. Where the land remained unmolested by man, the fields and pastures regenerated to the coverts many of my generation remember in their early years. And then the forests gradually took over.

Being off the beaten path, I am thankful that there is no development surrounding my ancestral lands; and it probably won't happen in the foreseeable future. With one of the largest gaming casinos in the world—Mohegan Sun—within a distance of four to five miles, it may be just a matter of time. For the moment, we are part of the last green belt between New York and Boston and continue to be "rural." (An interesting note: high-speed Internet is not yet available to me through AT&T!)

Upon reaching my property line, I marveled over the changes that had occurred as a result of my earlier vision. A one-acre clearcut, bulldozed ten years ago into a woodcock singing ground, is now an open field that we bush hog once per year in the summer. The woodlands to the south, east and north surrounding this maintained area are continually disturbed by my chainsaw—I enjoy central wood heat in my home—from which I harvest a modest six to seven cords annually, hickory (*Carya*) preferred, thank you. In addition to my needs, a friend removed all the swamp maple (*Acer rubrum*) out of a large wet area over many seasons. "Free" wood will be offered to others for bartered services. Where we started cutting, the woodcock moved in almost immediately. I wish I could say the same for grouse.

Young Jing and I moved nine woodcock—one a triple flush. We make this run about every other day with the blank pistol and always find birds during that roughly six-week window in late February and March, the time of the annual migration. If the ground is frozen, we look for open wet areas. As a result of our frequent excursions this year, Jing is now steady to wing and shot. What a great way to field train a young bird dog!

The basics of "Wildlife Management 101" is a message that needs to be disseminated to rural landowners, especially those who have an interest in developing the types of habitat that are best suited to game bird and song bird species. Many landowners have been led to believe by certain environmental organizations, tree huggers, and the media that cutting a tree is sacrilege; clearcuts are anathema. Through their inaction they believe that doing nothing is an accepted—even desirable—option. Yes, worst things could happen, such as selling the land for development or some other enterprise. A cash-generating forest dominated by mature timber is great for deer, the prevalent hardwood in Connecticut being the various species of acorn-producing oaks (*Quercus*), primarily white, red, and black (desirable for mast in that order). It's no wonder that Connecticut is overrun with white tailed deer. (There are other reasons.) Mature forests produce minimum value to other wildlife species because there is not enough light in the understory for the growth of food-producing forbs and flora, the shrubby cover that protects wildlife from predators. Clearcuts, in addition to providing habitat diversity, quickly regenerate to produce the food and cover necessary for wildlife survival and propagation. Ideally, an ecosystem should be all about habitat diversity.

Hunters who are interested in habitat improvement for game species should consider joining The Ruffed Grouse Society. Money raised from banquets sponsored by this worthy organization is diverted to various habitat management projects in several states. In cooperation with the UConn Cooperative Extension System, The Ruffed Grouse Society and other state organizations, The Coverts Project in Connecticut is an ongoing program to educate landowners about wildlife and forest management. This weekend educational seminar, held at Yale Forest in Norfolk, Connecticut, is free (including meals and lodging!). You don't have to own the minimum acreage—ten or so I believe. Just be a member of a club that does.

Lost Covert

Recently, one of my long-time haunts and a favorite game covert was deeded from the Federal Deposit Insurance Corporation to the present owner, acting on his own behalf at an auction. The news of the transfer of this large and habitat-diverse parcel of 243 acres was, for the most part, welcome, but somewhat bittersweet. Let me explain.

In my teens, the tillable fields were teeming with woodchucks. The tenant farmer, with his modest herd of Holsteins, allowed me unlimited access. Once, with my scoped .22 Browning autoloader, I nailed a big fat chuck through the head at a measured one hundred and twenty yards, holding over about one-foot. I guess that was pure luck. Those cool June evenings were tranquil times on the L. Raymond farm, an escape perhaps, but more pleasurable for me than doing more socially acceptable, *de rigueur,* teen stuff.

More memorable were the grouse and woodcock hunts and earlier frog forays in the old cow pond, or the time, as in a dream, my setter bumped a literal score of grouse. We followed up the wild flush in all directions but never found even a single bird. I always wondered whether this sighting of grouse was two or three families joined together, or possibly one large covey.

The back-lying regenerating fields were ideal singing grounds for woodcock, and the cutover saw timber forests, intermingled with innumerable wetlands surrounded by a meandering, centrally located brook, produced great holding cover for the longbills. I experienced hundreds of woodcock flushes here over the years and fair numbers of grouse sightings. Back in the days of five-bird woodcock limits, securing a full game bag was not that difficult in a morning or afternoon hunt.

Dreams and memories were made from boyhood to middle age. But then, ownership changed several times, and finally the infinite greed of duplicitous developers and bankers just about sealed the fate of my Shangri-la. Seventy houses were planned. My neighbors and I voiced our vehement disapproval, mostly for different reasons, such as increased traffic and other costly infrastructure needs. I'm sure my personal objection, based on ruination of an ecosystem fell on deaf ears. In actuality, much of this vast covert was wetlands.

I don't seem to remember if the town's planning & zoning board approved the subdivision. Fortunately, from my neighbors' and my perspective, the economy soured, the realty group went bankrupt and the bank failed. The Federal deposit Insurance Corporation ended up with the property who then auctioned it to a Norwich businessman for about $1000 per acre. He (presumably with his wife) then spent upwards of $100,000—offset somewhat by a timber harvest—clearing and stumping the regenerating fields, removing all the surface stone, enlarging the pond, regrading the pond watershed, and building several hundred feet of extra fine, dry-laid stonewalls. As a lover of New England fieldstone walls, I appreciate that they are very well made and beautiful. The new owners, Joe and Lois, built two luxurious homes, one for them and the other for their married son on the opposite end of the property. No question, it's a beautiful setting and one of the nicest properties in the whole town. We see Joe and Lois occasionally around Christmastime, and they're great people, in fact Joe is an avid fly-fisherman and occasional hunter.

I have no reasonable right not to be pleased with the outcome. After all, there are only two houses, not seventy. There will be no development and the rural atmosphere of the countryside will be maintained. I should be ecstatic.

But I know what I lost. I lost the best local covert I have ever known. Yes, it's still there, and Joe has invited me on a few occasions to hunt with him. I haven't taken him up on his offer yet. I don't recognize it anymore. I've even walked the property alone a couple of times with Molly and Jing looking for the apple tree where a grouse always flushed and the little wet run where I achieved my one and only double on woodcock. I think both are part of the scrupulously-maintained cow pond watershed now. And somehow I can't seem to find the little farm wall that seemed to go nowhere and the copse of black walnuts that grew either side of it. Maybe the round rocks from it were bulldozed and buried in a big hole where the old rock dump used to be.

On Roots and Quiet Places

I will always be a New Englander at heart even if fate takes me elsewhere upon retirement. In any event, put me out of the mainstream of life in a little corner of any of these places (except maybe the seashore of Rhode Island), and I probably would be happier than swine in wallow—to paraphrase the proverbial. On many occasions I have tried, mostly in vain, to rationalize why I am attached to the place where I live, especially since there are other more desirable sections of this continent where I probably would rather be, aesthetically speaking. But there is a reason. For sure, living outside of nature's bosom—in a city or suburbia—is not an option.

World traveler I am not, but I have been in most of the states and provinces of Canada. I love Alaska's grandeur and have many fond memories of our forty-ninth state, having spent two and one-half months there during my college years, fishing by day and sleeping in a stove-heated tent to recharge the batteries. Many a sportsman has been attracted to Alaska's big fish and game opportunities. For that matter,

British Columbia or the Yukon Territory would do just as well. But to quote a title of the late University of South Carolina English professor, sportsman, and writer, Havilah Babcock, *I Don't Want to Shoot an Elephant,* my hunting and fishing pursuits are limited to upland game and stream fish.

Vermont, with its idyllic countryside and rugged hills, is my favorite New England state. Driving along I-91 in Central and Northern Vermont is a great visual experience in all four seasons. From what I've heard though, living there in the winter can be a challenge!

Maine has everything, from its quaint seacoast villages to the North Woods. I could even compromise with New Hampshire with its rugged White Mountains (and its inherent tax advantages?). Actually, there's little difference between the three, especially when you focus on the White Mountains of Western Maine. Obviously, the rugged Maine coastline is somewhat unique to the three states—along with its summer "touristas!"

Massachusetts is where it all started, and for the history buff and those seeking employment opportunities, Boston and surroundings can be a jumping off place to outdoor adventure. In that context, Ben Ames Williams comes to mind, writing in Boston and fishing and hunting in Maine in the early to mid twentieth century. Western Massachusetts is beautiful. Rhode Island, a sun worshipper's haven, is best known for its sandy beaches and Newport mansions.

But do you know what? My roots are in the rolling hills and stonewalls of Connecticut, and Connecticut is where I will remain. Not just in this state, but where I actually "hang my hat" on a rocky hill in the Last Green Valley between D.C. and Boston where my forebears have lived for countless generations.

Never mind that grouse are scarce in my state. Only pockets here and there remain. Grouse require regenerating fields and farmland, young growth, and minimum fragmentation. There's now too much of the latter and not enough of the former. But there may be more to the equation, and I will keep trying to learn what I can do to attract *Bonasa umbellus* to my "disturbed" fields and woodlots. I digress.

To have roots is to have a special sense of *déjà vu* when I commune with the land, tear-stained from the joys and sorrows of my ancestors, knowing that literally I follow in their footsteps. I view the world from the same vantage point as they, because nothing has really changed—away from the well-traveled byways. My quiet corner of earth is still aesthetically bountiful, and I am special to this land; it is my niche.

To have roots is to be born of and buried in the same earth as those who have gone before me. To have roots is to experience an ineffable and sublime kinship, to feel that I am being watched over, and to go on living my time expecting tacit endorsement for life's decisions from ancestral lineage, somehow transmuted across the ages.

To have roots is to have a connection—some would argue too much—with mundane events and common everyday people of the past, for which I do not apologize.

To have roots is to never sell the land no matter what its appreciated value and to be motivated to instill the continuum in successive generations.

There are some silent places still in my little corner of earth. These little nooks, unaffected by the din and clutter of a busy and often unfair social community, comfort the soul and soothe the pain of emotions stripped raw from human interaction. Why is it that the milk of human kindness, fairness, and common decency are ideals too seldom encountered? I try to ignore unfettered greed, mean spiritedness and the "what's-in-it-for-me attitude" that is so prevalent. Are these the attributes of our modern-day world that simply cause us to need vacations? I guess...

I spend thought-provoked and pleasure-filled New Year's days in surrounding hills and valleys isolated from my fellow man, accompanied by my setter(s) of the time. These are moments to reflect the joys and ponder the sorrows of the past year, a time to be swept up and healed by the visual power manifest in the bosom of the Heavenly Maker. This is my celebration on this special day.

On top of the hill where I live, swept bare from man's indiscretions by searing winds but glorious in vernal awakening, is an ancient burial ground. It is a quiet place. On this crisp June day a canopy of purest blue firmament arcs the centuries-old stonewalls that enclose this roughly-kept resting place of my ancestors. Only a nascent stirring of an unceasing wind, common to this place, pleasantly wafts the solitude of early morning, diffusing the pungent sweetness emanating from that baneful invasive to path and pasture, euphemistically called wild rose.

I often wonder if my mind could really know the love of such quiet places were it not for the punitive social foibles of my peers and the real problems of life that I and all humankind face. They cause me to pause, reflect, and recoil.

The beauty of God's creation is all around me. It redeems my afflictions. It doesn't answer back and asks nothing in return. Do others know the feeling? Or are they too busy fighting day-to-day battles, living for selfish moments and to hell with tomorrow, too busy keeping up with the Joneses and living life to its fullest?

An eighteenth century marker of my matriarchal-descended ancestor stands among deteriorating memorials of others long forgotten, family names of early settlers—Allen, Bradford, Copp, Dolbeare, Hillhouse, Raymond, Vibber. A time-ravaged epitaph headed by the Angel of Death is barely legible in the spalling red sandstone: "Here lies the body of Lieut. Joseph Bradford who departed this life A.D. 1747 in the seventy-third year of his age." What circumstances forced him from historic Lebanon, Connecticut to my town in 1717—cheap farmland, financial opportunity?

Or just maybe he was such an emotionally sensitive soul that his fellow man caused him to yank up his roots and move south to the North Parish of New London.

Trash

O Lord, our Lord,
How majestic is your name in all
The earth!
When I consider your heavens,
The work of your fingers,
The moon and the stars,
which you have set in place,
what is man that you are mindful of
him?
The son of man that you care for him?
You made him a little lower than
the heavenly beings
and crowned him with glory and honor.

You made him ruler over the works
of your hands;
you put everything under his feet:
all flocks and herds,
and the beasts of the field,
the birds of the air,
and the fish of the sea,
all that swims the paths of the
seas.

From Psalm 8

I believe every living creature has its own particular sensitivity—
what man might consider appreciation—to its surroundings, not just
chosen solely for the sake of survival. It may be true that the higher
the order of intelligence, the more rational this bond of understanding,
at least theoretically. On a grand scale, without an environment that
protects all of earth's living beings, life, as we know it, would not exist.
Most would probably agree that the nexus is more profound in *Homo
sapiens*, and, as such, we of the highest order, according to Psalmist
above, exercise more control over the destructive forces that threaten
the world's environment and ecosystems, again, at least theoretically.

It is also accurate to say that man is the most hurtful of all God's
creatures and that his callous treatment of his habitat is repugnant.
I'm referring here to garbage—man-made garbage. Overt disposal of
trash, bottles, cans, plastic vessels (no matter how refined the bottle
bill in your state), and other fast food containers casually tossed out
of car windows is becoming an epidemic, from my observation.
Surreptitious dumping is a favorite way to avoid going to the town
landfill if it happens to be closed or if the annual fee hasn't been paid.
While these misdemeanors are not ruinous, they are indicative of man's
total lack of understanding of the much more difficult problems that
environmentalists and politicians vex. Even with penalties as high as
$1000, it does not appear that state and municipal coffers are exactly
overflowing from the collection of these fines.

I love the land and its beauty. It is more important to me than
all of life's toys, joys, and pleasures; in fact, the land is responsible for
many of the things we need and enjoy in life; right down to the air we

breathe. When some unthinking nut strews his Burger King breakfast remains replete with napkins and coffee cup across the countryside, the earth's visual quality is compromised. You have to doubt that the perpetrator is more responsible or is to be more respected than any of God's four-legged creatures. Is he the exception or the rule? I keep asking what kind of individual would profess no compunction about doing this, notwithstanding its illegality. Are these the people with whom we could otherwise have normal dealings in everyday venues? Are kids and teenagers responsible, as someone has suggested? Yes, in part, but I think the problem crosses generations.

Recently, I had the distinct pleasure of watching and listening to a video on www.youtube of a group of six very young ladies (ages eight to fourteen or so), The Cactus Cuties, performing the *Star-Spangled Banner* at the commencement of a sporting event. Listening carefully to the words and very special fine harmony—as I've never heard before in any rendition of our National Anthem—brought tears to my eyes. As these words were adopted to inspire pride in our beloved country, I asked myself: What possesses so many to tarnish its image?

My granddaughter and I spent a few hours recently collecting bottles, cans, and other detritus of humankind that had been discarded along a half-mile or so of my property's road frontage. And you know what? I found a new generation of beer cans and plastic bottles the very next day! How long will they last if not removed? How about ten years, or even twenty years?—longer in the case of plastics.

I have a name for these polluters—"The Dirty Americans." Of all the criteria by which I judge a man, one of the most important is his ppp—propensity to purposefully pollute. Unfortunately, you can never know of his abominable intentions unless you catch him in the act.

Cleaned up one day by city public works officials and possibly store employees, the wooded acreage east of Wal-Mart in Norwich became a mass garbage pit within a short time. It's too bad that enforcement of existing fines is not exactly high priority with local *gendarmes.* Sadly, the indifference of polluters does not bode well for the future of our visual environment.

I respect our Native American Indians for the religion of their forefathers. Hold on, don't get me wrong; this is not a quasi-repudiation of our Judeo-Christian heritage. It's just a statement of my admiration for our native tribes who revered the manifestations of the natural world. Admittedly, I must remember that they were not forced to contend with the trash of modern day civilization—the residue of McDonald's or myriad other fast food vendors, for example.

A family member became incensed by a plethora of strewn McDonald's debris in front of his home, which he carefully bagged and deposited on the countertop of the local Golden Arches' franchise. Although his solution was misplaced, it symbolized a mounting frustration with a growing problem in this country.

When bird hunting, it's been my unfortunate experience to come across dumped trash in remote sections of rural northern New England. I guess uncaring Americans exist everywhere, but where there are more people, more trash is evident.

As fishermen and hunters using the land, we have an obligation to preach proper disposal of trash and to police the litter of "civilized" society.

Splendor

My spirit gets a lift in the spring of each year when nature unfolds its colorful montage on the New England landscape. The fast-moving sequence never ceases to be a source of inspiration and therapy from the impersonal and spurious world. Beheld with awe and admiration, and not just seen, this floral transformation can soothe a man's weary soul. Its cathartic reflex is to fix one's life into proper perspective, or at the very least, assuage the travails of present day living that force us to be out of touch with the splendor of His mighty works.

There are a few native trees and shrubs of the New England landscape that are special. I have known them since youthful wanderings, and while some are well known, others are not. My mother had a passion for wild flowers, and searching for them was her excuse to be in the woods that she loved so much. She taught me where to find the secretive trailing arbutus in early spring; the seldom-seen lady's slipper in May; the showy cardinal flower of damp places in late July and early August.

I first look for the white sprinkling of shadblow (*Amelanchia*) when the shad are spawning. Also known as serviceberry and Juneberry, it is common to native landscapes. It appears in a stark panorama just awakening from winter's slumber in late April to early May, just as leaf buds of most trees are starting to open. Picture an overcast day overlooking an open expanse of intermittent lowlands and highlands. Serviceberry blossoms stand out in an otherwise bleak but soon-to-be unfolding glory of spring. At this time, the inconspicuous yellow-flowered spicebush (*Lindera*) of wet places has long since joined the pleadings of peep frogs. Pinch the twigs and the wonderful aroma of spice is released. Where it forms a thicket, sometimes I find migrating woodcock under the branches of this low growing shrub. Because it is muted in bloom, I suspect that many casual observers are immune to its presence.

Toward the tail end of shadblow's fleeting spectacle, the opening bracts of the indigenous dogwoods (*Cornus florida*) slowly open to a pure showy white that personifies the New England landscape. Although pink and red cultivars are common in the nursery trade, the long-lasting flower bracts of the native white, when fully open, are a joy to behold. I cannot conjure our regenerating fields and woods openings in May without this splendid tree whose flowers appear before the leaves. The later blooming June variety (Cornus kousa) of suburbia is a notably beautiful dogwood. Although not a native species, the June cream-to-white flowers of mature specimens are extremely floriferous and breathtaking. It is pest free and of longer life than our native species.

When fishing a favorite trout stream, the sight and smell of our native pinxterbloom (*Rhod. nudiflorum*), pink and resplendent in sylvan settings, is captivating. Better yet, leave the rod in the car for an hour and make this wild azalea the object of your search in the dewy early day. Its presence will be betrayed by its sweet pungency. Later, in July, look for its close cousin, *Rhod. Viscosum*, or swamp azalea. Fragrant and pure white, it provides contrast to summer's greenery. We flyfishers, fully occupied and devoted to studying the hatch on the water, sometimes fail to take note of God's blessings all around us.

How many late spring fishermen are aware of the awe-inspiring yellow, green and orange blossoms of the common tulip tree (*Liriodendron*)? Although not showy from a distance, when viewed from a within several inches they are truly one of nature's marvels. Also called tulip poplar (by foresters) or whitewood (by old-timers), this clear grained, straight-as-an-arrow hardwood was once popularly harvested for barn siding because of its light weight. Many outdoorsmen are unaware that this high-branched forest giant of the eastern U.S. produces gorgeous early to mid-June flowers, perhaps because it generates few lower branches upon which its blossoms can readily be seen in a heavily wooded environment. Growing in the open, the beautiful (but small) June flowers become readily apparent on lower branches.

Liriodendron Tulipifera, Tulip Tree

Along about graduation time, long after most of the myriad, non-native, spring flowering ornamentals and just after the lordly rhoddys have burst forth in spectacular profusion, the state flower of Connecticut, mountain laurel (*Kalmia*), is almost alone in flower. Growing best in partial shade in a woodsy setting and producing white to deep pink flowers and good foliage, mountain laurel is also a popular shrub for homeowners. Once I pushed a grouse into a laurel thicket. Forget it! The bird's flush was visible, but I couldn't bring the gun up through the unyielding branches.

Closing out the native landscape in late fall is a personal favorite—black alder (*Ilex*). Not to be confused with speckled alder (*Alnus*), a preferred haunt of the American woodcock in northern climes, this eight to ten foot tall shrub is also known as winterberry or Christmas berry. After the yellow fall leaves drop in November its bright red berries stand out in the stark, leafless landscape otherwise void of color. In cutting the brush around my Connecticut stonewalls, I am careful to leave this exceptional plant, which I don't consider "brush." Its solitary red berries last into January.

And so we have come through a full cycle of seasonal interest, not to mention the spectacular New England fall foliage.

Letters From a Sportsman

Part I

    Dick Curriden, of Greenville, Maine and Griswold, Connecticut has been a friend, occasional hunting companion and correspondent for over thirty years. When putting these letters together, I tried to recollect where and when I first met Dick. It probably was on the skeet fields of the Quaker Hill Rod & Gun Club in Montville, Connecticut in the early 1970s. In his letters that follow, Dick addresses me sometimes as Cap'n because I was captain of a skeet team sponsored by that club for several years. Dick was a member of that team, the Quaker Hill Puritans. We weren't world-class skeet shooters, as I recall, but we competed consistently in the higher divisions—Division I in 1973-74—and had a lot of fun. The other team members were Jay Buckley, Bill Clarke, Bill Downie, Manfred Schact von Wittenau (who, along with Dick, taught me why I should love German shotguns, especially Merkels) and Harry Warner.

    I came to know Dick as representing the epitome of the word "sportsman." I think you will find this to be evident in the following letters. Whereas my sporting endeavors evolved to include only upland hunting and a smattering of fly-fishing, Dick has done it all. Dick's and Lee's lovely home on the shores of Moosehead Lake in Greenville, Maine allows him quick access to fishing opportunities, but I sense that as Dick approaches his eighth decade, he favors the upland shooting life over all other types of outdoor activity.

    As to the upland shooting life, the team (or Dick alone) presented me with a couple of books over those skeet shooting years, both inscribed by Dick. George Bird Evans' *The Upland Shooting Life* and William Harnden Foster's *New England Grouse Shooting* were to be instrumental in advancing my future bird hunting and book collecting interests. My library of upland books now numbers in excess of 325 collectible volumes, attributable to those early gifts and foresight of Dick Curriden.

Greenville, ME 04441
Sept. 6, 1993
Hi Cap'n,

    This ad in the RGS magazine caught my eye. I've been to Cochrane (Ontario) before, flew out there on a moose and goose hunt back in '72. But I like the prospects of a Sept. 15th bird hunt. Rest assured the leaves will be pretty well down in that latitude by that time. Ten flushes per hour? I don't think I could stand it. Not only that but after the birding how about dropping in at friend Rikhoff's little duck pond; hell, it's on the way home! I sent for the poop. We can talk it over this fall.

    Also, look out! I got into a gun trade with old Doc Blanchard up here and ended up with a Prussian Sauer 20 gauge, 25" barrels; cylinder & improved chokes cover a bed sheet at twenty-five yards with my skeet loads. Get this—14½" LOP, 1 5/8" drop at comb and 3 3/8" at heel with some cast off, and it fits like a dream. Doc says this gun should be outlawed for woodcock. We'll see.

    I hate to tell you what I had to trade to get it, but I can say it was so severe that I had to change my will afterwards. Some of the jewels that were supposed to go with me in the box had to be sacrificed!!

Dick

    P.S. Bilinski's choice of the P.W.G. in *Come October* shows that he is a man of very great knowledge, indifferent to "trend" and of great taste and class! Oh how I love those 16s, especially Foxes and the ever-so-rare Hopkins & Allen of the Rose City of old.

    Ed. note: Dick refers to our upcoming trip to Patten River Camp, Cochrane, Ontario. Obviously, he prefers crooked stocks that were popular at the turn of the twentieth century (1900!). P.W.G. refers to Perfect Woodcock Gun. The "Rose City" is Norwich, Connecticut, home of many gun manufacturers in the nineteenth and early twentieth centuries

Greenville, ME 04441
April 5, 1994
Maine Dept. of Inland Fisheries & Wildlife (copy to author for opinion)
Attn: Commissioner
Dear Commissioner:

As a lifelong hunter and fisherman (started in Maine in 1941), I would like to pass along a few of my observations, particularly about the decline of the ruffed grouse.

I have hunted the Moosehead region, the western mountains and the North Woods above Moosehead with good dogs, and I am finding the grouse population diminished more and more each year. Yes, I know about cycles, but I think this scarcity is more than merely cyclic.

I go back to the days of great abundance when using a shotgun was considered "unsporting." A .22 pistol was all that was required as there were a great many, and tame at that. That was before the great network of roads that began to appear in the North Woods.

This grand bird's weakness is to come to the side of the road and peck for gravel, making it vulnerable to the road hunter. Without getting into the ethics of this type of hunting and after observing the great decline in numbers of these birds, I conclude that the pressure of frequent traffic and the unnecessarily high limit four (4) per day is rapidly leading to the near extinction of the species. Let's not wait until the horse has been stolen before we lock the barn door, as we have in the case of trout and salmon. Possibly we can restore the latter, but not so the grouse. I don't see the need for a four-bird limit in this day and age. Two should be sufficient.

Enclosed is a clipping showing that a neighboring state (Massachusetts) recognizes this problem and is moving to do something about it.

Also: POSSUM!! This critter does not deserve the status of a game animal or even furbearer—not in this part of the country, anyway!

The possum began showing up in southern New England soon after WWII. Prior to this sad event, there was good hunting for quail, grouse, rabbit and pheasant. The possum has proven to be as bad a PREDATOR on small game as the fox, coyote and house cat combined. They vacuum the ground at night and will consume any egg-laying or ground-nesting animal, even skunks. The latter have all but disappeared too, along with those mentioned above. I know the idea is unpopular, but there ought to be a bounty on them. Keep an eye on the southern portions of the state where these critters have already become established, and watch and see if your small game numbers don't drop off drastically. The trouble is that by the time it's noticed it may already be too late.

Sincerely,
Curriden

Greenville, ME 04441
May 18, 1994
Hi Cap'n,

Thanks for your note and "epistle." Maine Fisheries and Wildlife acknowledged my comments re: grouse and possums and passed it to some regional head for "further study."

It has been quite cool and wet so far here this month but still managed to get out for some of the spring activities as mentioned by (Tom) Hennessey. Dog flushed a grouse by the gravel road last evening. Don't know how it could have survived the winter. Nature sure is miraculous.

Best regards,
Dick

Greenville, ME 04441
Oct. 18, 1994
Hi Cap'n,

Talked to Fred (Maine guide) and heard you aborted the New Hampshire trip. Good choice. Sometimes you can go wrong by getting something for nothing, which is probably what you would have gotten in NH. All bird reports are way off here this year.

I went up to the Jackman border this a.m. Got thoroughly frustrated as I entered the Duty Store to find the clerks attending to no less than a whole busload (100 or so) of octogenarians of many mixed nationalities all trying to cash in their receipts of reimbursable tax! Oh woe is me. Quite ugly! I attempted to convince the dingy clerk that we received no guiding at Patten River Camp, (Cochrane, Ontario); all was for food and lodging, as we were rained out. I produced the copy of Robert's statement to that effect. Anyway, they came up with a rebate of $58 (Canadian), which included one motel slip for a total of around $54. I have to send to Ottawa (like you) for my other rebate for the caribou hunt, because of the time delay. Also, one must appear in person to receive this rebate. I had to show my driver's license, and because I didn't have my Social Security card on me, I had to produce my blood donor record for sufficient I.D! I thought they would also ask for the equivalency of a blood donation by that time.

After all that, I went on to hunt the whole Jackman area, found where a great emigration of woodcock took place during the full moon last night—splash only. Went on to flush one bird, which I missed cleanly, thus keeping my record quite well intact. Hopefully it will go on to breed, as we need all the survivors we can get now! Just talked to Fred, and he hasn't done anything on birds on his own the last two days either.

Dick

Greenville, ME
Jan. 1, 1995
Dear Paul,

A year ago last July, I sold this fellow a 16 gauge Merkel Model 201E through an ad in the *Gun List*. Coming from the Chicago environment, he had an awful "I'm-getting-screwed" complex, and although he dearly wanted the gun, he was hesitant. After the deal was made, he wrote back saying he didn't think such "honesty" was still existent. Recently I received a nice card thanking me again and recounting his pleasures with the Merkel. Of course, I had to respond—copy enclosed. It's remarkable how Bodio agrees.

See ya,
Dick

Ed. Note: In his book, *Good Guns Again*, Steve Bodio opines about the value of a 16 gauge O/U or S/S with 28-inch barrels, double triggers and a wide spread between chokes.

Greenville, ME
March 16, 1995. (The day after the Ides of March, beware. The day before St. Patrick's Day, rejoice!)
Hi Cap'n,

Was reading the latest RGS magazine and came across an article by Joe Arnette, a Mainer and a bird hunter. He espouses on the grand bird hunting he enjoyed in one of my world-favorite places, Cape Breton Island, Nova Scotia. The best thing of all is that partridge haven't got scare there yet! If you don't have the issue, I'll send you a copy. Very interesting.

Winter is coming to an end here, and it's getting slushy. I'll be down to spend April in Connecticut.

See ya,
Dick

Greenville, ME
June 3, 1995 (wet & buggy)
Dear Paul,

Received your recent letter and club news; always good to hear.

It's raining this morning; otherwise the reply might be a little later in coming.

You must have read Michael McIntosh's article regarding the "16" in the last issue of *Sporting Classics*, especially the last paragraph where he refers to the "wizened silver hairs" who recognize the inherent value of the gauge. Glad you got out of Jim Austin's clutches without financing his trip to Europe. Keep looking. Eventually you'll do better. We all must have a "Holy Grail!"

How was I ever so lucky to get Trevallion to take the time to bend my stock, since he is so pre-occupied with employment by the Japanese. Do they hunt? I thought it was golf.

Enjoyed your nostalgic story in the newsletter. A couple generations back and amongst my earliest memories of my agrarian heritage, I can remember often those stories about the men who were gored by their barnyard bulls. It's a known fact that they have killed more men than all the wild beasts ever. It was a fact of the times.

I haven't done much fishing here so far; too rainy. I have gone beyond the point of suffering misery to enjoy my sport. I'd just as soon leave it for another day. Got a couple of trout (very nice) and small salmon so far.

I wrote to Joe Arnette regarding Cape Breton, but no answer as yet. I have also been pondering a western hunt before the CRP lands disappear and the abundance of birds with it, as happened before.

Your story "No Finer Tribute" in RGS was good, a nice way to go, probably better than bag pipes. Keep 'em coming.

Best regards,
Dick

Greenville, ME
June 4, 1995 (Sunny, wind N.W.)
Dear Paul,

Just getting back from mailing your letter yesterday, the phone was ringing, and it was David Trevallion. I had previously told him not to take a chance on shipping my gun, and that I would be around the 1st of June to pick it up. Due to complications, I didn't make it. He wanted to know if he should ship it. I said no, that I'd be down week after next on my way to Connecticut for dental surgery. He sympathized, having just suffered a root canal. So much for modern dentistry. He wanted me to be sure and call before I came down as at present he was escorting a "Japanese gentleman" and that would be taking him away from his shop and around to the various sites in the state of Maine. No more carving gunstocks!!!

I passed on my regards from you and commented that you passed on a 16 gauge at Austin's. Further commenting that you might be interested in hearing about a nice one with GOOD WOOD, he replied that he had just acquired a nice collection from New York (ahh sooo!) I should look it over for a nice 16.

I get the feeling that there is no love lost between him and Austin, so don't be surprised to hear that we have a fine new "London West" gun shop sprouting up in the hinterland.

Will talk to you when I come down in mid-June, that is, if I am able to talk.

Best regards,
Dick

Part II

Greenville, ME
June 8, 1995
Hi Cap'n,

Things sure happen in strange ways, don't they? Sometimes when you throw your hat at the ceiling, it sticks!

Due to extraordinary good luck, my young friend and co-hunter was picked in the Maine Moose Lottery. The odds were only 100 chances out of 17,799, and he got it!

This means that I am obliged to go moose hunting the first week of October in the Northeast Zone (unfortunately), which is Northern Aroostook County. It's too far to consider hunting out of here or even our camp at Elm Pond. Therefore, we have to hire a camp, and the best deal I can find so far—there aren't many in that area—is $80 per day per person plus other expenses I must share.

I am afraid this blows the fuse on my limited funds for bird hunting this fall. I have already incurred considerable medical expenses for this year already—enough to pay for a damned good hunt—and I am in for more of it as I am headed down to Connecticut next week for dental surgery (no insurance) to dentists that I already owe $1,300 going in.

In view of this, I think I'll be forced to cancel my part of the hunt with Fred Westerberg this fall. It would put me too much in the hole, I'm afraid. I won't be going anywhere but here, so you would be welcome to come up and kick around the alders in this territory with me for whatever.

I also received a reply from Joe Arnette. Cape Breton Island sounds good—maybe next year if my rim-racked old body holds together.

Best regards,
Dick

Greenville. ME
Sept. 22, 1995 (fall is here)
Dear Paul,

I received your letter and "epistle" yesterday. Good to hear from you. Sounds to me that you have been quite busy around the old homestead this summer, but it must be a great satisfaction to see the land coming back according to your plan.

It has been very dry here too. We have a "no fire" ban, but they have stopped short of closing the woods for the time being. We sure could use some of that beautiful rain that keeps on going out to sea with the hurricanes. I don't know for sure what that will do to the woodcock flights, but I'm inclined to think if they can't find food in the usual coverts they will just keep on going after a brief rest. (Your Russells will be just fine, in fact, sandals will do.) On the plus side, partridge sightings have been up. They may be on the incline from the cyclic low, I hope, and that will be just fine with me.

George Finch, an old friend from the Groton Sportsman's Club, is working up here with Gentle Ben's as a bear guide. Last Sunday we went down to the Big Pine Club in Dover-Foxcroft and shot five-stand sporting clays for the first time. It's a real departure from conventional skeet and very much a challenge—and good fun.

Sorry to hear about your unexpected heavy home improvement expenses. A lot of the old homesteads were lost to chimney fires, including my ancestors'. Better to spend the money. See ya on the fifteenth.

Dick

Greenville, ME
July 8, 1996
Dear Paul

Reading the Bangor paper yesterday, Tom Hennessey's article on the "birds" (enclosed) gets one's mind off the fishing, what little there was, and on to the more important subjects.

Al Airey, Pete Lamey and I had planned a trip to West Texas for quail last February, but the killing ice storm there caused the guide to cancel on the eve of our departure. And now, the wet spring doesn't bode well for here either. We are, however planning a trip to South Dakota the last of September for sharptail grouse, Huns, and of course, pheasant, then on to Wisconsin for grouse. We'll see what happens there.

As ever a friend,
Dick

Greenville, ME
10-17-96
Dear Paul,

How's it going? We're winding down up here for the season.

No doubt you got a good earful about what a wanderlust bum I am. Of course, it's all too true!

I hooked up with Al Airey for a long awaited trip to South Dakota for prairie chicken, sharptail grouse and pheasant the last week of September. Then on to Wisconsin for ruffed grouse and woodcock.

The hunting in S.D. was most rigorous, as they figure seven and one-half miles to the bird—forced march, no lollygagging! By the time you get your three birds, you've done, by simple arithmetic, twenty + miles. That's only the morning hunt! In the afternoon you go for pheasants in the brushy draws—real buggery holes. And do they RUN! We hunted with Labs who both flushed and retrieved. As many as there were, it would have been impossible without the dogs. We didn't do any "driving and blocking" (gang shoot) as is done later in the season.

Here, this year, birds are scarce and the weather violently terrible, gale winds and cold. I've been out a half dozen times without getting a single bird, having neither seen nor heard but few. Will go through the motions again this afternoon.

See ya in a couple of weeks.

Dick

Greenville, October 23, 1996   (included with previous)

Have been out a few more times since, only to confirm the earlier report of no partridge and damn few woodcock. This past weekend we found other hunters in all our previously "secret" covers. Some even left their spent Orvis cases lying about. We've been discovered! One must now go to the ends of the earth to get what little is left of hunting.

How did your trip to "new ground" go?

Oh yes, regarding Wisconsin: We hunted three days in beautiful cover, but too much foliage. We seemed to be in between native birds (woodcock) moving out and before the migratory flights moved in. Flushed a few but only got a couple. The rest of it was twenty miles to the partridge, same as here. We hunted over drathaars—good dogs, good pointers, close workers and good retrievers as well.

Greenville
3/22/97
Paul:

Here's the latest Hennessey column.

We came up to get our annual taste of winter this month, and there's plenty of it this year—three to five feet of snow on the level. Drifts and banks are mountainous. Plenty of ice on Moosehead Lake, but there's nobody ice fishing as it's nineteen degrees with a northwest wind twenty-five to forty mph. It was five degrees above this morning. Been like this all month.

Enough already. We're heading back to Connecticut ahead of the mud and flood.

This "spring" does not bode well for returning birds.

Dick

Greenville
10-28-97, snowing and snowing
Hi Paul,

Enclosed is Hennessey's lament. I thought we were doing badly until I read his report.

The first couple of weeks were warm with heavy foliage. Last two weeks snow, wind and cold. Only a few birds early, none since.

How'd you do? Glad not to have gone out West this year.

My response.....

Oakdale, CT
Oct. 31, 1997
Hi Dick,

Thanks for Hennessey's doom and gloom. Regardless of the content, I always enjoy reading his stuff. Relative to the matter of bird scarcity, here are my thoughts and experience to date this year.

The annual Maine hunt was good. We moved thirty to thirty-five woodcock. Our shooting averages were on the high side—about forty-five % for both Greg and me. We shot sixteen woodcock, two shy of a two-man, three-day limit. Greg also shot a grouse. This is far from a record in terms of birds moved and bagged, but we were satisfied. Yes, we saw fewer birds, but we expected that.

Vermont was sort of a disaster. The first day, October 23, was OK. We saw few woodcock, but Dave Smith, my guide, and I shot four. Lots of grouse, but I think we just happened to disturb a couple of families for the first time since spring. Beautiful dog work (Blaze), but the birds were too wily in their running tactics for us to have had any success in bringing any to bag.

I awoke the next day to four to five inches of snow—and still coming. With the forecast for the white stuff to continue, I packed it up and came home. Have not been out since but will be taking a week off soon to hit a few local coverts.

I can't argue against the evidence that woodcock numbers are down. But from year to year it's sometimes hard to tell because of weather and timing, meaning one year may be better than the last if you hit the flights. That's been my experience.

I think you know me well enough to realize that pride in my setter bitch, Blaze, should not be construed as boasting—and she isn't perfect by a long shot. But I have to say that she covers her ground well and stretches out to find birds. If there's a bird in a big cover, she'll find it and hold it for you. This is what we need, especially in times of bird scarcity. W.H. Foster said essentially the same thing sixty years ago, meaning if you want to find birds, you'll need more than a boot licker. Not all agree on this of course. A highly trained bird dog is essential.

Fred told me that he guided Ken Dugas in Maine and New Hampshire over the Columbus Day weekend and he shot two birds in three days. I have no other details.

Paul

(no date)
Griswold, CT
Hi Paul,

This is my "grouse and gun" story for the year. Do you think it will sell? Pictured is a horny hen between my size twelve boots! It's been five or more years since I've seen a grouse in our Connecticut woodlands—walking, running or flying, and here she comes to keep me company on my solitary deer stand. Do you suppose the "boss" grouse is trying to send us a message?

Also, the 20-gauge Fox Sterlingworth is a "State of Maine Special." Firing hi-brass sixes in those 2½ inch chambers was the cause of the fractured stock and dislodged teeth of the former owner.

Dick

Ed. note: I suspect Dick's "horny hen" was actually a male protecting his hallowed ground, this pronouncement according to the editor of RGS magazine.

June 14, 1998, Flag Day
Greenville, ME
Hi Paul,

It looks like Greg Sepic has gone on to the Happy Hunting Ground where maybe, at last, he can solve the riddle of the mysterious woodcock.

Partridge very scarce to non-existent due to the ravages of multiple ice storms last winter.

On Wisconsin! Great Lake states supposed to be good this year.

Best regards,
Dick

Greenville, ME
July 16, 1998
Hi Paul,

Of all you've ever written, your "obituaries" are the best! Consider yourself hired to do mine, but please remember that good men do live after them and the bad are interred with their bones.

Hang in there,
Dick

No place
September 18, 1998
Hi Paul,

Thanks for the report on Jim Austin—just when I placed an order for a 20-gauge Arietta. I might have to collect it from the Feds! How could a guy, as smart as he is, be that stupid—although I could say the same for our revered president.

Nice woodchuck story, well done, but eighteen pounds? Wow!

Grouse prospects here are terrible—what with all the crust we had last winter and a wet, rainy June. We hunted rabbits last March on top of three to three and one-half feet of snow without snowshoes. I wonder how many partridge we walked over?

We'll hunt Wisconsin the last three days of October, then on to South Dakota for pheasants and ducks. Birds are supposed to be up this year in the northern lake states.

Regards,
Dick

80 Sheldon Rd.
Voluntown, CT 06384
December 9, 1998
Dear Doc, Duddy & everyone,

We left Greenville on October 25. It was snowing. Time to go.

Headed out to Wisconsin. Northern part is much like Maine. Had three good days of grouse and woodcock hunting; then to South Dakota for pheasants and ducks. The ducks were plentiful with "pot hole" shooting being the method, which I prefer. There was an assortment of mallards, pintails, widgeon and gadwall, the latter being a new one on me as it is seen on the Mississippi and Central Flyways but rare in the East.

The pheasants were another story. The same dogs, drathaars, that were so good on grouse and woodcock in Wisconsin, were wild as hell on South Dakota pheasants. Can't blame the dog when he gets into a mile-long slough full of running bird scent and he doesn't hold point. The birds eventually flush ½ mile ahead, with a gone-crazy dog right under them. If you can get the dog to come back, you may pick up a few stragglers. We got birds, but it was long, tough and HARD going. We didn't do the cornfield drives that are so popular—with good reason.

We picked up this "errant" bear cub (pictures enclosed) that got separated from his mother after he had a lumberjack "treed" all that morning. We didn't have a dog at that time, so we took him along and he hunted for us as good as most dogs.

How were your trips?

Best regards,
Dick

Part III

Greenville, ME
6-29-99
Hi Paul,

Received your newsletter and I laud you on your stand for the NRA. We are in the fight of our lives right now. With your permission I'd like to send copies to the Groton and Mystic clubs, also the County League. I will urge all the membership to get in on this effort as we have long passed the time of "let the other guy do it." The recent attempt that was rammed through the Senate—that fortunately had the Congress choking—didn't fly (infuriating Slick). But never fear; they will be back, more determined than ever.

I see you got _____ in your club. Did you know he's a full-automatic buff? Also, _____ is a new millionaire now, so he can afford the Double Gun Journal and your club's membership price. When he and Al Airey were younger, they hunted on trips together, until recently when _____ discovered there were so many women and so little time left.

We have a saying around here that if you want to catch trout you've got to go way back, and if you don't get 'em there, save your dough and go on up to Quebec or Labrador. But bring your BUG suit!

Jim Austin got me to buy one of those $3600 Arrietas—20-gauge sidelock with a few extra accoutrements—just previous to his incarceration. He's a good salesman as you know, but nonetheless the gun is a honey and shoots as good as it looks. It's unfortunate that something like this didn't come along earlier in my lifetime so I could enjoy it more.

Dick

Greenville, ME 04441
July 7, 1999
Double Gun Journal
5014 Rockery School Rd.
East Jordan, MI
Attn: Daniel Cote—the most humble and down-to-earth man (besides myself) that Paul Chase has ever known

Dear Daniel Cote,

Somehow my renewal of DGJ slipped through the cracks—a thousand *mea culpas*. My renewal check for $39 is enclosed. Please start me up where I left off, as Paul Chase politely admonished me for missing his feature article in the last issue. Also, I happen to have a few choice shotguns for sale at this time. Please be so kind as to place them in your "For Sale" list of the next available issue.

Sincerely,
Richard Curriden

P.S. Paul (Daniel sent a copy of the above to me.) I, like you, get all the mags. *Sporting Classics* and *Shooting Sportsman* are also my favorites, and I read all the gun articles, of course. Wieland's piece on Arrietas was timely as I just received mine—my first custom gun since the Merkel O&U in '65—and am well pleased. Looking forward to this year's grouse hunt in Wisconsin again. It's supposed to be a peak year. Good luck with your new dog. Maybe she'll turn out as nice as Bess. Congratulations on getting Jon out of law school and into "the law" in time for your retirement.

Best regards,
Dick

Greenville, ME
October 6, 1999 (woodcock season opens today)
Hi Paul,

Got your "communiqué"—thanks, always good to hear from you.
Grouse hunting off to a slow start. According to the "experts," they should be "raining out of the trees." But with gun and dog in the woods, it's still the same old story—twenty miles to the partridge.
Glad to see you made it around to the "elitists rendezvous" last month. I guess Addieville took a back seat to Sandanona. New England Arms didn't show at any of the Maine gun shows this year either.

My acquisitions for the year include a nice Arrieta 20 gauge made to my specs. And surprisingly, delivered as ordered from New England Arms.

I purchased a very nice I. Rizzini 28-gauge O&U from Cubetas at an irresistible price, also a 28-gauge Luciano Rota from the *Gun List*—a very nice gun for the price. I didn't mind having Trevallion bend the Rizzini stock down for the "ultimate fit." It's still a little straight but I'll hold off using the wood rasp for a while.

Hunted the wily bird this a.m. with Bogey, now nine, and casting nicely within range, sight and sound. Like old Harry Allyn used to say, "About the time they get good, they go and die on ya." Used old "Hundred Percent," my aged Hopkins & Allen sawed off to twenty-five inches with three-inch drop—DEADLY! The old rainy day gun outshoots them all!

Will rendezvous with Al Airey in South Dakota for ducks and pheasants the last of October. Then we're on to Wisconsin for grouse and a few bothersome woodcock.

Best regards,
Dick

P.S. A word to the bank regarding your proposed "retirement" gifts might be in order—much more preferable than the usual Rolex!

Greenville, ME
Sept. 29, 2001
Hi Cap'n,

Good seeing you and Greg at Sandanona.

Did you get that Lindner Daly?

Congratulations on winning the Concours with your pristine Daly. Class will tell!

I participated in the Cape Gun Event and scored twenty-one out of thirty, a respectable score. When a seventy-four-year-old gent shoots a seventy-year-old gun in competition in a "world class event," it don't get no better than that (sic).

I'm delighted with your editing of my "epistle." Somehow I thought you would. Your copy is so neat I'm going to frame it. You have my permission, of course, to do whatever with it.

I'll get in touch when I start to write my book! I could start it off with "The Cape Gun Story." Quite unique.

Best regards,
Dick

Vintagers
Order of Edwardian Gunners
Hawley, MA 01339
September 26,2001
Richard Curriden
Greenville, Maine 04441
Dear Dick,

Congratulations! Your fine shooting earned you second place in the Cape-Gun Event! Enclosed you'll find your trophy. We hope you enjoyed yourself at this year's Vintage Cup and look forward to having you back again next year, September 19-22, 2002 at Sandanona.

Hammers Back
Ray Poudrier, President
The Vintagers

Hi Paul,

And a very handsome bit or sterling silver! What a nice surprise when I got back here. I had no idea where I placed. Good show!

Dick

Griswold, CT   (Mailing address changed from Voluntown to Griswold)
October 31, 2001
Hi Cap'n,

Regarding the Cape gun, it's a J.P. Sauer, 1931 vintage with hammers but modern steel barrels (double barrel), 16 gauge on the left and 7 X 57 on the right. This opposed to a drilling which has two shotgun barrels on top and a rifle barrel underneath. There are other configurations with various Germanic names. The reason for the existence of these guns, beside their inherent versatility, was the Krauts heavily taxed all guns owned in excess of one, so many shooters only needed to own one gun—a tribute to German ingenuity. We shot thirty targets. I scored 21/30; good for second place, but wait 'til next year!

As to the hunting: Never killed a partridge, although I put in my regulation twenty + miles afoot. Road hunters mopped up as usual. One hunter with a $1,000,000 dog did much better. The woodcock numbers were only a trickle before I left for Wisconsin on October 20. We had one good day of hunting grouse on Wednesday the 24th, then the Great Western Blizzard hit and we were wiped out for the rest of the week.

Glad to hear that Molly is coming along so good. Hard to believe Blaze is ten already. My old Brit is eleven and can still put up a pheasant now and then, as long as I don't hunt her more than a couple of hours. That's enough for me too.

Keep those cards and letters coming.

Dick

Greenville, ME
Oct. 22, 2003
Hi Grandpa,

Congratulations on the perpetuation of your fine family.

I received an interesting note from DGJ that my subscription had expired. I replied that I had sent in my renewal check along with my

"Cape Gun Story," and that it was probably in the bottom of the round file. Indeed it was, as they pawed through their backlog of stories to find my renewal check!

Couldn't get to Sandanona this year. Too tied up. Will try for next year.

The bird hunting here this fall has been an absolute DISASTER! We started out with very heavy foliage and warm weather. The coverts were impossibly thick—too much for these old and tired legs to penetrate. What few native woodcock were here were impossible to approach and shoot. Forget what few grouse we flushed. The weather changed mid-month following Columbus Day. Even though conditions were better, the flight birds hadn't arrived and the grouse were even wilder.

Then the rains came with very high winds (even a twister) on top of already flooded ground. The last two years the coverts were bone dry, this year flooded.

I hunted the grassy roads for grouse Monday afternoon sans dog—thirteen-years-old and lame (I got her on the same joint medicine I'm on). Score: three (flushes), hunter zero. I'm too slow now for those buzz bombs. I'll have to settle for those slow, lumbering pheasants.

The weather on that p.m. hunt was cold, raw and damp and I thought I could smell snow. Indeed it did, all that night. Woke up to four to six inches of the wettest and heaviest snow I ever saw. The trees were all bent over, and we lost power for the day. It rained on top of that wet heavy mess all day. The prediction is for another like amount tonight, high winds with rain and snow mix for Thursday.

Last summer Pete Lampasona's life-long hunting partner died. They had made plans to hunt at McNally's, up in the Allagash, one hundred miles north of here. They did well there last year. I was invited to go in Paul Wood's place. We leave tonight in the teeth of a blizzard! In my long past duck hunting days I'd pray for just such weather. Right now I'd just as soon stay home and stoke my three wood stoves.

How did you find things this year?

Sorry about Molly. Hope she'll be able to hunt some. It's slim pickings with a good dog and pure hell without.

Best regards,
Dick

Paul E. Chase

Greenville, ME
June 28, 2004
Hi Cap'n,

Just returned from a trip cruising the Inside Passage of the Alaskan coast on a "paddle wheel" steamboat. There aren't enough adjectives to properly describe this area, as it has to be one of the ten most spectacular places in the whole world. The enclosed photos are pitifully inadequate. Accommodations on this unique mode of travel were all above expectations.

I know you once went to the interior of Alaska years ago, but you must make this trip with your fair bride while you are still able. When you get an advertisement in the mail regarding this unparalleled trip, look it over carefully before consigning it to the can. I requested they send you all the info.

Say, how about that photo that appeared in the last pages in the summer edition of *DGJ*! They didn't do the whole story, just the photo of me, the big moose and mention of the Buschflinte 7 X 57/16 gauge. I thought they'd at least mention the ptarmigan part. Maybe later.

Best regards,
Dick

Griswold, CT
November 10, 2005
Hi Cap'n,

Am breathlessly awaiting your tales and adventures of the uplands, this year of *EXTREMES*. Only got out once myself—no more dog. Going for nerve (sciatic) test and MRI tomorrow to see if I can reclaim my hind legs again.

Dick

Greenville, ME
June 8, 2006, rain, rain, rain
Hi Cap'n,

Am in receipt of your latest epistle.

Man, what a fish story! I used to do that forty + years ago, so I can relate. Our best was a 300-lb. swordfish in 1961 and a 500-lb. tuna a year later (before the Japs were buying them). There were many offshore trips after that.

Regarding "Changing Habitat," I can also relate. I remember years ago when you escorted me around your "hallowed haunts." Nice while it lasted, huh? Up here, the usual woodcock numbers seem to be showing up each year, but their habitat keeps changing; now you have to go find them.

As to grouse, there should be a plethora due to all the clear cutting, but they have been declining dramatically. This is the fourth year of late, wet and cold springs. This one has been the worst of all! I suggest that the Dept. of Fish & Game put a moratorium on hunting until the populations recover. I haven't shot one in about three years now.

Otherwise, my knee and back operations were successful, and I'm back walking again. It sure was hell the last couple of years when I couldn't.

Best regards,
Dick

Greenville, ME
June 26, 2006
Hi Cap'n,

How are you coming along with "the book?"

Enclosed is my latest "epistle," which I wrote in 1946.

Recently, The Northern Forest Canoe Trail was formed connecting 740 miles of rivers and lakes, of which Moosehead is a part.

The only campsites in the southwest portion of the lake are threatened by development and I, a very small voice, like Paul Revere, have been trying to get something started to offset this disaster. Apathy prevails. The above outfit is directly involved. There may be hope.

In my correspondence with NFCT, I mentioned that I go back to '46 here and had a great time camping with three other chums, all from WWII. We got lost, soaking wet, starved, and nearly drowned. Had a great time, nonetheless.

Jennifer Lamphere, assistant director of NFCT, wrote back thanking me for my input and asked to know more about the starvation and near drowning, and I complied thus.

Dick

Griswold, CT
December 8, 2008
Hi Cap'n,

Just received Snake Meadow Happenings. Sorry to hear of Tim Brennan's passing. He lived well and, merciful God, died well. That was a noble eulogy you delivered. He deserved the best and will be long remembered.

I'm astonished at the sheer numbers of birds you flushed in the Maine coverts!—although conditions were wet; good for holding birds. Glad to hear the F.lli Rizzini is waterproof, but another trip up to Trevallion's to have that right barrel opened up to cylinder might improve your score. Otherwise leave it for sake of "conservation."

Dick

Miscellaneous

A Long Sporting Life

A few years ago, I offered the following tribute to an old family friend at a testimonial in his honor in the little chapel down the road from my home:

"As you celebrate your ninetieth birthday, Raymond Scholfield, I look anew and with ever increasing admiration upon the simple, wholesome life that you have lived. You have been true to family and friends, all of whom are immensely proud to be with you on this momentous occasion. I know I speak for everyone in that we all desire to attain age 90, but only if we can arrive there in a healthy condition like you.

I have known our honored guest all my life. He was a friend of my mother's side of the family, and he and Marion visited frequently at our "Homestead on the Hill." But in my youth, I came to know Ray as a hunter and one who shared with me sensitive feelings about our great out-of-doors.

Borrowing the words of Archibald Rutledge, the first poet laureate of the state of South Carolina, best conveys my thoughts of you, Ray.

'If the sentimentalists were right, hunting would develop in men a cruelty of character. But I have found it inculcates patience, demands discipline, and develops a serenity of spirit and iron nerve that makes for long life and long love of life. And it is my fixed conviction that if a parent can give his children a passionate and wholesome devotion to the outdoors, the fact that he cannot leave them a fortune does not really matter so much. They will always worship the Creator in His mighty works. And because they know and love the natural world, they will always feel at home in the wild, sweet habitations of the ancient Mother.'

Along this same outdoor theme, my first lasting impression of our celebrated guest occurred when I was about sixteen. I had been hunting woodcock unsuccessfully in our "Rogers Pasture," when late in the day, out of the gloaming, appeared a ghostlike figure in the fading light. It was Ray. A little cocker spaniel held closely to heel and a 20-gauge Marlin Model 90 over and under was tucked under arm. In hand and just recently brought to bag was a brace of woodcock. He said but few words and we parted. He never asked for permission to hunt there; he never had to. From that day forward, I held this poignant scene in my memory and this gentleman in awe because, you see, in the eyes of a sixteen-year-old youth this man was to be worshipped, because he was an old-time woodcock hunter.

In later years when Ray no longer could hunt, I wondered if he really knew about all the times I hunted his land. It was a favorite little corner to chase woodcock and the occasional grouse with one or two of my setters. No one else hunted there, and I was curious if anyone ever noticed that 'his' birds were not as plentiful after a season of gunning. That little regenerating field out back of the barn beyond the swamp always held birds. If I had a successful hunt there or elsewhere, I would bring the contents of my game bag to Ray, and Marion would always say: "We luv' 'em. We luv' 'em on toast for breakfast." But I would not always tell them that the birds came from out back of his barn! Most of the time they did. Ray would then take the birds out to the shed and hang them from the rafters for several days until they became, well, quite ripe.

Enough. Getting to the other pleasure filled business at hand, may I propose a toast to you and to your long and happy life? We wish you many more years of good health and happiness. And may we continue to have the benefit of your wise counsel and judgment. Happy ninetieth birthday!"

As I look back on that memorable celebration of Ray's birthday, I think of the changes that have taken place in back of Ray's place. He certainly knows of the little trailer park that now sits adjacent to the land that he sold several years ago. He remembers the land where he and I hunted woodchucks before the town bought it and converted it into a sports complex. I hunted birds just west of the football field when there were no games being played—great woodcock and quail cover. When quail were plentiful, I got into a big bevy once with my setter, Liberty. I was kneeling and placing one in my game bag when I looked up to see a couple fellows menacingly staring down at me as if I had committed the ultimate crime. To them, the football coach and the director of athletics of the town high school, I guess I did, for I was summarily ordered off!

Annual Hunt & Banquet

A.L. Ripley etching, *Pheasant Shooting*

The Annual Hunt & Banquet at Snake Meadow Club is a gala affair that would tickle the trigger finger of any upland hunter and cause the gastronomical juices to flow for anyone who enjoys excellent cuisine. No, it's not about wingshooting wild game, but it is as good as it gets with released birds. And no, Snake Meadow Club is not a Four-Star restaurant employing area-renown chefs, but it's an acceptable substitute using in-house, member talent. This function has been an annual event for as long as I can remember and probably dates back to the early 1970s.

The day starts very early with most participants arriving around 7:00 a.m. Travel distances are occasionally great, sometimes as long as two hours of driving time, although most members live within two to thirty miles from the club. Breakfast is simple, usually coffee and donuts, unlike weekends during the two and one-half month regular season when the morning meal is complete and hearty (also cholesterol filled!). The reason for this disparity is the addition of a full-fledged bill of fare for the noon meal on the day of the Annual Hunt.

Although the club membership is less than 100 individuals, normal attendance for the regular weekend bird hunts—Saturday and Sunday—probably averages only eight to twelve hunters with dogs per day. There are 10 designated hunting areas—each composed of several acres—in which one hunter with a dog has sole "ownership" during his hunt. There could be two or more hunters per area if a member invites a guest or agrees to share the area with another member. Five birds are usually released per area. During the Annual Hunt, forty-five to fifty-five participants enjoy the day. These numbers indicate a very special occasion.

Like any club, Snake Meadow has rules and regulations governing daily and weekly limits for birds shot and fish caught, although there are no season limits. There is no per-bird charge. Each member and guest is allowed two birds—usually pheasant—in the bag per day. Sometimes chukar partridge and occasionally, Hungarian partridge are an added bonus. At the Annual Hunt, Hunting Chairman Tom Dufficy invariably will bend the rules somewhat to allow for greater indulgence. This is one reason why this special day is probably unique and exclusive to Snake Meadow Club. To many, including this writer, it seems too good to be true.

Obviously, with ten hunting areas and an increased number of participants, the organized—what we call formal—hunts must be accommodated in "waves," on a first come first served basis. As with any "checkerboard" hunt (or any hunt for that matter), safety is always the primary concern. There will be several stockings to accommodate participation of members and guests. Incidentally, hunting takes place during the week, but no stocking of birds is allowed unless members, by prior arrangement, choose to buy birds (private hunts) at a price that basically represents cost to the club.

But ah, the camaraderie! For those who don't have specific jobs, such as cooking and stocking, the Annual Hunt and Banquet is an occasion to renew past acquaintances and to talk the talk that sportsmen are wont to do on such occasions. The discussion around the flaming open hearth is both animated and festive. Of course, bird-hunting topics seem to be the most popular. At the last Annual Hunt, I overheard conversations regarding dogs, shotguns, sporting art, sporting books, deer hunting, hunting trips, an up-coming gun show, and fishing for Snake Meadow's giant trout. The list goes on, but by and large, it's all sporting related.

One of main attractions of the day is the banquet. This eminent and time-honored affair is a full-course meal prepared by the usual—and much-appreciated—coterie of club chefs and several come to mind. This year, Stan Ward prepared succulent roast pork with all the fixings. A selection of hors-d'oeuvres, including lobster dip, fresh shrimp, and myriad other equally delectable preparations, preceded the entrée. If anyone has the stomach capacity, a choice of mouth-watering desserts is available. Whew! But, it ain't over yet!

Care to hunt again? You could pursue the remaining ringnecks that, by word of mouth, for example, are known to exist in Area 2. You might succeed in convincing Tom to stock a few more birds in prairie-like Area 8, or for the lissome younger set, Area 11—Heart Attack Hill. You'll never know unless you ask!

The cost for participation in this annual event is obviously not included in membership dues, which are quite modest for the benefits available. Members are charged forty dollars for the day, eighty dollars if they bring a guest. What a deal!

Sandanona

Trying to follow up on the success of the Vintage Cup Double Gun championships held at Addieville East Farm, Mapleville, Rhode Island for the past two years, the local Rhode Islanders ventured to do their own thing September 24th through the 26th The Edwardians moved their venue to the Orvis Sandanona shooting grounds in Millbrook, New York—more on this later. My impression is that it was not successful in terms of the relatively sparse number of attendees, compared to the crowds of the previous two years under Vintager auspices. But the pundits were all there, with few exceptions, and I enjoyed the experience.

On loan from Gardone, Val Trompia in Italy and hanging around the Holland & Holland tent was Giacomo Fausti, a world-renown engraver from the firm of Creative Art. This firm engraves some of Tony Galazan's best guns and for Ithaca's recently resurrected NIDs (New Improved Double). Several gun magazine editors were present, such as John Gosselin from *Grouse Point Almanac* (now *Upland Almanac*) and Ralph Stuart, editor in chief of *Shooting Sportsman*. Advertising representative, Valerie Raba (a very attractive lady!), ably represented *Double Gun Journal.* (Daniel Cotè, editor-publisher of the Michigan-based *DGJ*, doesn't fly—somebody said he doesn't drive a car either!) I relished talking with these people because the common bond that exists between us is a big part of my life. On to Sandanona!

Just over the border from Sharon, Connecticut is the lovely little town of Millbrook, New York. When you get back on the main highway, which bypasses this quaint village throwback, you will come upon the Orvis Sandanona shooting grounds, site of the 1999 Vintagers side by side shooting championships (Vintage Cup). The gorgeous weather of the previous weekend repeated, and I can speculate, without much doubt, that the event was an unqualified success.

One of the main sponsors, Audi of America, had a number of upscale touring cars on display. The A6 model is about everything I would aspire to own in the luxury price range.

Purveyors of fine shotguns and double rifles found this to be the Mecca of the eastern U.S. and probably second only to the annual Las Vegas show. The shooting and the viewing of the various booths (under tents) took place simultaneously. More often than not, visitors to the various vendor tables carried double shotguns. Any problem with this arrangement? Of course not, and there never has been. No one even gives it a second thought. Admittedly, the attendees are the high end of the gun-coveting public and represent the epitome of the often-used words "legitimate, law-abiding gun owners." Many non-shooting visitors would probably react in horror at the <u>potential</u> for violence.

James Purdey and Sons of London was represented with some excellent new doubles and a fine pre-owned contingent of their world-famous sidelocks. One disciple of Purdeys was so impressed that he literally marched stock maker David Trevallion, a former Purdey employee, to the famous gunmaker's tent, presumable for a fitting, and ordered a matched pair on the spot at a cost exceeding $150,000, this according to David, who's been known to tell a few tall ones (I'm not questioning the money). Purdeys displayed some much understated gentlemen's ties at $100 each. Is there a subtle message here regarding their fine guns—in terms of price?

Representing the sporting art world, Peter Corbin displayed several original paintings that I recognized as being the basis for some of his prints. Corbin is very accommodating, although I found his blood-splattered game vest a bit tacky, especially among wannabe Edwardians exuding sartorial niceties.

What can I say about Vermont's famous engraver/sculptor Winston Churchill? Besides being one of the best engravers in the world, he is always the perfect gentleman, as those of you who know him can attest. I have found him to be a sensitive environmentalist who really cares about his land that has remained in his family for several generations.

Since my wife was with me, I hinted at a few Christmas remembrances that would be truly appreciated—any one of Winston's gorgeous bronzes, an Audi A6, and a pre-owned 20-gauge Westley Richards drop lock. I suggested that my gift requests were all-inclusive, not either/or, but that's it—absolutely no more. In return, I promised my wife that I would be more than willing to gift her with a whole day of shopping at the local Crystal Mall, away from household responsibilities!

Montville Gun Ordinance Withdrawn

Possibly more than a few club members followed the recent imbroglio in my town over the gun ordinance that was to have been presented by Mayor Jaskiewicz to the Montville Town Council on August 14. A few days prior, I went to see the mayor seeking more information but was told that the ordinance language was not yet available from legal counsel. He assured me, however, that it was purely a safety measure and that citizens' rights under the Second Amendment would not be jeopardized in any way. Evidentially, Avon and West Hartford had adopted similar regulations.

Briefly, NRA member John Dufrat, evidentially on behalf of his position as chief warden at the Milo Light Nature Preserve (in Bozrah) complained to the chief of police or to the mayor directly that Guy

Flatley, who lives on Route 82 in Montville, established a shooting range in his back yard—purportedly with adequate safety provisions—and that pedestrians walking on the Milo Light Preserve to the northwest could be at risk from gunfire.

Curiosity got the best of me and I drove to Flatley's address. It is a rural section of town but there are several houses in a line set back from the state highway. A sign alongside his driveway warns of a shooting range on the property. There is no listing in the telephone directory for John Dufrat; only a listing for A.M. Dufrat at 519 Route 82.

I suspect the truth is that Dufrat is Flatley's adjacent neighbor and this ordinance came about as a result of a dispute between the two. I had read that Flatley alerts his neighbors when he commences shooting in the afternoon and that he does this two or three times in the course of a week. Evidentially Dufrat took exception to this practice because of the noise, or because of some other unrelated altercation between the two neighbors.

The proposed ordinance's ostensible purpose, in part, was to bring regulations regarding target shooting in line with state <u>hunting</u> regulations relating to the 500 feet minimum distance requirement from buildings occupied by people or livestock. In addition, parks and nature preserves would have been subject to the same requirement. Regulated shooting ranges were mandated along with onerous restrictions as to the relationship of the relative instructing the shooter and to the shooter himself, sixteen being the minimum age of the latter.

The NRA Web site/emails (with a few misstatements) alerted members to the upcoming Town Council meeting and urged members to attend in protest. Some 175 citizens did just that. (I was in Maine, but my son attended.) Since that number exceeded legal room capacity, all were ordered to leave. Nobody did, and so action on the proposal was postponed for another time and place, commensurate with the potential size of the gathering. A few days later, the mayor withdrew the ordinance. Case closed.

The primary objection of the NRA and those attending the meeting was "infringement" of Second Amendment rights. Under the ordinance, I would have retained my right to own a firearm for protection (in spite of New Orleans Mayor Nagin's contrary view), indulge in hunting and target shooting but with unreasonable restrictions regarding the latter, so I think "infringement" is the proper term.

From the time I (finally) saw the proposed language, I kept asking, "how does this affect me?" The ordinance would have foreclosed the shooting of marauding woodchucks—pest management, not hunting—in my garden and patterning a shotgun down the farm lane—a lifelong practice—because my neighbor's house is less than 500 feet (barely) distant (that's 100 feet shy of 200 yards—two football fields back to back) and because it is not a "regulated" shooting range. Shooting elsewhere on my property, even with the minimum distance requirement satisfied, I would have been prohibited from instructing my granddaughters—reserved for a parent or "duly qualified instructor" only—how to shoot a BB gun, .22 rifle or whatever, other than at an "authorized range." In an op-ed by the often-wrong *Norwich Bulletin* August 24, these were pronounced to be reasonable restrictions.

In truth, I suspect this ordinance was all about a neighborly dispute and power politics in a small, essentially rural, town. Contrary to the needs of West Hartford and Avon, and the opinion of the *Norwich Bulletin*, a vanguard of Montville citizenry said no. I'm relatively certain that had not the NRA and another organization within Connecticut alerted its members to attend the meeting, this badly written ordinance—even Norwich exempts shooting vermin within their fifty-rod (800 feet) restriction—would have been passed by the town council and put out to referendum.

Poaching

Over the years, I readily admit to having done my share of poaching. When it comes to fish and game limits and all other legalities in regard to the taking of same, I am fastidious in upholding the law. I suppose I profess a somewhat uncommon sense, in that the features of the coverts that I hunt and fish seem to be imbued in my soul. My ancestors used these lands freely. You never needed permission back then. But times change.

Every so often in my youthful years there were a few incidents when my "neighbors" confronted me with their diatribe as to why I shouldn't be on their land. "Why didn't you seek my permission?" they asked. My muttered retorts usually had something to do with God-given rights and precedence established by my forefathers or, the land is for all to enjoy; you're only a steward of the land for a short time. I could cast a fly line away from dwellings without being detected; shooting a grouse presented a problem that, to this day, caused me to favor small bore shotguns because of the perceived lower noise level—obviously a bunch of malarkey!

Several years ago, five hunters bedecked in blaze orange from head to foot—why do so many folks hate this color; is it because they hate hunters?—were heard and seen nonchalantly ambulating down the lane not fifty yards in back of our family homestead. I was ripping mad. What was wrong they asked, and why was I offended? Was it because they could hardly converse—for an interesting parallel spoof, read Ray Holland's *Now Listen Warden*—in English, their arrogance, their gang-like numbers? Would I have given permission if they had asked? The answer is an emphatic NO! I guess I just didn't like these people. More to the point, this incident changed my thinking about poaching. Or did it?

Over time, in a far-away place, we were questioned on a few occasions about trespassing. In all cases, our Maine guide should have done his homework. In most instances, permission would have been readily granted. Last time it happened, I had to give over two fat birds out of my game bag for "public relations," but future opportunities made the sacrifice well worth it. My hunting partner and I had to awkwardly pretend being busy along the wooded sideline as our guide smoothed over our—rather his—transgression.

No doubt, incidents such as the foregoing caused much privately owned land to be posted. We have nobody to blame but ourselves and, of course, other flagrant, non-hunting types who despoil private lands.

We always considered a couple of favorite coverts in the vicinity of Andover, Maine to be the Mecca of opportunity for flight woodcock. Encompassed by meandering streams and an ideal mixture of regenerating hardwoods and brush, they always produced an ample number of woodcock and grouse alike. After hunting these "end-all" lands for upwards of twenty years, the axe finally fell in 2004 when we found the all-too-familiar "No Trespassing" signs posted by the non-resident owner. It was patently obvious that dumped garbage was the reason for posting. We suggested to our guide that he get in touch with the owner, a New Jersey resident, to seek hunting permission, but we've not heard that he ever made the call.

The domestic scene was not without its shame in an encounter with a local landowner. I was in a little corner that I had hunted for the past thirty years, knew the then landowner well and always had standing permission. Unbeknown to me, this little regenerating lot was sold a few years ago to a lady who operated a small mobile home park, and it appeared she was expanding into "my" cover, judging by the very gradual clearing operation. I got the drift that she now owned this piece.

"We love 'em on toast for breakfast," the former owner's wife always remarked when I handed over my birds after hunting the "trailer cover." He would hang them in the attached shed and let them "season" for about a week until they were just on the verge of becoming ......, well, never mind.

Anyway, birds still hung along the edges. I approached this field on Veteran's Day, and I could hear her small bulldozer working in the distance. My setter, Blaze, slid into a point, but I was nervous about the company and missed on the rise. Time to make tracks, I thought. All of a sudden, a stentorian hail rang out loud and clear, "Stop where you are!" I froze—when I probably should have kept on going. Well, this lady crawler operator laid into me like I was a hardened criminal. When I attempted to state my name and where I lived, she cut me off like a bull in China closet. "Just think," she said in her hyperventilated voice, "I take my little dog for a walk in this lot every morning. What if you had been hunting here?" I began to formulate a statement to the effect that I did not make it a practice of shooting lap dogs, but I thought better of adding insult to injury. She ordered me off, and I finally said, "Ma'am, I'm sorry about this incident, and I apologize."

Have I gone full circle? Yes, and by virtue of an embarrassing lesson learned.

Sporting Guides

When planning a hunting or fishing trip, one very important detail is choosing a competent guide. Many sporting camps have several available, and if it's a reputable outfit, capable and skilled guides are probably part of the reason. In the situation where accommodations—a lodge—are not available, and you must provide your own arrangements for sleeping and eating, guide selection becomes all-important. When you find a good one, and your hunting or fishing experience was enjoyable and productive, always book for the next year before you leave. Otherwise your choice of time may not be available. Whenever possible, you would be wise to obtain references before booking a new guide.

I have had little experience staying at lodges, presumably because my focus has been on the guide rather than the accommodations. In all but a few instances, the guides that I chose over the years, and continue to do so, are independent of a complete package. In other words, we stay at an inn (preferable), a private summer cabin, or a motel of choice. We—I'm almost always with a partner—are not tied into any one venue, meaning we can take evening meals at various local restaurants (when available) depending on our culinary desires (and capacity) of the particular day. Our guides always provide lunch in the field, and we frequently enjoy hot meals and home-baked goods—sometimes even brazed woodcock! Admittedly, we don't get to "talk the talk" with fellow bird-hunters in the evening and watching the lodge's fireplace embers burn down with glazed eyes, so I have to listen to my partner's oft-repeated stories!

On a bird-hunting trip to New Brunswick several years ago, Ken and I had to settle for an idiot who, after transporting us to a regimen of supposedly desirable coverts, sat in the camp van reading girlie magazines—not a camp guide's most endearing quality! In defense of this particular camp, accommodations were very good and the cuisine was outstanding. We very much liked the owner and his wife.

A good guide will stay with the hunters and dogs, or with the anglers on lake or stream, pointing out a hot corner for grouse here or a good "lie" for trout there. If you are unfamiliar with the country or water, a guide's value can be immeasurable. To simply point "sports" in the right direction is not what good guiding is all about.

Since our trips throughout New England and Canada are usually repeat offerings with little variation in venue year after year, we often discuss the need for a guide (U.S. only). Even though we know how to get the most out of the covers, our experience is that guides become friends. If we chose not to employ their services, we often shudder when thinking about what would happen if we ran into a former guide in the field. Now that would be embarrassing!

The subject of guides is well covered in an enriching and captivating, privately printed book, *Along the Trail,* written by Marshal Stearns in 1936. Evidently Stearns, an attorney from Hartford's environs, made annual fishing excursions to the Dead River area of Maine, specifically around Spencer Lake and the Enchanted Region—King and Bartlett Lake is located several miles to the southwest. Not really a guide but a camp owner and hermit, the author introduces the reader to "Tommy," who ran a small camp at Little Enchanted Lake around 1905. A French Canadian, Tommy Giroux (or Gerard) had a post office named after him—Gerard, Maine in Somerset County. The author thought so highly of this wonderful little man with extraordinary culinary talents that he made an unannounced, off-season trip in February to visit his reclusive friend. To Jackman by rail was easy. The eighteen miles to Spencer Lake in frigid temperatures was doable. Stearns took to skis—with which he was not experienced—on the final leg of his journey over the mountain and down to Little Enchanted—we call this cross-country skiing nowadays—while his companions labored on snowshoes in six feet of the powdery white stuff. Tommy was elated to see his friends, the first humans to cross his path since September of the previous year. Sadly, the two friends never met again, as Tommy died soon after their reunion.

Having established good rapport with guides, I too have found myself wanting to make social calls during the off-season, and perhaps partake of a collation or dinner with wives (guides included of course!) at one of the local restaurants. I have done this on a few occasions with guides in two New England states, not to mention frequent telephone calls and e-mails. Valued guides do indeed become friends.

World Champion Lumberjack

I have had the pleasure of knowing H. David Geer for many years. While not exactly a club member (although he was in past years), Dave is a permanent fixture at Snake Meadow Club, that is, at all the steak dinners—no steak-loving patron would ever dare sit in his seat in the dining room in front of the fireplace. There are nine public suppers held during the year (excluding July, August, and September). Why do I single out Dave Geer? He is the consummate world champion lumberjack, a terrific guy, and an extraordinary gentleman to boot. Dave is 5' 8" tall and weighs 210 lbs.—and handsome! Everybody seems to take Dave for granted around here on his home turf, but step back a moment and review his achievements.

At age eighty, he recently beat all the younger competition—the first eighty-year-old to win a World Championship in Lumberjacking—at Lake Haywood, Wisconsin in 2005 to win the Axe Throwing contest— 15/15 bull's eyes—for the eighth time! While attending a recent steak dinner at Snake Meadow Club, I asked Dave if he planned to compete at Lake Haywood this coming summer. I half expected him to say no and that he was finally "hanging it up." He looked at me with a rather quizzical look as if to say, "Why not?" He assured me that he would participate, and then commenced to rattle off the other major events that he will enter.

Dave has won the following *World Championships:*
....5 times Champion Woodchopper
....5 times Champion Power Sawyer
...22 times Champion Double Sawing
....1 time Champion Single Sawing
....8 times Champion Axe Thrower
....4 times Best All Around Lumberjack
Whew! That's a total of forty-five World Championships! In addition, Dave has won over 600 state and regional championships.

When competing in New York State, he tells of the time when he continually bested a bruising 6'4" lumberjack. Dave says he was a good-looking physical specimen but not a very good woodsman. After being humbled by Dave several times, he quit competition.

Presidents Ford, Carter, Truman, and Nixon decorated Dave. Additionally, Nelson Rockefeller, John D. Rockefeller IV of West Virginia, and Norman Vincent Peale recognized him for his extraordinary achievements.

He appeared on many television shows over the years, such as *I've Got a Secret, To Tell the Truth, What's My Line ?, Who Do You Trust ?, Hobby Lobby and Today Show.* Joining him the last time he appeared on the Johnny Carson Show in 1970 were Lauren Bacall and Dr.

Spock. The Prime Minister of England acknowledged Dave as the first American lumberjack to compete in Australia.

In a picture-rich brochure, Dave is shown receiving the National Champion Best All-Around Lumberjack plaque from President Harry S. Truman. He appeared on major sport shows in New York, Chicago, Milwaukee, Minneapolis, Kansas City, Anaheim, Fort Wayne, Charleston and Hartford, Connecticut. Last, but not least, Dave performed a major exhibition in Japan.

Several years ago, Dave did an exhibition at the Brooklyn (Connecticut) Fair. He carved out a chair from a stump of wood with his chainsaw, a feat he performed often. My granddaughter, Brittany, was selected to receive the chair but I recall she was too shy to retrieve it from Dave in front of the grandstand crowd. Yours truly did the honors.

In addition to his exceptional success in his long-time hobby, Dave is a well-known businessman in Griswold and surrounding towns, sand/gravel and Christmas trees being his vocational pursuits. As a life-long banker, I always wondered why Dave was never elected to the board of directors of my bank—although he has served as a corporator for many years. He and his wife live in a lovely, picture-perfect, eighteenth century country home between undulating fields and woods.

Why not come out to the February steak supper, bring a guest, and chat with Dave? He's easy going, unaffected by fame and achievement, and a pleasure to talk with. Autographs will be freely given. An autographed, double bit throwing axe actually used by Dave in competition will be raffled for five dollar ticket. Here's a chance to own a valuable piece of history with guaranteed collector value.

So there you have it. Come one and all to greet Dave and at the same time, enjoy the best steak dinner in eastern Connecticut.

Tale of a Puma

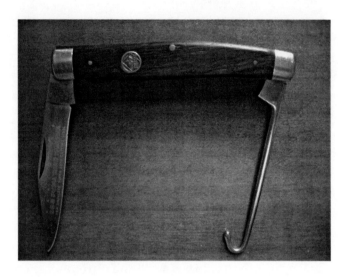

Fishing for Artic grayling in the Yukon Territory's Trout River many years ago, I came face to face with a puma. I froze in my footsteps, and for a moment we squared off and just stared at each other. And then came wise decisions. We both turned around and ran like hell! However, this little memoir is not about that puma, the animal.

I have been "accused" of professing too strong a penchant for coveting sporting treasures, justified in my own mind by the inherent pleasure of owning these toys and what I consider to be the obvious tendency toward rampant appreciation. This proclivity to possess never extended itself to the collecting of knives, that is, until recent years, but I do have a story to relate about a special knife and a very precious possession.

Back in the 1970s I received a birthday gift from one of "my" girls at work, no doubt inspired by my interest in an ad appearing in a copy of *Gray's Sporting Journal*—back when Ed Gray was running the show—that just happened to be reposing on the lunch room table. You can imagine my exhilaration upon opening the green and yellow box to discover the knife of my dreams—a Puma Bird Hunter. As I recall, it was an expensive little tool. Of stainless steel construction with jacaranda handles, it served this sportsman admirably over the next fifteen or so years—not to the mention five times that it had eluded my retrieval after doing its job of field dressing in the uplands.

Most of the time I discovered the loss when emptying my pockets upon retirement during the evening hours, too late to physically retrace the day's activity. The L. Raymond covert—Lawrence Raymond has been dead for a hundred years, so I don't worry about the name giving away its whereabouts—claimed my knife 11/5/77 after an exciting day in which my English setter, Troubles, and I moved thirty-five birds in the biggest "fall" of 'cock that I have ever witnessed in my native haunts. Can you blame me for being excited? None the worst after an overnight rain, the Puma was readily found the next day at the site of the last ritual.

My upland diary relates that the knife was missing 10/27/79 but found the following day in the Old Car Covert where I had shot my last woodcock—more important to soothe ruffled feathers before securely placing this grand bird in the game pocket of my coat. (I am extra careful now when placing birds in my game pocket because on a few occasions I missed the opening. What a surprise to find you're shy a woodcock or two when emptying your game bag at day's end.)

Once I retraced my steps several hundred yards after missing the familiar bulge in my back pocket when sitting down for a breather. I found the Puma next to the leaf-covered entrails of a cock grouse I had shot in the Dead-End Street Covert.

Another time it had been lost one whole week when, after a day's hunt, the glint from the sun's rays betrayed its presence mashed in the ground by the old well curb where I had paused for a cold, sweet refresher.

A hen pheasant in Carl Anderson's Voluntown bailiwick separated me from my Puma. On Carl's second try he found it on horseback on the Sunday following Friday's hunt, right where I told him it would surely be found.

A few years later I started to collect bird knives with gut hooks, all sizes and shapes. A favorite was a yellow-handled Case, which I liked because of its slim construction. I say, "liked," because I lost this little knife after field dressing a woodcock in western Maine a few years ago. I retraced my steps several times but couldn't find it, as it obviously lay hidden among the fallen yellowed birch and popple leaves. So much for the yellow handles! But it had a great feel for the smaller game birds up to the size of grouse, unlike my stag-handled, Italian-made Orvis that, due to its substantial size, works well on the larger birds, such as pheasants.

Back to the Puma. Still razor sharp—its only blemish is a burn mark on the back of the blade—and in fine condition, the old warhorse was retired in the interest of collector value (first year production) after the 1989 season. My new Böker has a shackle so I can attach a lanyard and tie it around my fool neck!

The burn mark? Occasionally it saw extracurricular service. Two weeks before Christmas, 1988, I was shortening an extension cord for our window candles with my knife. One problem—I forgot to unplug the cord!

Ted's Deer

Along Route 12 in the lovely little rural town of Plainfield, Connecticut the land slopes off toward the west, providing one of the most captivating landscapes in all of the Nutmeg State. The long-time steward of this enthralling panorama, Ted Boskovich, saw the beauty of the scene and envisioned the house of his dreams overlooking a wildlife sanctuary that had become a reality over the years.

Just below the house, a small duck-laden pond immediately draws the viewer's focus down into the valley where a larger pond, teaming with pampered trout, connects a wooded strip and then levels off to fertile corn-planted fields. Gradually, an inclining oak-dominated forest joins the horizon several miles distant. It is hard not to love this place. I had been here before and enjoyed a fine luncheon prepared by Anne, Ted's companion of several years.

Ted was a deer hunter in his early years. He also hunted birds over his English setters. He loved fly-fishing and saltwater fishing. Time has been kind to Ted, as his life was the sporting life. Now getting on in years, Ted has slowed down a bit, but his passion for the well-being of animals is evident. But this is not a story about Ted, the consummate sportsman. It's the story of "Spiro" and how he came to be.

A few months ago, Ted, on behalf of his late wife Christine, donated sixteen sets of deer antlers to the Snake Meadow Club, where he had hunted and fished since he was a teenager. I am a member of this club also and became interested as a result of the display of these antlers at a members' night function recently.

In the mid-to-late 1960s, Ted purchased two does from a game farm in Wyoming, Rhode Island that were chosen because they were raised in a small enclosure and were tame as a result. The does were placed in a two-acre enclosure in back of Ted's house. After a careful search for a buck with the desired conformation and size, and after many rejections, "Bucky" was brought to Plainfield from Wilmington, in Northwestern Connecticut. Bucky lived to be ten and one-half and produced nine sets of antlers that were donated to the Howard Bigelow Club in Hampton, Connecticut.

Actually, Bucky was given to Ted, a brick mason by trade. A patron, after many turndowns, finally persuaded Ted to construct a fireplace in his home, for which Ted accepted Bucky in payment.

Spiro, named after Spiro Agnew (both were contentious), was born in 1969, the offspring of Bucky and one of the Rhode Island does. He lived to be over eighteen and produced some magnificent racks, easily explained by his varied diet supplied by Ted's friends over the years.

Dietary favors consisted of corn and apples, of which Red Delicious was the obvious favorite, with lettuce, celery, melons, pumpkins, donuts and bread proffered on a less frequent basis. It pays to have a lot of friends, especially those in the retail food, orchard, and restaurant businesses.

What fun Ted and Chris enjoyed with visiting Sunday school children! During the Christmas season they would come to see "Rudolph" and the other reindeer. The *Norwich* (Conn.) *Bulletin* ran a story with photos of the famous herd. They had to agree not to divulge the names of their benefactors or where they were located for fear they might end up on someone's dinner table. Ted and Chris could be described as overly protective parents.

Bucky and Spiro lived in the same enclosure and often fought for the attention of the other female residents. The two bucks sparred and mashed antlers frequently. One such clash, early in Spiro's long life, left him without an antler. This probably had some effect on future racks as a result of the left pedicel being damaged. Chris astutely noted that when stomachs are full, there's no fighting!

Of course, as both bucks were raised in the two-acre enclosure, it was possible to document all dropped antlers each year. Spiro grew his best shaped and largest antlers at ages four, five and six, with an outward spread of approximately two feet. Generally there were eight points. But at age five, a "drop tine" developed, making Spiro a nine-pointer. From this period on, Spiro maintained this basic eight-point structure, with drop tines increasing the number of points from nine to eleven. Later years were marked by smaller mass and increasing deformity in the left antler. In 1987, the left antler had become nothing more than a stunted nub but the right antler still maintained 4 points.

Ted never sold any deer. Limited space meant that offspring had to be culled and given away from time to time.

Spiro's long life ended on a frustrating day in late 1987 when he was attacked by roaming dogs. Even though the police were contacted, their unfamiliarity with the legalities of whether to shoot the dogs or whether to allow Ted to protect his pet ultimately led to Spiro's death. Ted and Chris were crushed. Ted feels that Spiro would have lived another couple of years if it had not been for this unfortunate incident.

And so, twenty-seven years of raising deer in captivity came to an inglorious closing. Yet Ted says he would do it again without hesitation. After all, in addition to the enjoyment of being with the animals, two complete sets of antlers were carefully collected, documented, and given away to recipients, who, more than anyone else appreciated the relationship that developed between this kind man and his pet deer.

What will be remembered over time, above all, is the simple fact that Spiro lived to be eighteen and one-half, which Ted believes to be a longevity record for a buck in captivity. Together, father and son produced twenty-five sets of recovered antlers, which, if not a record, is highly unusual.

Even though the fences are gone, the deer remain. They keep coming back to the daily feast of apples transported from nearby orchards and spread out under a canopy of cedars. Waving corn grows in the valleys just like before. The does come and lie in the clover especially planted for them, keeping watch over their napping "Bambis." Mighty bucks kick their heels and paw the earth. All is well.

The Meadows

As I write this (January 25), I contemplate the long winter ahead. It's this time of year when the wood cutting chores need to be addressed. Once over that hump though, spring cannot be far behind, and you know that ravenous trout will be impatiently awaiting the woolybugger, hornburg, and other inciting offerings of the fishing coterie. This anticipatory activity makes me forgive winter's bane.

Actually I like the cold months. Every Saturday morning, weather permitting, finds me doing my favorite work—cutting firewood for the next heating season. My grandfather taught me about wood when I was a kid, how to identify trees by bark, leaf, branch structure, smell when split, and aroma when burned. He encouraged me to love the forest in those formative years, and I came to respect the simple, wholesome life that he lived. I learned about the scourge that extirpated the American chestnut and came to know the redolence of white oak imprinted on my olfactory memory as I witnessed the saffron glow of sunset on the way home from the woods. My grandfather, on a "good" day, could cut and stack four honest cords of mixed hardwood working from dawn to dusk—that's 512 cubic feet—using hand tools! Anyway, my dalliance with spring fishing is dependent on the frugal pursuit of other activities on winter's Saturdays—the woods beg for my presence. May these Saturdays always be sunny and brisk.

In my grade-school youth, long before I started to fish for trout in the spring months, I spent many pleasant hours at Lowthorpe Meadows in historic Norwichtown. The Meadows were at the mid point on the way home from Samuel Huntington (grammar) School, and they became my playground, sledding on steep trails ending in the Meadows and ice-skating on the pond with its center island where late-day fires kept toes from freezing—but still you wondered if you could survive the pain of frozen extremities on the long walk home.

I remember the BB gunfights (hard to believe but true) in the adjacent cemetery—resting place of Benedict Arnold's father and mother—where ancient gravestones served as ramparts deflecting live BBs. This nefarious behavior came to an inglorious end when Robert "Jughead" Jones supposedly scored a direct hit to the white of the eye of an "adversary," or so the latter claimed. Boy, were we some scared and right well we should have been! The inflicted youth never seemed any the worst for his ordeal, and nothing ever came of it—except a good lesson learned by all.

At a much later time, The Meadows was the venue for a rendezvous with English setter puppies—a litter of Chief setters to be exact— belonging to hunting partner, Ken Dugas. I finally chose Blaze (now fourteen), who has given me many years of devotion and bird hunting thrills. I ogled at those puppies between the sledding run and the pond on that spring-like sunny day in February.

In addition to the foregoing incidents, the most memorable occasion was the explosion of spring in The Meadows. While attending the eighth grade I penned some juvenile poetry, some of which I still remember:

In The Meadows on a spring day warm,
A Heavenly world in God's own form,
A glimpse of Life.
Trees and flowers all so fair
Made me laugh and carefree there.

Such was the result of youth's social truculence that prompted me to spend many hours alone in The Meadows. Most alluring to me at that time was an inscription on the upright of a stone bench tucked beneath the end of a sledding run:

"They ne'er grow old who gather gold
Where spring awakes and flowers unfold..."

Several years later I discovered that Colonel George L. Perkins, a prominent Norwich native, on the occasion of his 100th birthday in 1888, wrote these lines. Successful in business and associated with U.S. presidents, Col. Perkins was a man of means and influence. A bit of research at the local library turned up the rest of his poem. I think, after reading it, you will know what kind of a man Perkins was, that success did not engross his life and that the two lines on The Meadows bench are appropriate for all times. Here is the rest of his poem:

"They soon grow old who grope for gold
In marts where all is bought and sold;
Who live for self and on some shelf
In darkened vaults hoard up their pelf
Cankered and crusted o'er with mold;
For them, their youth itself is old.
They ne'er grow old who gather gold
Where spring awakes and flowers unfold;
Where suns arise in joyous skies;
And fill the soul within their eyes;
For them, the immortal bards have sung;
For them, old age itself is young."
Amen.

Close Call

I like to build stonewalls. In recent years though, moving heavy rocks long distances has not exactly been my cup of tea, and my son has pretty much taken over this chore on the retired family farm. Of all man's constructive talents, a properly laid dry wall, in my eyes, is the epitome of craftsmanship. Unfortunately, it's a disappearing art.

Recently we came upon a source of flat stone. My land abuts a local reservoir that supplies water for two adjacent towns. It had been recently drained for upgrading. Never, to my knowledge, had it been at such a low level since it was built in 1912. And thus was revealed a sight that would warm the cockles of any stone mason's heart. Flat rock was everywhere.

Old roads replete with a stone bridge and stonewalls intersecting feeder streams were once landmarks probably not seen by man in more than four-score years. This rock-laden, moon-like landscape probably had been a grazing ground for cattle and other livestock, evidenced by an old house foundation up on the northern rim. But no green grass grows now; just rock and mud. What water remained in the center and along the eastern portion was teaming with largemouth bass, attested to by a few of my poaching neighbors.

As is usually the case with public water supplies, trespassing is not allowed. But, I always rationalized (incorrectly) that since my family had sold thirty acres to the municipality to allow for the construction of the reservoir, my transgression would be overlooked.

The reconnaissance long since completed, we zeroed in on a near perfect 8½ x 1½ x 7" granite slab that had not been cut. We estimated the weight at one-half to three-quarter ton. Aided by three strong backs and a 1950s vintage U-haul trailing my four-wheel-drive, L-Series Kubota, we set about our task. The clear stillness of the cool August evening was pierced by plaintive and foreboding cries of a Killdeer plover exalting in his new-found ground.

We followed the main road (the "road to Norwich") down into the depths, turned left on the "road to Asa Maple's," (as is recorded in eighteenth century deeds) across the stone bridge, gingerly forded the main stone-strewn feeder stream and climbed up to the brink on the far shore where the object of our pursuit reposed.

Fighting darkness, it took longer than anticipated to pry loose and jack up the recalcitrant megalith to the required loading height. That task accomplished, we searched for a shorter way out along the shoreline rather than retrace out route back into the bowels of Time. No such luck. A thirty degree grade frustrated the back-weighted tractor/trailer from gaining the necessary traction, so we attempted to retrace our original route.

A more direct course seemed feasible where rocks were less concentrated at the stream crossing. As I drew nearer, the front wheels began to sink. The Killdeer tocsin reverberated in my brain, but a reactive revving of the engine brought me to my senses. I slowly pulled the tractor away from danger in the nick of time.

The night was upon us now and my son Jon, our point man, wended a roadway along the oblique and rock-studded route on which we had come. Finally we reached a chosen crossing upstream, but the last shafts of daylight had all but faded, and soon we became hopelessly locked in the grips of unseen stone and mud. I had no tools to unhook the trailer—I forgot there was a wrench in the toolbox—so we concentrated on offloading our prize, which now was solidly wedged between the ground and the trailer bed.

I sent Jon home with my English setter, Blaze, to alert our families that we were in no danger, but it would be almost an hour before he would arrive home and return with flashlights and other tools. Without my belled setter leading the way, he never could have found his way alone in the pitch-black night.

By some miracle, my neighbor Mike and I worked the stone off with the crow bar and were halfway home when we met Jon. I believe he was somewhat surprised to see us, tractor with trailer, and only lacking our granite slab.

Back home and much relieved, we relaxed a few minutes with refreshments and talked about our exploits. I couldn't help but ponder the potential problems and embarrassment that might have resulted if we had to abandon the tractor. I visualized the local newspaper headlines—"MEN ARRESTED; TRACTOR FOUND IN LOCAL RESERVOIR."

The Second Amendment Revisited

> "A well regulated Militia, being necessary
> to the security of a free State, the right of
> the people to keep and bear Arms, shall
> not be infringed."

The argument: Does a militia refer to a formal, organized group such as a state-ordered National Guard (as we know it today) or, to take the strict constructionist's approach, any group of able bodied men?

And so, the argument continues. It is particularly poignant in the aftermath of the horrific Columbine High School massacre, and I suppose it is sometimes natural for emotion rather than reason to prevail, as witnessed by the multitude of "solutions" to the problem being offered by the media and the pending Senate and House legislation.

To the sportsman, of course, these entail real and scary ramifications. Waterford (Conn.) First Selectman Tony Sheridan recently offered his police department as a storage facility for gun owners. Although he envisioned this as voluntary, one has to question the criminal or ill-intentioned gun owner's participation in this program.

Columnist Jim Conrad, writing in the *Norwich Bulletin* May 25, in his usual anti-sportsman, anti-gun diatribe, pontificated, "like drunk driving, wife beating, and racism, guns have no place in civilized society." To say I take exception to this is a gross understatement! This kind of mentality is the very best reason I know not to be a complacent, sideline viewer of the gradual but inexorable erosion of the right to keep and bear arms.

In response to Mr. Konrad's statement, Mr. R.J. Phillips in his letter to the *Bulletin* editor, told of his youthful days when he would carry his .22 target rifle to school for late-day rifle team practice and store it in his locker—unlocked.

Obviously, times have changed, and money alone won't solve all the enumerated problems that have caused modern-day society to run amok. That's why gun ownership is an easy target, and everyone knows Slick Willy's take on gun control.

I advocate reasonable gun control measures, and it's possible that I will take a stand that is sometimes contrary to that of the NRA. In all candor, though, we probably have enough gun control laws on the books already. What we need is more enforcement of existing laws. But I choose to support the leadership of Charlton Heston, Konrad's "the most vile man in the country" and the NRA.

Some of my compatriots have said to me, "it's not your war, and it does not affect us." This is the crux of the elitist position. History may record this head-in-the-sand attitude as being the major contributing factor to the virtual extinction of private gun ownership as we know it.

On the front page of the 5/4/99 edition of *The Wall Street Journal,* author James P. Sterba produced a stunning revelation of high-end gun-coveting or, stated more accurately, the politically correct arena of gun usage—if there is one currently connected to gun ownership—that tends to disconnect from the ordinary gun-owning world. He referred to pricey double-barrel shotguns, their accoutrements, and the socially acceptable game of sporting clays, which has been described as "golf with a gun." The upscale folks who can afford a shotgun priced at $50 thou or more, once the shooting toys of the landed English gentry, more than likely support the NRA but probably won't admit it. My take is that many do not, and they are less inclined to vocally support the organization that is the prime protector of the Second Amendment.

I believe that NRA ownership is somewhat akin to supporting your political party. You cannot be so blind as to know that they are right all the time, but you still lend your support. After all, we are a gun club, and if our members don't support our "national association," how can we expect other non-gun owners to speak for us?

I would like to know which activist pro-gun organizations you non-NRA members support financially? There are a few other major players of course, and they deserve your support also. But how many of these organizations, such as the Second Amendment Foundation, and the Citizens Committee for the Right to Keep and Bear Arms, to name a few, have the financial and political clout of the NRA?

Why NRA Membership Should Be Required

"A gun cannot harm anyone unless there is a human being to pull the trigger. Ten million guns would be harmless unless some human became stimulated by hate, greed, or prejudice. So, the gun controversy becomes a spiritual problem. While strict gun laws might have some effect in showing the world that we are concerned about the violence, violence is really a thing of the human heart and conscience. If men harbor the desire to kill and maim, they will find a way, guns or no guns."

Rev. Billy Graham

NRA membership is optional at Snake Meadow Club. It shouldn't be. We are a sportsman's club that needs to support the pro-gun agenda of the organization recently rated as the most highly effective lobbying group in the nation's Capitol. We should not be complacent with this strength. Sportsmen need to continue, indeed increase, their support of the NRA if they are to invalidate a United Nations resolution to disarm the world. Yes, you read right.

We would do well to follow the lead of sportsman's clubs like Fin Fur & Feather. NRA membership is required of their 400+ members, no exceptions. Or, at the very least, require membership during the probationary period, as does Bozrah Rod & Gun Club. They are ninety percent NRA, a much higher percentage than presently exists at Snake Meadow Club.

When the treasurer moved to make NRA membership mandatory for all prospective club joiners—present non-members would be grand fathered—at the December, 2004 board of directors meeting, a lively discussion ensued. In the end, it was decided to defer the vote until the annual meeting in April.

Gun ownership is a controversial subject in the U.S., especially among those who have no connection with the hunting or shooting sports and those who refuse to believe that they or others, who may not reside in ivory tower neighborhoods, have a need to defend themselves with a firearm. Make no mistake; read the writings of our forefathers, not the twisted rhetoric of modern day interpreters. The right to keep and bear arms was clearly drafted by our forefathers as an individual right in the Second Amendment of the U.S. Constitution.

The club spends several thousand dollars a year for NRA liability insurance, commercial property insurance and other incidental insurance. In exchange, the club itself is required to maintain affiliate NRA membership at an annual cost of thirty-five dollars. Further, under the NRA rules, a modest fifty percent of our members are required to be NRA members, as are three club officers. Four of our current officers are card-carrying NRA members. Presently, the secretary's records indicate that only sixty-three percent of Snake Meadow's membership belongs (we don't know for sure without an annual survey). More disturbing is that only ten of nineteen current provisional members, fifty-three percent, belong to the NRA. If this trend is indicative as to the NRA status of new club applicants, we're obviously headed in the wrong direction. In addition, we could have a problem attracting the most qualified officers if they don't support the NRA, to say nothing about the club's eligibility for affiliate membership in the first place. The Nominating Committee should well keep this in mind when they deliberate a slate of officers for the annual meetings.

I heard a few notably fragile objections to mandatory NRA membership at the December board meeting:

- It's a political thing. Fact: The NRA does not support Democrats or Republicans as such. They support the pro-gun views of politicians of both parties. Incidentally, no longer is an anti-gun agenda part of the Democratic Party plank.
- Affordability. An individual membership costs thirty-five dollars per annum, or four percent of the cost of joining Snake Meadow Club. I don't think this is excessive or beyond the

means of a new member, after laying out $850 to join our club.

- Irritating. Some complain of too many phone calls asking for prepaid dues and other financial support. Fact: The NRA has extensive and far-reaching programs; it just doesn't publish monthly magazines. Unfortunately, the NRA can't claim an ultra-wealthy individual like billionaire George Soros, who provides much of the funding for the "anti" organizations.
- I'm a fisherman only. I don't shoot or hunt. My guess is that most, if not all, fisherman in our club own firearms. We're not a golf club, a ping-pong club, or a book club. We hunt, fish, and shoot (with shotguns, rifles, and bows); that's what brings us together, and these enjoyments should not be considered distinctly in a vacuum. On July 4, 1776, a gentleman by the name of Franklin wrote, "We must all hang together or assuredly we shall hang separately."

In the past, other reproaches have been offered. One is the "elitist" argument—"Hey, I only shoot 2-barrel shotguns, and the government will never take these away from me. So why should I support the NRA? And what's wrong with going after the 'automatics' (the true 'assault weapons')? I have no interest in these." Fact is, ownership of fully automatic firearms has been prohibited since the early 1930s. Semi-autos, the so-called "assault weapons" of the uninformed—and a clay target shooter's favorite—would be clearly outlawed under the U.N. mandate espoused by Australian Rebecca Peters, head of IANSA (International Action Network on Small Arms). Can you guess who spearheaded the half-billion dollar program of personal arms destruction in her native land?

Ms. Peters would also outlaw pump shotguns, i.e. the venerable Winchester Model 12 and the like. In fact, she inferred, unequivocally, in a recent debate with NRA EVP Wayne LaPierre in the King's College library in London (perceptibly won by LaPierre before a mixed audience), that individuals have no right—forget the U.S. Bill of Rights—to defend themselves; that is the responsibility of police. (Yeah!) Further, the only personal firearms that should be allowed in the world, under the U.N. mandate, are single-shot-capable firearms belonging to *hunters* (only). If her restrictions are too onerous, she added, "Take up another sport."

The purpose of the debate was to address the question: Should the U.S. Senate support the proposed U.N. Resolution as promoted by IANSA? Recall that the U.S. Senate negotiates international treaties, and if the composition of this body is anti-Second Amendment, the chances for the success of the U.N. Resolution is eminently enhanced.

Scary? Yet there are those sportsmen who pay no attention to reality and scornfully deny that the scenario presented above could never happen in the U.S. It's hard to accept that some hunters embrace outspoken distain for the NRA. The freedoms that these people enjoy are largely the result of 4 million plus NRA members contributing millions of dollars annually to fight for the right to keep and bear arms and hunt. To not support this right, *but reap the benefits*, is not only divisive but, in my mind, the apex of hypocrisy. Hunters and shooters seem to have two adversaries—those who would disarm us and those within our own ranks, who, perhaps unknowingly, buttress the urbane liberalism of Ms. Peters.

Training Collars, Bells and Beepers

There has been a sea change in the past several years regarding the usage of field aids for better control of bird dogs. I'm referring to the technology allowing the manufacture of smaller and more sophisticated electronic collars. No doubt that not too far in near future we will look at today's improvements as just part of the evolution toward smaller and more technologically advanced communication devices no bigger than a large button,

Not long ago I remarked to our Maine guide that a dog we were running at the time was decorated like a Christmas tree. Around her neck were strapped 1) a regular collar, 2) a bell collar, 3) an electronic training collar and, 4) a beeper collar (pointing mode only), all different colors, of course! I said to Fred, our guide, wouldn't it be great if the electronic gurus could combine the training and beeper collars.

Well, in a few months it happened. Such equipment does not come cheap, but it is affordable for most hunters. Several makers now produce combination units. First was Innotec with the Model 1600 Track 'N Train, followed by Tri-Tronics' Upland Special. I used the two-dog Innotec Track 'N Train for a few years and then switched to the Dogtra T&B. I find the latter to be the most reliable of the e-collar units that I have used. DT Systems and Sport Dog are other well-known competitors.

Tri-Tronics had been the undisputed industry leader since day one until Innotec made the quantum leap with its combination unit. I used the Tri-Tronics A1-80 remote trainer for several years until it failed. My sense is that Tri-Tronics is still the industry's most well known brand.

Not everyone is a fan of electronic collars, whether used for training or tracking, or both. Discount the oft-heard statement that stimulation usage is akin to animal cruelty. However, don't ignore the fact that some trainers/hunters are idiots and don't know when and how much to stimulate the trainee. First lesson: Don't use the e-collar for reinforcement until the dog has learned the command in conventional ways. In other words, first do your backyard training without the collar. Then, and secondly, if he misbehaves, use only as much stimulation as is necessary to reinforce the command.

The tried and traditional bell sounds great in the uplands and for the most part does the job of keeping track of your canine partner effectively. Some hunters will never use any device other than a bell regardless of future electronic enhancements. However, as pointing dogs are wont to do, they point game (and sometimes other things). I have spent far too much time searching for my dogs on point, as no sound comes from an unmoving bell. This sometimes happens in the heavy and rank understory growth of New England coverts where your dog could be on point under your nose but go undetected, or out thirty yards—many hunters insist on close-working pointing dogs ranging like flushers—snuggled up to an unmoving woodcock. This occurs more often in the early season before the foliage starts to drop.

Beepers allow the hunter to avoid this anguish. I like my dogs to be "out there" and ranging for game, à la William Harnden Foster's English pointers, not underfoot. But we all know that even the best dogs slow down after eight or nine years, and this is when bells usually are just the ticket.

In the end, only you can decide if a five dollar bell will continue to meet your tracking needs in this electronic age. I use both, depending on the dog and the terrain. For example, the tracking function of my combination beeper, which can be turned on and off remotely, is not necessary when hunting the small patchwork covers of Snake Meadow Club. I am strongly convinced, however, that an electronic training device, with adjustable stimulation, measurably shortens the training period for young dogs. It is one of the most important aids available to the dog trainer.

One of the unresolved issues is deafness in dogs caused by bells and beepers. The horn of a beeper supposedly is positioned above and between the ears. Obviously, a bell hangs under the dog's head. Is one device or positioning more injurious to hearing than the other? A bell is constant; a beeper is sporadic, depending on the mode in which it is set—it could be silent if the beeper is set for point only mode. One of my four-legged partners is a very deaf fourteen-year-old setter who has had a bell hanging from her neck during most of her hunts and when loose on my property. I believe the bell helped cause her deafness.

Consider this also: The electronic reprimand could possibly save your dog's life, or prevent serious injury in an encounter with a porcupine. The best-behaved dogs usually will not pay attention to verbal commands—as in screaming—when the nemesis is a porky or a skunk. Dogs go after these critters—either of which can ruin a 3-day hunt for differing reasons—with a vengeance! Returning from my walk with Jing last Monday, I took a shortcut home through my property. Leaving the blacktop, Jing immediately started trailing. Soon I saw the unmistakable black form and long tail of a fisher cat. One little tap on my Dogtra, accompanied by the "come" command, prevented what could have been a disaster. My friend Steve, a friend of Lyme sporting artist Chet Reneson, told me of the time when Chet lost a young setter to a logging truck in Maine when chasing a woodcock across the highway. It could have been prevented with an e-collar. Now, Chet will not be without one.

My advice: When walking your dog in the woods or when you embark on a hunting trip, don't leave home without an e-collar!

"Moose"

I lost contact with a good friend once, back around 1985 when I joined Snake Meadow Club. I loved this guy partly because he was always doing stuff for me, like buying little sporting tokens that he knew I would appreciate. Most were related to bird hunting. On one occasion he gave me an inexpensive print—two setters pointing birds by a no-name artist in a cheap frame. It didn't cost very much. But it wasn't the value that mattered; he owed me nothing. Another time he favored me with a little dog-training book, *Modern Breaking,* by William Bruette chock-full of Edmund Osthaus illustrations. Perhaps he knew how much I loved the images of this early twentieth century artist. It was published as a tenth edition in 1920—I think it cost my friend fifty cents. There were other little things over the years, small keepsakes. There was always a note signed:

"From your pal, Moose."

I guess I knew him for about twenty years when he and I both were members of the Quaker Hill Rod & Gun Club in Oakdale (originally in the Quaker Hill section of Waterford, hence the name). I was president of that club for two years and Moose served on the Executive Committee with me; I got to know him pretty well. He was a well-rounded sportsman who collected, well, "stuff." Mostly, he enjoyed shooting rifles, but he did a fair share of shotgunning and fishing also.

Four years ago I saw his obituary in the local papers. I was shocked. If my memory is accurate, he was only in his early sixties. The diabetes I knew he had was what did him in, according to his son. I had good intentions of going to his funeral, but something came up—I had planned to be out of town on bank business—and I missed it. Many are the times I felt remorse since then because I chose—I could have easily gone—to ignore the chance to honor my friend for his last earthly celebration. Looking back, I learned a valuable lesson that day: Friendship is far more important than being AWOL from prescribed duties of the day.

Bervin M. Nelson, universally known as "Moose," was a retired Navy master chief. Southern born, he was a big guy, tall, robust, and handsome, too. Kind, gentle, and forever smiling his warm smile, I was honored to be his friend. He was always saying, "I'm from Missouri—show me," so I guessed he really was from Missouri. There wasn't anything he wouldn't do for anyone. As I said, I loved this guy, and I'm sure all others who knew him felt the same way about Moose.

A few months ago my wife saw an ad in *The Day* describing a yard sale at his family residence. I went, and the good memories of this big-hearted man engulfed my soul. His son, much like his father in stature and mannerisms, was checking out patrons' low-priced bargains outside the garage. I didn't buy much—just a few tools, but there were a lot of sporting giveaways—a bamboo fly rod and other miscellaneous fishing rods (some unused), sporting books and art—that represented a lifetime of collecting. We chatted a bit, his son and I, and when I asked to buy a sign reposing on the shelf just inside the door to his basement for my ammo reloading room, he smiled and just handed it to me. On the rough backside of this 12" x 5" piece of sheet paneling was Moose's neat, unmistakable one-inch-tall block printing burned into the wood:

B M NELSON
USN RET

In a strange but positive way, I felt redeemed from my guilt because maybe now he knows how much I esteemed his friendship. The value of these simple but personal treasures is that they bring back the memory of a gentleman and friend I so much admired and respected. I will never forget him.

About the Author

The author is a life-long Connecticut Yankee with family roots tracing back to the Mayflower. A retired bank official, he has lived most of his life on and around acreage farmed by his ancestors since the early 1700s. His life passions are the outdoors, the English setters he trains and loves, the native birds he hunts in New England and eastern Canada, and the scarce and coveted upland books and art that can be found in his extensive library.

He helps us understand his hunting ethic by giving us insight into his heritage and who his heroes are. Through these descriptions, we see the basis for his standards. There was never a question as to why he believes in this sport and how it is to be played.

When he speaks of the land, he recalls an earlier ethic. This ethic, born on early New England hillsides, is still practiced by the author. He talks of the husbandry and devotion to his own land, and what it means for the birds. He decries the loss of open land and begrudgingly accepts the emasculation of it where birds are ever increasingly betrayed by development.

In describing his trips out of Connecticut, there seems to be a bittersweet acknowledgement that not long ago there was an abundance of birds in his lower lot and travel was not necessary. It's not that he doesn't love the uplands of Maine and Vermont but is perhaps saddened that his own house is no longer filled.

Breinigsville, PA USA
28 January 2010

231535BV00001B/4/P